THE TERRORIST

THE TERRORIST

Nigel Harris

Book Guild Publishing
Sussex, England

First published in Great Britain in 2007 by
The Book Guild Ltd,
Pavilion View,
19 New Road
Brighton, BN1 1UF

Typesetting in Baskerville by
IML Typographers, Birkenhead, Merseyside

Printed in Great Britain by
CPI Antony Rowe

A catalogue record for this book is available from
The British Library.

ISBN 978 1 84624 084 3

'The revolutionary is a doomed man. He has neither his own interests, nor affairs, nor feelings, nor attitudes, nor property, nor even name. Everything in him is absorbed by a single exclusive interest, by a total concept, a total passion – revolution.'

S.N. Nechaev: *Catechism of a Revolutionary*, 1870.

'They acted in accordance with their convictions and did not shrink from the prospect of sacrificing their lives for the cause in which they believed. Their devotion to something that they thought was right to the point of self-sacrifice was the positive side of Nechaevism and it quite naturally led many to follow their example ... After long consideration, we too have come to the conclusion that the realisation of an end that is good justifies the use of every means.'

Debagory-Mokrievich, *Reminiscences*, 1902.

Contents

1	Arrivals	1
2	Cairo	13
3	Lunch with the Cyprians	22
4	Letter 1	39
5	Letter 2	44
6	Leila I	49
7	Letter 3	52
8	Letter 4	56
9	Khaled I	59
10	Letter 5	62
11	Letter 6	65
12	Khaled II	68
13	Letter 7	83
14	Letter 8	85
15	Leila II	87
16	Letter 9	97
17	Letter 10	100
18	Leila III	103
19	Letter 11	114
20	Letter 12	116
21	Mona	118
22	Letter 13	123
23	Letter 14	125
24	Khaled in Flight	127

25   The Horror   133
26   Into the Gulag   148
27   Letter 15   171
28   Letter 16   174
29   Letter 17   176
30   Epilogue   180
Appendix   187
The Characters, Events and References   195

The Terrorist

To 'the women of my household' – and all who
helped to make this little craft more seaworthy –
Ruth Balogh, John Charlton, Ibrahim Fathy,
Nigel Fountain, Tirril Harris, Kate Thompson,
Mary McAuley, Helen Nichols, David Steel,
Hana Suleyman.

1

Arrivals

Michael dug his fingers deeper in the soil. The sweat on his forehead was chill. The nettle root ran deep. The roses were old. There was not much point in weeding round them. Everyone said so; better to cut them down and plant new ones. He could hear faraway, crows cawing in the churchyard.

He was old too, ready to be cut down to make way for the new. He didn't feel old. The roses probably didn't either. Only, in his case, the frame showed wear and tear, the lungs puffed on quite slight inclines, the joints creaked. He stood up, and caught himself standing with his palms flat against the small of his back, slightly stooped, just as he had seen countless old men standing. One learned, he supposed, to do that, to practise being old.

The early November sun was already cooling. It had been warm for the time of year. He looked up and caught sight of a cloud of birds winging across the sky. The shadows were lengthening across the lawn. Roses, *wardh* in Arabic, with such delicate petals and that scent. How shockingly beautiful she had been. Everyone stole glances at her to avoid just staring, not believing anyone could be like that, could be so perfect. He remembered hoping she would speak in Arabic for a long time so that then he could just stare at the movement of her face without having to pay attention to anything she said or appear rude.

He remembered the first time they had met. It was in her father-in-law's apartment. She was demure in a grey lace *hijab*. Her father-in-law's reproof was like a whiplash across her face.

'Take that thing off your head. The women of my house are not ashamed to show their face and their hair. They are free women and take pride in showing themselves.'

The shock of it, like a blow striking her. She paled, angry red

1

patches rising on her white face. Her hand trembled as she pulled the veil over her forehead protectively.

He was dreaming again, he reflected ruefully, standing in the garden with his old roses, old men's dreams. He must finish and get the cottage ready. Jane and the children would arrive from London very soon.

Yet he stayed, motionless, abstracted. How stealthily time had crept up on him, ambushing him with old age, stealing the years. Like everyone else, he had squandered his time as if there would never be an end. Until, to his astonishment, he was eased out of the normal into that parking space, called retirement, awaiting the end.

Yet being old – and with some application, practising the condition – had not stopped him lusting after Khaled's beautiful wife. Or had it just been melancholy at what could never be? He heard her voice, low, almost gruff, with that Arabic lilt and the pause – '*yanny*' – that caught his heart. He saw the long stare of those green eyes, fixing him in their gaze; and the great black gown, like a bell tent. He had scarcely known her, yet her existence had, like the scent of those roses on a summer evening, seeped through the pores of his skin.

He remembered dozing in the early morning sunlight of the Cairo flat, recollecting those secret hints of femaleness that the black tent could not completely conceal – the glimpse of an olive ankle, a wisp of hair slipping out of her *hijab*, the hint of breast or buttock. Islamic dress incited unlawful fantasy. He smiled ruefully. Old men lusting over the young were always ridiculous – or disgusting.

He caught a sudden movement out of the corner of his eye – and froze. He stood very still, his heart pounding, sweat cold at his temples. He turned very slowly as if to give no sign of movement, to fool the sniper. There was a gap in the hedge leading into the field beyond. A cow had crossed the gap and now, munching slowly, stared at him impassively.

Relief flooded him and he laughed aloud. It was a vanity to think he was important enough to be reached by the long arm of Islamic justice, here in the sleepy fields of Hampshire.

It was ironic that he, of all people, and so late in life, might be a target of terror. He had spent his life telling people about terrorism – from Samson, the first suicide bomber, to Robespierre with a guillotine on every corner to cleanse a world of filth, to the IRA or the

Tamil Tigers or Hammas: the thousands of young men and women who put their lives in the balance in the struggle for freedom.

There had been so many fine heroes in his life, straight and unbending, fire in their eyes, steeled to accept no compromise, no 'buts'.

Many had been women. For men, it was a cult to be brave; but women were allowed to be honourable cowards. But there had been plenty of them – Joan of Arcs. Charlotte Corday, murdering Marat in his bath, and when asked what she had to say at her trial, crying: 'Nothing, except that I have succeeded' and would join Brutus in the Elysian Fields. Vera Zasulich who stood before the crowd and shot the monster General Trepov in full view; and then, so profound was the hatred of the Tsar, she was found innocent by her jury. Or the women of the Baader-Meinhof group – throwing away comfortable lives to cleanse the dishonour of Germany and its brash new capitalism. Or Fusako Shigenobu, finally found after a quarter of a century on the run; at 24, she led the most daring attacks of the Japan Red Army round the world. They bet their all on the wager. With his cult of brave women, he was a sucker for Leila Cyprian.

He smiled suddenly, as he looked up at the sun, remembering the frivolity of an old friend, Fernando, standing in the middle of a dirt road in Managua – it was 1979 and the Sandinistas had just come to power in Nicaragua: 'I can't bear it,' he shouted to nobody in particular. 'Women in khaki with machine-guns are just *so* sexy!'

Helen always said he only married her because she was a war correspondent, a pseudo-terrorist, always in khaki bush shirts. For 30 years she had zoomed in and out of crises round the world, ripping pictures of horror out of the world for the breakfast front pages and a second cup of tea. Neither bullet nor bomb had finally caught her, but a bug, a circumstantial detail, eating her away on an old-fashioned iron bedstead, in Winchester General Hospital, smelling of disinfectant and brown Windsor soup. He had held her hand for so long, willing her not to go. And then stared dry-eyed as she slipped away without glance or wince. The light of his life had gone with her, leaving only a ghost.

Most of his heroines and heroes perished – or, worst still, ended in bewildered or frightened old age, unable to understand how the world had deserted them. He remembered playing pool in a Catholic pub in Belfast, and thinking that most of these young heroes were certainly doomed in the ancient struggle to win a free

3

Ireland. They made no money out of it, spent lives permanently on the run. If lucky, they met early deaths and 'martyrdom'. Their lovers were one-night stands, snatched between secret hideaways, and stolen cars, leaving fatherless young to bring themselves up. Like the others who put their lives on the line – in Palestine, in Sri Lanka, in Kashmir, in Colombia, in Chechnya. So much blood, so much butchery. For much of his life, butchery and nobility went hand in hand. And now it was all overlaid with the imagery of the New York twin towers crashing. There was no end to it, no relief or compassion.

His dreaming was broken by a shout from the hedge. Bernard leant on his bike by the garden gate. Michael started and stood, smiling broadly.

'You're back,' he said. 'How good to see you. I missed you.'

Bernard was a tall thin man, with greying hair and a stoop. His face, caught at rest, was long and gaunt.

'I've just got in. Been down to the shop to get some food – and some rat poison. They've made a terrible mess while I was away.'

Bernard had been to visit his son in Sydney.

'They're all fine there,' he said. 'The weather was marvellous and I swam with the grandkids every day.

'But it's a relief to be home at last. I don't know whether I can face that trip again. And you – are you back from Cairo permanently? Or dashing off again?'

'I'm back for good – though missing it,' Michael said.

'I bet you do. We must meet and swap stories over a Scotch or two. I want to hear more about those letters you got before you went away.'

'Why don't you come to supper tonight? Jane's coming down so the food will be a cut above bachelor scraps.'

'But you'll want a bit of time with her – she isn't coming from London to feed another boring old fart. We can meet next week in the pub.'

'Come, and no more nonsense,' Michael insisted. 'She'd love to see you – and so would I. And it'll save you cooking after being away so long.'

It was settled. Bernard got on his bike awkwardly, and with a wave, peddled off, up the track, dodging the ruts and heaps of rotting leaves. Michael was glad – having Bernard back would break his awful isolation, his habit of talking to himself.

4

Mention of Jane reminded him he must get ready – open the gates for the car, lay the fire in the sitting-room, bring in the logs, air the beds for the children, put out the towels.

As he went in the door to the cottage, he glanced at the picture of Helen over the fireplace. It was a silly pretension. It had kept such a prominent position only out of inertia – the war correspondent uniformed in ballgown and jewellery. Her father had paid for it though he had long gone. The face was a good likeness. It still had the power in the right light to catch his heart. But she looked uncomfortable, defying anyone to think this was really her. The body beneath the silk was too angular, too full of peremptory action to fit comfortably within a leisured class.

On the opposite wall were her trophies. Her satchel hung there, khaki, stained and frayed. The binding of the water bottle was torn in one corner and the metal below glittered. The gash was a souvenir of Sierra Leone, a deflected bullet, the closest she came to an end before the end. He passed on to the photographs further down the room: Helen shaking hands with Nasser; in a group with Kennedy at the time of the Cuban missile crisis; meeting Sukarno. No ball dress here, but bush shirts and trousers. He recollected her very scent in her shirts, streaked and stained with hard wear in a hot climate. He stopped himself – that way lay disaster, depression. He took down the photograph of Nasser and gazed at it as if it held some secret message – that square spade face, not unlike Kirk Douglas. Helen looked like delicate china beside the monumental Egyptian pharaoh.

As he knelt at the fireplace, crumpling paper to lay kindling, he heard Jane's car in the drive and the sound of the horn. The doors slammed and there were children's feet on the gravel path and excited shouts. Then they were through the open door and on him, knocking him to one side on his arm as they clambered like boisterous puppies. Tom and Jack, faces shining as they hugged him, were a gale of noise and action. He levered himself to his feet, stooping to kiss them. But he still felt remote.

Jane followed. She was loaded with plastic bags, things to bribe the children to put up with grandpa's eccentricities. She dumped the bags on the rug and kissed him, shooing the boys into the garden.

She held him for a moment at arm's length, staring hard.

'Dad, how *are* you?' she asked. 'Are you on the mend after all that?'

'Oh, yes,' he said neutrally. 'I'm thawing out.' And then with a self-deprecating laugh, 'But it is a long way out of that deep freeze.'

In the evening, he helped Jane bath the boys, and read them a story. They were still young enough to accept a story from their grandfather, a reminder of the time before they could read. He tucked them up with a hug and a kiss, and told them not to talk too long, leaving a side light glowing. The wind had got up and as he came down the stairs, he could hear the trees thrashing outside.

Bernard arrived. He had put on a tie and, Michael thought, brushed his shoes. He was sitting upright on the sofa before the fire, looking at the drawings Jane had laid out for inspection.

Jane called from the kitchen, asking him where the tin opener was, and he went to get it.

'See what I'm doing in Stuttgart,' she said gaily. 'I've put it on the table. And get a drink for Bernard – supper won't be long.'

Michael did as he was told, and sat on the sofa to share Jane's drawings. The top one was the museum for Stuttgart.

'It's great,' Michael called out. 'It looks like a revision of Swansea.'

'It is but also I've rethought the inside so you've got much more space for big exhibitions – that's what they asked for. And do you like the way I've allowed for the water?'

'Splendid,' Michael said.

There was a pause while they continued to look at the drawings. The fire crackled as the alcohol warmed their stomachs.

'I read your article again on the plane,' Bernard said tentatively. 'On those letters. What an amazing find that was. Weren't you astonished?'

Michael got off the sofa with difficulty, laying the drawings carefully on a side table, and moved to a chair opposite Bernard.

'Very,' Michael said. 'It was such a stroke of luck.'

'Think if someone had found them and thrown them in the rubbish,' Bernard said.

'It would have been easy enough,' Michael agreed, relaxing now with the warmth of the fire and the Scotch.

'How did you come by them?'

'I had a French doctoral student, André Caudet. His father was an antique dealer and bought the little cabinet in a market in Cambrai;

6

his cabinet-maker found the letters. Knowing my interests, André asked me to look at them.'

'And you bought them?'

'No, no. André's father wouldn't hear of it. What's more, when he heard how important it was, he made me a present of the cabinet as well. Of course, it might have looked like a bribe to get his son through the hurdles. If it was, it was a poor investment. His son dropped out even before the cabinet arrived and, ran away with a Colombian girl to fight for the Palestinians or something like that.'

Michael and Bernard smiled at the madness of the young.

'Didn't anyone doubt their authenticity? Forgeries? It is odd there is no other trace of this woman.'

'Professor Janna Métier of Grenoble tried. It is the way we academics make our name,' Michael smiled wryly. 'But people have now had a good chance to go over them. The detail is right, the paper is right, the ink, the style and the circumstantial evidence, so generally I think they have come to be accepted as authentic.'

'And what happened to the cupboard?'

'It's here, now marvellously restored by a London cabinet-maker.'

Michael stood up. He lifted a table lamp to shine the light on a small upright cupboard, flat against the wall. There were three drawers with brass handles at the base, and a fold-down top, covered by a marble slab. The veneer glowed like honey in the light.

'It's a lady's writing desk,' Michael said as Bernard followed him. 'It's now been restored, and the restorer did a beautiful job in patching up the veneer – Brazilian tulip wood, he said. He guessed that it was probably made for a lady's boudoir, an *escritoire*, mid-eighteenth century but renovated in the nineteenth, when the letters would have been left there.'

Michael opened the top flap to show a shabby stained leather writing surface, fringed with faded gold tooling, before a set of small inner drawers for ink and pens.

'You'll have to show me the secret drawer,' Bernard said.

Michael rummaged in the top drawer and took out a small iron rod and a little torch.

'It's not built for rapid concealment,' he said, stooping to take out the bottom drawer of the cupboard. He went on his knees awkwardly as he groped in the space, shining the torch in the hole and finally locating the keyhole at the back. It clicked quite easily.

7

'Then,' he said, struggling to his feet, holding on to the cupboard, 'you remove the locking rod by sliding aside this little panel at the top and drawing it out.'

He turned the cupboard and reached down the back. 'And, you slide aside this panel at the base and, hey presto, you have the secret space.'

'But it is so small,' Bernard said, 'so easy to miss.'

'Only a fractional difference in the size of the drawers gives it away – it is so small, you could never get much in.'

At that moment, Jane came into the room, carrying steaming dishes. She was dressed in brilliant crimson, showing off her pale skin, a dramatic change from the frayed jeans. She was wearing a necklace and bracelets. Michael marvelled at how much she resembled her mother.

'You look stunning, my dear,' Michael said in slow admiration, with Bernard murmuring his agreement. 'And put me to shame in my old clothes.'

Jane smiled in delight at her effect. She was still a strikingly handsome woman, he reflected, though now her skin was tempered by the trials of late motherhood and an intense career – and a husband, Michael grumbled, who travelled too much.

Jane put the dishes down on the table.

'You're looking at the *escritoire*,' she said, 'where Dad found Marx's daughter's letters?'

'Not Marx's daughter,' Michael said gravely. 'Her French teacher.'

'Come and eat,' Jane commanded, 'and tell me how much you love my museum in Stuttgart.'

It was an excellent meal, prepared in London to cheer a lonely father.

Afterwards, the two old men left Jane drinking her wine in front of the television news while they cleared the table and washed up. When they returned, she was sound asleep, her face flushed with wine and the warmth of the fire.

Michael turned off the television and got the two of them a brandy. As he returned, Jane woke with a start, disconcerted.

'I'm always doing that,' she said. 'It makes me a wash-out at dinner parties.'

'Why not just go to bed and get a good sleep? You've earned it,

8

making all that marvellous food on top of a working day. We'll be all right, sitting here, chewing the cud,' Michael said.

Without too much persuasion, she agreed.

When she had gone, the two men sat in silence for a while, gazing into the fire.

'And what finally became of that Russian terrorist that so frightened Natalie in your letters?' Bernard asked abruptly, as if resuming an interrupted discussion.

'Nechaev? He died in 1882 in the Peter and Paul Fortress in St Petersburg, aged about thirty-five.'

'So he never got out again?'

'No, sentenced to hard labour for life in Siberia, but they kept him in St Petersburg – in case, I guess, he might escape from Siberia. People say he convinced all his gaolers of the need for a revolution.'

'And did he really murder someone in cold blood?'

'I think so. A student and member of his group, Ivanov.'

'But why? Was he a psychopath?'

'I don't think so, but perhaps he needed to prove he was above conventional morality, to bind the other members of his group into a conspiracy. Who knows? But that was a tremendous shock to the dilettante leftist students of Russia. Even more when it was discovered he was drawing up lists of all those in the establishment and the opposition who were to be murdered.'

'Some more brandy?' Michael offered, but Bernard, staring into the fire, declined. 'I shall fall off my bike in this wind if I have any more,' he said.

'What was Nechaev's background?' he asked finally.

'European Russian, provincial working class. He came from the main textile town of Russia. His father was a bit of an odd-job man – sign-painter, waiter, labourer. His mother, I think, washed clothes.

'He basically educated himself, with a bit of help from church schools, and finally got a job as a religious teacher in a St Petersburg parish school. I suppose he fell in with a student crowd there. He would have been impressively proletarian among those children of the lower nobility – as well as having an amazing chip on his shoulder.'

'And why was he so famous?' Bernard asked.

'I suppose because of the murder, showing his complete single-mindedness, ruthlessness – and his hotline to Russia's most famous revolutionary, Bakunin, then in exile in Geneva. Russia's students were always talking revolution, the need to act and so on, but they never did anything. Then they ended up as doctors or lawyers or bureaucrats in some provincial town. Nechaev stood out as someone who did not just talk but dedicated himself completely to the overthrow of the Tsar. Nothing else counted and he seemed happy to die to achieve it, a real potential suicide-bomber.

'His zeal even impressed Lenin thirty-five years later. When they opened the Tsarist police archives after the 1917 revolution, he read the dossier, and told the Bolsheviks they had got Nechaev wrong – he was a real revolutionary. Until then the Bolsheviks had denounced him as an anarchist, so it was quite a turn round.'

'Lenin was a bit of an anarchist, wasn't he?' Bernard asked.

'He was. His brother was executed for being in the plot that killed the Tsar. And you know, after the revolution, Lenin invited Kropotkin, one of the famous founding fathers of Russian anarchism, to come back to Russia, and promised to republish his collected works when the country settled down. Who knows, maybe he would have republished the other great Russian anarchist, Bakunin. That would have set the cat among the Bolshevik pigeons. After Lenin's death, the Communists treated anarchists as police agents; they gunned them down in the Spanish Civil War.'

'And what happened to the girl who wrote the letters? I forget her name,' Bernard asked.

'Natalie. I didn't discover a lot. She married a local farmer three years after she got back to Cambrai; had three sons. Her brother, Jean, got back to France under the amnesty of 1881 and settled in Paris. But then it all went wrong. You may remember there was a conspiracy of former *communards* to assassinate General Mercier, the general in charge of much of the butchery of the Commune. Jean Kolakowski was caught up in that, arrested and sentenced to hard labour for life in New Caledonia. He died there of a fever in 1886. I think he was probably innocent of doing anything practical but was a useful scapegoat for the regime.'

They paused, the silence broken only by the wind in the trees and wood in the fire quietly singing to itself.

'How did you ever get started, working on terrorism?' Bernard said slowly, looking into the fire.

'Ah, that's a long story,' Michael replied, 'too long for this late at night. Just three headlines. First, my father was an anarchist and, for his pains, fought in the Spanish Civil War. It's a wonder he escaped given his politics. But I think he brought home some bug and died from it when I was about five. I remember him as a sad man. I always thought the sadness was due to the double defeat – of the Spanish Republic by Franco and the Right, and of the anarchists by the Communists.

'Second, my mother, a strong fierce woman who was not political in the ordinary sense. She made radio programmes. Her best one, made in my teens, was a series of three under the title *Here I Stand* on people who risked their lives to assassinate former heroes who had become tyrants: Brutus who killed Julius Caesar; Edward Sexby who wanted to kill Cromwell after the English Civil War; and Count Stauffenberg who conspired to murder Hitler in 1944. As a young teenager, I lived through all the obsessive preparation of the programmes.

'My mother died while I was a student – in 1958 – and I spent a long summer vacation going through the family papers. I discovered how little I knew about my parents. I skimmed my father's marvellous library of anarchism, which I'd never paid attention to. It was just in time for all the giddy politics of the sixties when we thought the revolution was due in the next twenty minutes. So there you have it – parentage and the times.'

Bernard finished his drink.

'It is such a long time ago now, a different age – whether the 1860s for Natalie and Nechaev or the 1960s for us,' Bernard said, struggling to his feet. 'All those passions and furies seem very remote.'

'Ah, but think of the Islamists, the fundamentalists,' Michael said with a smile, as he got up to help his friend and see him out. 'They keep the flame alive.'

'Yes, but what flame?' Bernard said as he wrapped his coat round himself and prepared to plunge into the wind.

After he had gone, Michael sat for a while, watching the dying fire, listening to the wind. It was a long time since he had thought of his mother. He tried to recall her face but could not. It was too late to search for a photograph. Only the tune 'Waltzing Matilda' seemed stuck in his mind. Perhaps it had been a favourite of hers, but he could no longer remember.

*　*　*

He woke only once, in a panic as usual at nearly three o'clock. Someone was breaking in downstairs. There were clear sounds – footsteps in the gravel, breaking glass. It lasted only a second until he heard the silence, the now light wind, stirring the trees. It was the normal panic. The alarms were set downstairs and had not gone off. He relaxed.

2

Cairo

It began with the start of his two-year contract at the American University in Cairo, the AUC, and his meeting with Sameh Cyprian. There was a party on the roof of the AUC student hostel on Zamalek island to welcome new staff.

The weather was balmy, the night sky black velvet with a dusting of stars, mimicking the lights from the massed buildings below, a painter's urban landscape of squares and oblongs, planes and shadows. A slender moon lay on her back, kicking her heels for joy. Occasionally, the lights of an aircraft moved across the dark, like a giant blind animal, nosing aside the few thin clouds, groaning with the effort to find its lair on the far side of the city. For a moment, he thought he caught sight of the moon's reflection in the river, but the buildings blocked any glimpse of either arm of the Nile.

There were ululations far below, from the great doors of the cathedral, and the cars that streamed down Ma'arashli, hooted the same rhythm; boasting the wedding of the children of some Coptic grandees. The car horns reminded him of the honking of the French Algerians, the *pieds noirs*, beating out *Algérie française* before they fled back to France. He and Helen had been there on one of their rare trips together.

He stood with his drink looking over the city, wondering again why he was in Cairo at all. Jane had laughed when he told her he was going:

'At your age? How bizarre! But you've always had a love affair with Islam, and there's enough terrorism there to keep you busy. There might be another book out of it.'

And then, with a frown of anxiety, 'But you will be careful, won't you. And keep in touch – an e-mail at least once a week.'

He was pulled away from the balcony and the vista of Zamalek to join the cluster of people. It was then that the American woman from the English department accosted him.

'Mordant!' she said loudly, her puffy face flushed with drink. 'That's what I thought the moment I saw you.' She swayed a little. She was large and her dress, some chintz pattern, bulged with rolls of surplus flesh, riding up her square thighs. Behind her lurked a slight young man with a crew cut, in a check shirt and jeans.

Was there such a word? He replied lamely, 'I'm sorry; next time I'll try to be less dant.'

She glared at him suspiciously, coughed her disapproval and turned away abruptly. That was a pity, he thought. She was probably a famous poet or a brilliant cook. Now he was on his own for two years in this strange city, he needed all the friends he could get.

A small professor from Kerala, smiling shyly through his thick glasses, introduced himself, and in turn, introduced an older woman who had just joined them.

'And this is Sheila Whittaker in Archeology. She has been here since 1963.'

'That is astonishing,' Michael said. 'You've seen the whole story of modern Egypt – Nasserism, Arab socialism, war on Israel and the alliance with Russia; and then the exact opposite – free markets, peace with Israel, the collapse of the Soviet Union – a new world.'

'Some new world,' the woman muttered. 'You don't get any feel for the big events when you live your daily life here, hanging on, and in my case, obsessed with life three thousand years ago. We're like ants living under an elephant.'

They were joined by others. A German anthropologist was earnestly explaining that the Islamic veil, the *hijab*, was not one garment, but many different statements about the world, from the religious to the flirty. An older American said he had just come from China. He had been to the centenary celebrations of his old school in Ningbo. His parents had been missionaries.

An older man with a stoop and a giggle, dressed rather foppishly, introduced himself as George, head of History. Michael noted the English accent.

'And what are you working on these days, Dr James?' he asked after the preliminaries were over.

'I've just finished editing a set of letters, discovered in an old bureau, between a French girl, a sort of *au pair*, living in Marx's house in London in 1872, and her brother, an ex-*communard* exiled in Geneva.'

'How exciting,' George responded. 'Just after the collapse of the Paris Commune.'

'Yes, and the Franco-Prussian War – a patriotic French girl, living in the home of the enemy, Marx the Prussian, just when Bakunin's anarchists were taking over his International.'

'George, don't monopolise all the interesting guests.'

The voice was low and gravelly, a smoker's voice, and close to Michael's ear.

'I think you must be Dr James. Allow me to introduce myself – Mohammed Mahmoud. I work mainly at the University of Cairo, but also do a little teaching at the American University – in management.'

Michael started with surprise. Surely he knew this man? He warmed to him at first but then felt a sense of foreboding, almost hatred. But wasn't he an Australian?

Mohammed Mahmoud was not Australian, but definitely Egyptian. He was a bear of a man and stooped over Michael. Perhaps he had been a boxer when he was young. He might have been in his late fifties, with grey close-cropped hair and a thick greying moustache. He was elegant in a well-tailored suit and what in England would have been a regimental tie. His English was carefully modulated. Sandhurst?

But then Michael involuntarily stiffened. Mahmoud must be military security. It was almost a uniform.

They shook hands with some show of affability. Mahmoud slipped his hand under Michael's elbow and drew him away from the group. He was obviously used to getting his way. Michael suppressed his irritation and allowed himself to be guided away from the crowd.

'I am proud to meet you,' he said. 'Your work is of course well known here among those with a serious interest. It is a great coup for the AUC to capture one of the leading authorities on political terrorism for its faculty. I hope they exploit the opportunity to the full. I've read a lot of your work and always found it most instructive.'

Michael was alerted by the outrageous flattery, and allowed himself no more than a curt nod of acknowledgement. Why was a teacher in management so interested in terrorism?

15

'May we expect, after your stay here, your thoughts on our home-grown political terrorism? For the moment, we have mastered the worst at home – Luxor, you remember? – and, I fear, started exporting our terrorists to the rest of the world. As you probably know, the second in command of Al-Qaeda in Afghanistan was the leader of Al-Jihad here, a Cairo surgeon.'

Michael was surprised at the sudden rush of information.

'Oh, I have no ambitions to contribute,' he replied. 'I'm here just to learn, and from a fairly basic starting point. I'm just beginning to learn some elementary Arabic – with much pain – but it will never be good enough to do serious work.'

Michael paused before continuing, trying to regain the initiative.

'But tell me, why is someone who teaches management so interested in political terrorism?'

Mahmoud looked irritated.

'I used to be involved with these matters, and keep an intellectual interest in the field. But I am sure you are being too modest about your possible work. We have much to learn from your immensely wide experience. I would have liked to sit in on your graduate class, but I fear it clashes with another engagement.'

They paused while a waiter brought round a plate of snacks.

'In fact, I was wondering,' Mahmoud continued, 'whether you might consider coming to address a little unofficial group of mine?'

Michael was alerted. He must be in the security services.

'It's a small group of committed enthusiasts,' Mahmoud went on, 'and includes many of the people who are centrally responsible for much of this country's security against terrorism. I think you might find it interesting to meet such a group of practitioners. We pay a small honorarium, of course. We tend to meet locally here in Zamalek – in the Officers' Club on July 26th Street. Do you know it?'

Michael knew it and nodded. Each time he passed it, he marvelled that the army could so shamelessly flaunt its power – a private club with gardens exclusively for its officers on some of the most expensive built-up land in the city.

'Well,' Michael said defensively. 'That is kind of you, but at the moment, I am rather run off my feet coping with courses at the AUC. Perhaps later on, when things have settled down, I might take you up.'

'I'm so glad,' Mahmoud beamed down at him, knowing Michael was refusing. 'Let me give you my card. Perhaps when you have a moment, we could meet again? Have you been on a felucca on the Nile, Dr James?' Michael had not. 'Then let me invite you to be my guest one of these evenings before it gets too cold. We can pick one up near the Meridien Hotel, just south of Garden City. The ideal time is sunset. You coast across that magnificent stretch of water in the heart of the city over to Giza. Of course, you ought to be with a pretty girl.'

Mahmoud bellowed with roguish laughter and wheezed. 'Which reminds me of another great sunset experience – riding across the desert to the pyramids at Giza. I have a couple of ponies out there, and maybe you would enjoy a ride? I'll give you a call later on, if you will allow me, and see if we can fix something up. And now,' Mahmoud continued abruptly, 'if you will forgive me, I really have to go. It was so charming meeting you, and I hope we meet again soon.'

He was smiling broadly as he bowed, taking Michael's now apparently small hand in his own bear's paw, and pumping it vigorously.

Michael watched him pass through the crowd, head and shoulders above everyone else, as if wading through a river of people. As a spy, he would not be easy to hide.

Michael looked at the card and noticed the 'Colonel' in front of the name, without even a 'rtd'.

Why did he have such a strong feeling that he ought to have been in the air force? It had been a hard sell, so many invitations. Did one or other of the security services have an eye on him? Or had the Egyptians been tipped off by British Intelligence?

Security in Egypt was big business. The downtown streets were populated by different varieties of policemen – from sheepish unshaven boys in ill-fitting black tunics who seemed not to know which way up to carry their Kalashnikovs, to meaner leaner men in red and black, to civilians, unmistakable, as if in uniform, in full suits, pastel shades, with dark glasses, mobile phones and a suspicious bulge under their jackets. Then there were others, high up, with sub machine-guns. Michael remembered his sense of slight shock outside the Cairo Museum, confronted by heavily armed paramilitary police, with fixed bayonets, steel helmets and flak jackets, some manning heavy machine guns. It was supposedly designed to sedate the nervous foreign tourist.

He then saw Sameh for the first time, threading his way through the crowds. He was an elderly man, handsome, tall, thin and straight, with a finely sculpted aquiline head, silver hair, a close-cropped beard and spectacles. He was dressed in a black polo neck shirt and jacket.

'Sameh Cyprian,' he said, holding out his hand. 'And you are, I think, Michael James, the terrorism authority? You see, news of your coming long preceded you. Everyone thinks you are a British spy, come to check up on what we're doing here! But, welcome to Cairo and the AUC.'

Sameh taught in the History department – modern Egyptian politics. Michael brightened up. He might learn something. There were desultory courtesies, before, somewhat too eagerly, Michael took the plunge.

'What sort of modern history do you teach?' Michael asked.

Sameh taught modern Egyptian nationalism – the post British period after the army Free Officers seized power in 1952. The regime was dominated by Colonel Nasser and his Arab socialism. Sameh's special interest was the Egyptian Communist Party. The party splintered into sects when Nasser seemed to adopt much of their programme – alliance with the Soviet Union and support for the Palestinians abroad; nationalization and land reform at home. Many Communists went over to Nasser and many more to gaol. Sameh admitted he had gone to gaol in 1958.

'It was not an experience I like to remember – prisons in Egypt are something very special. When I came out, it seemed, the party and all it stood for had become meaningless. I was lucky – relatives in high places. I went off to California, to Berkeley to do a Ph.D. Instead of the Free Officers, I got the Free Speech movement – if you go to San Francisco, wear a flower in your hair!'

Michael smiled. 'They were great times.'

'Yes, and it changed me completely. We don't have any liberation tradition in Egypt. The Left here was always as authoritarian as the Right; it was pharaohs all the way. So California just blew my mind. American anarchism was a revelation.'

He changed the subject quickly. 'But I had a special reason for wanting to meet you,' he said. 'I hope you won't think it out of order? My younger son, Bulus, is a new graduate student in your department. He's put himself down for one of your courses. His

18

educational background is tangled. We thought he was dyslexic for a long time and put him through a special school. We rather despaired of him ever being able to lead a normal life. But once past twelve, to everybody's delight, he began to make great progress and came in with a respectable degree. But you'll understand the worries of his parents, Dr James, that he might now, with graduate work, be trying to fly too high. It would be a terrible disappointment, if whatever was wrong with him before, came back.'

Sameh was visibly relieved that Michael was sympathetic and not offended at his special pleading.

'And how are you liking Cairo, Dr James? Is it your first visit?'

'Please,' Michael said, 'Michael.'

'We would say Dr Michael in Egypt,' Sameh replied.

Michael said he was loving Cairo, tramping the streets to get to know it – and especially walking to the centre each morning along the western bank of the Nile, and back in the evening on the other bank to see the crowds taking the sunset air and the breeze from Alexandria. Or he sat on his balcony watching the world. His apartment overlooked the glassed-in verandah of the mansion of some great landlord pasha of the old days. One evening, the lights were on and a butler was serving drinks.

'What fun,' Sameh said. 'So many foreigners get stuck being expatriates, longing all the time to be somewhere else. Or else they can't get over the poverty. Either way, they see only the problems of living here.

'But, on a different subject, are you ever free for luncheon one day. Ramadan is coming – when all good Muslims must fast in the hours of daylight. The greatest thing we Copts can do for non-Muslims like you, is invite you for lunch. Could you make it in a couple of weeks' time – say, the twenty-seventh?'

* * *

Michael learned, and his new life settled into routines. AUC graduate classes were held in the late afternoon because so many had jobs during the day. It meant people were often tired and difficult to interest.

As the autumn progressed, the evening light faded into twilight and sunset during classes. Once the sun disappeared, the chill in the air became noticeable. At some stage, someone switched on the lights.

The sheer youth of the class overwhelmed him, the grace and enthusiasm of some of them was infectious. It made him forget the other glazed eyes, bored or thinking of other things. Most of them were peculiarly prejudiced about political terrorism.

'You have to empathise if you are to understand, though understanding does not mean forgiving,' he urged them patiently. 'You have to enter into the mind of the person who throws the bomb or fires the pistol. What could be the cause of such an uncompromising zeal that almost certainly leads to their own death, sooner or later? What measure of idealism leads to self-destruction? They are, after all, usually people like you – roughly the same age, and often with university education. What drives them?

'Remember also that the very term "terrorist" is politically biased – governments use it to mean their *unofficial* enemies, non-State enemies. But if we define terrorism in neutral terms, as the use of violence or its threat to achieve political ends, then governments are everywhere easily the biggest terrorists. What governments call terrorism is almost always a reaction to the greater use of violence by governments themselves. And it may be impossible to end what governments call terrorism without governments themselves giving up the use of violence.'

In the first class, Michael picked out someone he thought might be the Cyprian boy. He was taller than most of the students, slim and good-looking, with large eyes and a mop of thick glossy hair. He seemed to concentrate intensely, taking copious notes.

After the class, the boy gravely introduced himself:

'My father asked me to give you this map, sir, so you can find your way to our apartment. It is quite easy.'

Michael thanked him as he gathered up his papers and the student papers. He cleaned the board and cleared up the chalk. Then together they walked in the gathering dusk across what was called the 'Greek campus' of the university. In the street, people hurried home at the end of the day. The boy relaxed and began to chat.

'Do you teach at Cambridge, sir?' he asked.

'No, at London, the London School of Economics. Or at least I used to – I am supposed to be retired now, so I teach only occasionally. This year, I will go back to London once a month for two or three days to lecture.'

'My brother, Butrus, was at Cambridge. He loved it. He's brilliant. He did anthropology at the AUC, and then took a medical degree at the University of Cairo. He was a postgraduate at Cambridge. His wife, Leila, is also a medical doctor – she is the most beautiful woman you ever saw.'

Bulus' thoughts tumbled out like water from a new spring.

They parted at the edge of Tahrir Square, at just the moment when, as if on a signal, the call to prayer burst out from the loudspeakers of thousands of minarets across the city. So many bellowing voices – from the gravelly and hoarse to the falsetto. They joined the traffic, honking and coughing and roaring in a great chorus, as vehicles swirled round the square. It was impossible to hear the 'Allah Akbar'. London was like this once, Michael thought, in the days when churches rang their bells through the day. It was a competition to see who could make the most noise; get most attention from the faithful.

Across the square, now flooded with crimson and orange from the dying sun, the black shadows advanced almost perceptibly. The colours touched the cars streaming by, burnishing the windows as if with a furnace, as flocks of people tried gingerly to cross between the vehicles. Great crowds of office workers waited at the bus stops, spilling into the road and narrowing the channel for the flow of angry traffic. The buses lurched, belching smoke, people clinging to the sides as if to a sinking ship. High above, the neon signs flashed on and off, the visual cacophony of a great city. In the darkening crimson world, people hurried home.

The sun was dying in Cairo, pinched out in the chill darkness, but now travelling swiftly westwards, summoning the call to prayer across the Sahara to Timbuktu, silent sentinel of mud minarets amid the sands – to the restless Atlantic shores of Morocco, and then to the Americas.

Michael turned along the eastern bank of the river and made for home.

3

Lunch with the Cyprians

Michael settled in: to his AUC apartment, to the AUC, to the locality. He reorganised the furniture, put up a small picture of Helen in his bedroom, set up his laptop, recruited a cleaning lady. Um-ahmed was a rotund middle-aged and veiled lady, a migrant from the Delta, with almost no English so talk was limited. He found a shop for foreign newspapers, only one day out-of-date. He began, with some pain, his Arabic lessons.

On the Friday of his lunch date with the Cyprians, the city was in the throes of Ramadan, fasting by day, feasting by night. At midday prayers on Friday, the city was alive with bustle. The loudspeakers bellowed out their sermons to the city. Outside Al-Saud, the little local supermarket, those at prayer had spilled out of the tiny basement mosque over the crossroads, now laid with prayer mats. The Saudi owner of the shop, a massive figure in a grand purple gown and a white turban, normally stationed at the store entrance, counting his money or threading his prayer beads, was absent now in the mosque. The worshippers knelt, hands clasped, listening intently to the unseen preacher, impervious to passers-by, to waiting cars, to those standing and staring. In Ramadan, some believed they could make up for the year's sins with a month of single-minded devotion. Even the drivers, waiting in their cars, often had a tiny Koran before them, filling in the time earning merit.

The Cyprian apartment was not difficult to find. It was part of an old block, overlooking the main channel of the Nile, close to the vast green acres of the Gezira sports club. That was a relic of British times, and as shameless a demonstration of military status as was Mahmoud's Officers' Club on July 26th Street. Close by was another exhibition of power, the spectacular palace built for the visit of Eugénie, wife of Emperor Louis Napoleon of France, to open the

Suez Canal (and put the British out of joint), now a Marriott hotel. Paying for the palace helped bankrupt the Khedive, the king of Egypt, so Britain could take over the country to bail out its bankers. The city was littered with such shameless exhibitions of power, modern pyramids.

The Cyprian block of flats had seen better days. Once, it had had ambitions to be grand. But the years had chipped those hopes away, leaving it tired and seedy. The sands of the desert had blasted it, like all old buildings in the city, leaving the walls streaked with decay, with ancient scars and patches of loose plaster. The long struggle to keep the desert at bay had left it exhausted. Only hourly sweeping the city's streets kept alive the illusion of the city as something separate from the surrounding sands that threatened to engulf it. The desert had time to wait.

The lift worked. It was a grand Edwardian wrought iron cage, open to the air, lined where there were walls, with mirrors and shiny mahogany. It groaned and rattled as, yet again, like some ancient gentleman, it made the immense effort to lever itself upwards from floor to floor, slow and shuddering. Each arrival was a triumph.

Michael was excited. It was his first invitation to an Egyptian home, and to the house of an ex-Communist.

The door was massive with well-polished brass fittings and a nameplate in Arabic and Roman scripts. Bulus opened the door swiftly as if he had been awaiting Michael's arrival, and greeted him with ill-concealed excitement.

The hall of the apartment was vast and dark, with a white marble floor and thick rugs. There was a large chandelier in the centre and much dark, heavy, old-fashioned furniture, ornate carved sofas and polished tables. Long mirrors lined the walls, and large portraits of heavy men with moustaches in suits and red fezes, governors and judges. Cyprian ancestors, Michael supposed.

At that moment, Sameh strode into the room, smiling with hands extended, followed by a small pretty woman, in a well-tailored trouser suit, perhaps in her late fifties.

'How good to see you,' he said, advancing on Michael to seize both his hands. 'And this is Yasmine, my wife,' he announced. She was a small delicate woman with grey hair.

'Bulus you already know, and this,' he gestured beyond his wife to the doorway, 'is Samir, my younger brother, known everywhere in the AUC, where he teaches maths, as "Emile" because, I think, he wears a beret.'

Emile was square and, unlike his brother, broad and well-built with a large nose and a shock of black hair.

'Come in, come in, come in,' Sameh said gaily, waving to the inner room.

'Dr James,' he said, making way, and they all trooped into a large sitting-room.

The sitting-room was also vast, with high ceilings, ornate plaster cornices and elaborate chandeliers. It also was full of the same heavy furniture. There were more portraits of grandees, some in uniform with high collars and many medals; there were also some high-busted women in ballgowns, heavy with jewellery. The sitting-room ended in tall glass doors, framed in faded long green velvet curtains. Through the glass doors, Michael could see a balcony, loaded with greenery, shrubs and small trees in pots. Beyond, he could just glimpse through the wrought iron railings the grey ruffled waters of the Nile and a cluster of buildings on the opposite bank.

Sameh said it was their old family home, filled with ancient furniture and bric-a-brac that no one had the energy to throw away. The Cyprian grandfather had been a great landowner, a feudal lord with an army of retainers and endless villages under his control. The family had had vast lands in the Delta and in Upper Egypt – in Asyut, and palaces in Alexandria and Cairo. The apartment was one of the last fragments of the estate, a toehold in the city. The Cyprian father had been a lawyer who became a high court judge and had lived in Cairo far more than his father. Under Nasser, it all went, leaving only the apartment.

'Our father, like us,' Sameh concluded, 'could never face the job of clearing out all the junk. So, we are stuck with it.' He nodded at Emile and Yasmine, 'One-time Communists caught in a time warp of the old feudal class.'

A tall elderly black man in a suit, bearing a silver tray, glasses and a decanter entered the room. He was wearing white gloves.

'Now, some sherry?' Sameh asked. 'Bobune,' he smiled at the manservant as he poured out the sherry, 'is also a relic of our family past. He refused to escape when offered liberation by Colonel Nasser, or even to change his habits and his dress. As boys, we were forever trying to get him into jeans and a T-shirt, but he never would. We still tease him over his gloves, but he says he is too old to change now.' Bobune smiled uncertainly, knowing he was being discussed. 'He is Nubian,' Sameh continued, passing a glass from the tray to Michael. 'Originally from one of my grandfather's villages in the far south. He's been with us half a century.'

'Our middle brother, Hosni, may drop in to meet you after we've eaten,' Emile said. 'He's in the government, one of the token Copts, but like everybody else in the same position, frantically busy cheating and bullying the rest of Egypt.' He gave a cough of laughter.

'Really, Emile,' Yasmine interjected. 'What will Dr James make of us, at the same time boasting of feudal grandeur, Communist pretensions and corrupt relatives.'

'Well, this is Egypt,' Emile said. 'Full of contradictions.'

'How did your brother manage politically when you were Communists?' Michael asked, trying to get the conversation off that particular rock and into something more interesting.

Hosni, Sameh said, had also been a Communist in the forties and fifties. Most of the Communists came from the upper classes and minorities – it was rather fashionable to hate your parents and love Egypt. But Hosni recognised early on that Nasser was much the same as Stalin (whom Communists thought of as a god). Nasser was not a Marxist and had no time for workers, but he was fighting the Americans and taking over the landowners and capitalists, just what the Communists wanted. So Hosni crossed over to Nasser and was well rewarded. And he was always a great survivor – knew when the line was going to change and when to jump.

'And as far as we were concerned,' Sameh waved again at Emile and Yasmine, 'it was a lucky thing. He protected us. I spent six years in prison, not as bad as it might have been, and then he got me out and, to the delight of our parents, wangled it so we could run away to California out of harm's way.'

'I was arrested only briefly,' Yasmine said.

It seemed incredible to Michael that this small, frail woman, with her well-groomed hair and impeccable clothes, could have been in prison.

She said that, unlike the men's prisons, women prisoners were not segregated – Islamists and Communists were mixed. Islamist women were officially

25

supposed to be secluded at home, but some of the university women were also feminists and could not be prevented from being active. Yasmine said she learned a lot from the women activists of the Muslim Brotherhood, the Islamists. It was strange but often the politics were not very different, though the Communists regarded the Islamists as fascists. But they were ferociously opposed to British imperialism and anti-capitalist; for free education (especially for women) and a public health system for all – anyone might have thought them good socialists.

'I was lucky,' Emile muttered, 'and escaped altogether. I was too young and my brothers kept me on the straight and narrow.'

The doorbell rang faraway, and Michael assumed it was Hosni, the third brother.

'It must be Butrus,' Bulus said excitedly. He almost ran from the room.

Sameh rose, turning his back towards the door and moving to a desk against the wall. He stood, shuffling some papers there. His body movements, Michael noted, seemed hostile, wary, almost frightened. He caught Yasmine giving a worried glance to Emile.

'I thought I had an article here that I wanted you to look at, Michael,' Sameh said vaguely, 'but I can't find it.'

Bulus returned in high excitement, followed by a man, possibly in his early forties, thin and slightly above average height, good-looking but with an eye patch and a slight limp. The family resemblance was striking. Butrus was handsome like his mother and brother, but with the frank countenance of his father. Impulsive, even rash, Michael reflected.

'This is my eldest son, Butrus,' Sameh said to Michael in a low, curt tone. 'Butrus Cyprian – Dr Michael James, just arrived as visiting professor at the AUC.' Butrus shook Michael's hand with a distant smile, murmuring almost inaudibly, 'Actually my name is Khaled.'

Sameh's exuberance had left him. The old man was suddenly sullen. Indeed, a chill silence had descended on the company, a discomfort. Butrus – or Khaled – moved towards his father as if to embrace him, but Sameh gestured him away. Awkwardly, he arranged himself in a low chair, shuffling as if to fill in time.

'How have you been, father?' he asked in English in a low tone.

'As well as can be expected,' his father muttered.

There was a pause. Michael was embarrassed, searching for

26

something to say to break the intense stillness. Beyond the apartment, there were cries from the river, a radio playing somewhere and a car horn blaring, exaggerating the silence within.

'My son,' Sameh began at last, apparently making a great effort, 'has become a Muslim, Dr James.' His tone was bitter. 'He thinks that to be an Arab and an Egyptian, it is also necessary to be Muslim, and abandon the traditions in which he was raised, traditions far older than those of Islam. Do not Copts also have a right to be Egyptian?'

The little group was stunned, as much by the assault on the courtesies or discreet silences owed to a guest as by the display of raw aggression.

'Sameh!' Yasmine and Emile protested together.

From the corner of his eye, Michael saw the panic convulsing the face of the younger brother.

Yasmine continued in a rush: 'Please don't start any of that nonsense, especially now we have a guest with us. Dr James does not want to witness all these family squabbles. Butrus is an adult and has the right to make up his own mind.'

Sameh was not to be deflected. 'Nobody will believe him, of course,' he mused in a low tone, as if to himself. 'When his friends come to power – God forbid! – he will go to the guillotine along with the rest of us.'

'Did you bring Leila?' Yasmine said quickly before anyone had time to respond.

'Yes, indeed,' Khaled said. 'She's just changing.'

'I'll slip out and have a word with her,' Yasmine said, 'and check that Bobune has the lunch in hand. Please forgive me.' She nodded at Michael, rose from her chair and moved swiftly to the door, abandoning the men to the furies.

Emile tried to restore matters, 'Butrus,' and then apologetically, 'it is so difficult to remember a new name when you've been used to a different one all your life – Khaled is a distinguished surgeon at the national hospital, and teaches at the University of Cairo.'

'How long will you be in Egypt, Dr James?' Khaled asked Michael in a tone languid enough to suggest he was not much interested in the reply.

'Possibly four semesters. I am to do some teaching, but my main purpose is research,' Michael replied.

The little spurt of conversation was too weak to withstand Sameh's brooding silence.

27

'Butrus took his first degree at the AUC – in Anthropology,' Sameh said at last but without much connection. And then as if no longer able to control his cold rage, asked curtly: 'And will you have a drink with us, now you're here?' He nodded at the sherry decanter. The room froze.

'You know I cannot,' Khaled said shortly.

Michael reflected confusedly that the day, Friday, and the season, Ramadan, let alone the general ban on drinking alcohol at any time, made the invitation a brutal insult.

'Well, lunch is at two,' the old man said truculently.

'That is enough, Sameh,' Emile said sharply. 'Stop trying to bait the boy and give us some peace.'

Michael noted again the palpable anguish of Bulus; he seemed to be trembling.

Khaled stiffened, and said something in Arabic in a low voice to his father. Michael guessed he was reminding him – if reminder were needed – that it was Ramadan and he was fasting. In any case, even if it weren't, Michael reflected, Khaled presumably could eat only halal food, and never share food with Christians.

The silence returned, each, as it were, examining their finger nails with intense interest. Michael wondered that the father had so deliberately set out to provoke his son, to do it in English and in the presence of a stranger. He seemed to want to expose the wound in the heart of the family, to make a kind of confession of his failure as a father. Or was he looking for moral approval from an outsider, or some assurance that he was not completely wrong?

'Bulus tells me you spent time at Cambridge,' Michael at last asked brightly. Khaled looked grateful for the distraction, but at that moment, the door opened and a woman entered. Michael presumed this was Leila. He rose to his feet.

The moment of Leila's entry would remain with him forever. It had a theatrical quality. She was shockingly beautiful. His heart lurched at the sight of her face, and he had to fight the temptation just to stare at her, open-mouthed in wonder. He feared he would be caught snatching quick glances at her.

Her beauty was not one of vivacity: she was subdued, eyes cast down, as if withdrawn into herself. But even with all these signs of rejecting the gaze of others, her face was dramatic, pale with a fine bone structure, high cheek bones and a straight aquiline nose. The enormous green eyes were, Michael thought, straight from a Fayoum portrait.

She was slender, of medium height, her head covered with a shawl of plain grey lace, indoor wear he presumed. The shawl seemed to exaggerate, not hide, her beauty. Indeed, Michael reflected, whatever she did would only heighten the effect. The only way of dimming the sun would be a full *burka*, covering everything, with only a tiny slit in the tent for her to look out through.

She made as if to greet Sameh with some act of obeisance, but he stiffened and turned away.

'This is my wife, Leila, Dr James,' Khaled said gravely. Sameh glowered.

'Delighted to meet you,' Michael said weakly.

She did not look up at the introduction, eyes lowered to the rug. Nor did she shake his hand, but slightly lowered her head in acknowledgement.

Michael sat down. The only place for the newcomer to sit was on a low stool next to him. She lowered herself gracefully, carefully folding her long grey gown more closely round her and pulling her shawl forward to conceal more of her forehead. Michael noticed how full and finely shaped her lips were. Surely there was a hint of lipstick there? And kohl round the eyes?

Khaled and Emile were discussing something, half in Arabic, half in French and English, slipping between languages without noticing. Sameh was silent, slumped at his desk, as if half asleep yet with something of a scowl on his face. Leila seemed also to be listening but remote from the world.

'Are you also a doctor,' Michael asked her conversationally at last. Her body stiffened with resentment. He wondered whether she did not speak English.

She murmured, almost inaudibly, a curt 'Yes'. Michael reflected that that capacious grey garment, designed to conceal all body movements, did not at all hide her hostility, her discouragement of any further talk from him. She still did not raise her eyes. It seemed to him she was almost scowling in distaste. Perhaps she hated foreigners, he thought.

'And do you also teach at Cairo University?' He was surprised at his refusal to respond appropriately to the signs of hostility. It was then – he remembered later – he noticed her hands with fingers like willow wands, and on the inside of her left wrist, a kind of tattoo, perhaps a bird or a flower, where the pale blue veins rose to the surface of her skin. The wrist was strikingly slender, the skin translucent. He wondered whether the tattoo had ritual significance.

'At Ain Shams University,' she replied, and on the instant, as if making a decision, rose to her feet. 'Excuse me,' she said, still not raising her eyes to his. She turned to Sameh with a slight obeisance, and asked meekly in English:

'Dr Sameh, I would like to have a few words with Madame Yasmine. Would you permit it?' The voice was low and husky.

Sameh looked up, as if for the first time noticing his daughter-in-law. And then it happened: the scene he so often remembered later. Sameh's face darkened with rage as he gazed at Leila.

'Why is your head covered in my sitting-room?' he said roughly. 'Take that thing off your head. The women of my house are not ashamed to show their face or their hair – as free women, they take pride in them.'

Emile jumped up and shouted at his brother in English. 'Sameh, for God's sake, enough – stop! Why do you keep picking a fight with the boy? Live and let live. We are all Egyptians, after all, all in the same family – and we won't get another one.'

His voice trailed away. With icy control, Khaled now addressed his father slowly and carefully in Arabic. Michael guessed the drift – that Leila could not uncover her head in the presence of strangers. He finished in English, as if unaware that he had changed languages.

'And if you insist, we will be forced to leave. It is a matter of honour, father. And if we leave,' he said, almost pleading, 'we will not be able to return.'

Bulus stood up, as if to plead with his father. But Sameh turned away, refusing to be consoled or persuaded, black with rage and misery. Emile moved as if to embrace him, to pull him back from the abyss.

It was Leila who broke the crisis. 'Please excuse me, Dr Sameh,' she said again with cold self-control, and turned to go. Sameh ignored her. And she left – with more grace, energy and dignity, Michael reflected, than was consistent with someone supposed to be so meek.

After she had gone, Sameh mumbled something to his eldest son, and then miserably, 'If she has to cover her hair, why don't you have a beard like the other …'

Michael thought he was going to say 'lunatics', but he didn't.

Wearily, Khaled responded: 'We have been over this many times, father. As you know, wearing a beard for us is optional.'

'Not for the Taliban,' his father snapped.

'That is so,' Khaled replied. 'But they were raw *madrasah* boys in Afghanistan, and we are not. In any case, it is politically useful at the moment that I should be clean-shaven.'

'Ah,' his father said almost triumphantly. 'You're what used to be called a fellow-traveller, an undercover cadre. Beware – you know the Chinese proverb: after the deer, the hunting dogs go into the pot.'

Khaled gave no reply. He rose to his feet with quiet dignity, bowed to his father and said as if placating him:

'I am sorry we cannot stay to lunch, but I would like a few words with my mother before you eat. Do I have your permission to go?'

'Go,' Sameh said miserably. 'I suppose you cannot eat the food of your parents now, though it was good enough for you for most of your life.'

Khaled crossed to his father and endeavoured to kiss the old man, but Sameh turned his head away and Khaled gave up. He shook Michael's hand, gave a sad smile to Emile and Bulus, and then, limping slightly, left. Bulus after a quick glance at his father, jumped up and followed his brother.

The silence returned, broken only by the sound of music from a passing river craft and the waterside restaurants. Michael reflected that the violence of Egypt ran straight through this family. He slowly relaxed.

Emile shook himself like a dog leaving a pond, and brightened.

'Sameh, what about freshening Dr James's glass?' Michael thought what a silly phrase it was.

'Oh, Michael, yes, I'm sorry.' Sameh took the decanter and filled Michael's glass.

'You see, Michael,' Sameh said at last after a long intake of breath, 'we have a problem. As a teenager, Butrus was set upon becoming a monk or a priest. God forbid! In a house of evangelical atheists! Then as a student, he was a raving Marxist – even wrote a book on Egyptian capitalism. He plucked Leila – a seriously disturbed

31

woman – out of the gutter, and for his pains, she led a student revolt and tried to burn down Cairo University. And now she's persuaded him to this insanity, Islamic fundamentalism!'

He paused meditatively. 'Perhaps it was Cambridge that did it? Looking at King's College chapel too long?' He gave a hollow laugh.

'Anyway, when they came back from England, they both joined the lunatics – the Muslim Brotherhood or one of its offshoots.'

'But there was consistency,' Emile interjected. 'He was always dedicated to liberation – whether through Christianity, Marxism or Islam.'

'Great,' Sameh said derisively. 'But what a mess for everybody else.'

'Your family is Coptic, isn't it?' asked Michael, nodding at the crucifix on the wall.

'Don't be fooled by the cross. That's just decorative and doesn't mean anything. Yasmine put it there to please her mother when she called. But we would be counted as Christian here – you can't escape religious stupidities in this country. We were always against all religion, especially my father. So you can imagine how we felt about Butrus as a militant Christian teenager. The local priest even called to see him at one stage, and he knew very well that we had never stepped inside his wretched church – except for other people's weddings and funerals. And here was our son, demanding – at an advanced age – to be baptised, to our shame.'

He gave a guffaw of laughter at the memory, and continued. 'But even that was not half as bad as this.' He drank sadly, musing to himself.

'After all, neither of them are children any longer. You can't put it down to adolescent rebellion, peeing on mummy's carpet.' And then, as if waking to his duties, he turned to Michael. 'I am sorry, Dr James – Michael – to burden you with these family squabbles, but you can see what a misery it is – and dangerous too.'

'It must be fairly rare,' Michael said.

'Almost unprecedented. And does anyone really believe it? A double apostate! In any case, he's come too late. The Islamists are finished here. He's backing a dead horse, or at least a dying one. Sheer State violence has smashed the activists and demoralised the rest – poor devils. Last year, Michael, there were over thirty military trials, with over six hundred gaoled and nearly a hundred sentenced to death. Much of the leadership has run away to Afghanistan. The only people who take it seriously, apart from my son and his wife, are the Americans. They need it now the Cold War is over, to replace the Russians.'

At that moment, Yasmine reappeared. 'You must all be starving,' she said. 'Come and eat,' and she led the way into the dining-room.

And eat they did, a Ramadan feast, while all the world around fasted. The heavy mahogany table, covered in brilliant starched damask, was laid with fine china, heavy silver cutlery, napkins, glasses and flowers. Only half the table was laid since the party was small. There was splendid red wine and stuffed pigeons. Another set of solemn pashas stared down impassively on the sacrilege.

'What great wine,' Michael said, savouring it.

'This is always Emile's doing,' Yasmine replied.

'The thing about a government as powerful – as totalitarian – and shamelessly mean as the Egyptian,' Emile said, 'is that the system is full of holes, and if you stand at the right point, fine wines trickle through.' He paused, and added, 'But it helps to have good friends in the French Embassy.'

Sameh's spirits were restored by the good food, the wine and the listeners. He obviously loved to talk. As the meal wore on, the discussion could not fail to return to the fate of the Egyptian Communists. And the story went on after they left the table, leaving a wreckage of crumbs, dishes and red wine stains, and continued back in the sitting-room over coffee and brandy.

Bulus seemed half asleep with all this ancient history. Emile puffed a great cigar before he also dozed off. The shadows of a late autumn evening lengthened, and another call to prayer came and went.

Sameh had been at school at the time of the great demonstration of February 1946. It had been a wonderful time to be young, and they thought it would never end until the British were driven out and they had socialism. Egypt had industrialised; it now had a working class that was leading the country in a wave of anti-British strikes. The theory had seemed to fit and Communism was the most uncompromising opponent of British imperialism. Sameh and his friends had formed a communist discussion group at school. Not that they had known much about it – only that the British had to be got out, the Soviet Union was on their side and the working class was going to run the world. And then the British cracked in India! And two years later,

33

China went communist – could anyone doubt they were on the winning side? Sameh took Emile – then ten and in short pants – down to the great Misr textile mill strike in the autumn of 1947. It was something amazing, marvellous – a sea of workers, banners tossing, with a roar that could reach every corner of Egypt. And then the police went on strike, and then the hospitals. The whole country could no longer be controlled. The King kept his bags permanently packed ready to flee – remembering what happened to Louis XVI and the Tsar.

Nothing could stop them – except Colonel Nasser, and the failure to build a Communist party capable of controlling him. When the army mutinied, the Free Officers seized power in 1952 and threw out the King, the first thing they did was to crush the great textile strike in Alexandria. Sameh and his comrades could not believe it. The army executed two of the strike leaders. Then Nasser stamped on the unions, and turned what was left of them into police agencies to control the workers.

They were stunned. The patriotic military, the Communists said, were supposed to drive out the British and the King, and then make way for workers' power. How foolish they had been – and intellectually disarmed before the monster. The Communists swung into reverse and declared the Free Officers were fascists, working for the US! But again Nasser fooled them – he rejected Washington, kicked the British out of the Suez Canal and allied with Moscow. He seized the land of the old feudal landlords and distributed it to the peasants; he destroyed the Egyptian capitalist class, but he had no time at all for workers' power.

It made no kind of sense. Many of the comrades gave up and joined Nasser – after all, he was doing all the things they had demanded (except bringing in workers' power). They were well rewarded. The rest of them, Sameh and Yasmine included, who hung on to some idea of the working class liberating itself, went to gaol. Sameh was in Wahat Oasis and it wasn't so bad. But many had a much more terrible time. Many were killed, dumped in unmarked desert graves. Others were maimed with torture and, if they ever came out of gaol, permanently disabled. Their complete demoralisation made it much worse. Nasser had taken over half their programme, and reduced them to either just cheering him on or plotting treason.

Sameh still found it impossible to understand how they could have been so wrong. In the name of liberation and socialism, Nasser built a terrifying totalitarian State, another Stalinism.

Sameh paused, musing on the destruction of the radicals of his generation.

34

'More coffee,' he asked absently. 'Were you ever part of all that, Dr James – sorry, Michael?'

'No – I was always against Stalinism,' he said derisively. 'You would have called me "ultra-Left". But of course, we endlessly demonstrated for the third world – for Sukarno, Nehru, Nasser. And we all went mad in 1956 when the British, the French and the Israelis invaded the Canal.'

'Nasser didn't give us a chance to cheer him on,' Sameh continued. 'Egypt's gaols are something special when it comes to cruelty. The old Communists used to speak in awe of Tourah where prisoners wore permanent foot irons, working through the hottest days without food or drink, carrying blocks of basalt in their bare hands. Or Kharguo in the southern desert – forty-seven degrees in the shade; sandstorms, scorpions. Even the prison officers were posted there for only three months at a time.'

'You saw my son, Butrus? The eyepatch, the limp, the marks of graduation from Egypt's Gulag. He was lucky to escape alive – and only then through the good offices of his uncle Hosni whom he despises.'

'I had it quite easy by comparison – dear Hosni did his best even though he thought we were complete fools not to join the regime.

'By the time I got out of prison, the cause had become futile. What were we fighting for? The communists had intellectually defeated themselves long before they dissolved the party in 1965. Our concepts were twaddle. Nasser was not a fascist, even if he did suppress the unions. Moscow turned him into – what was that awful gobbledegook? – "a revolutionary leader of the national bourgeoisie, led by the working class in a new and unprecedented class formation that would lead inexorably to socialism". What complete bullshit as the Americans say. The Communists were the only people fooled.' He gave a hollow laugh.

'But California was my epiphany – is that the word? I went from the instinctive Stalinism of the Egyptian radicals to let it all hang out – the nineteen-sixties, the free speech movement, open all the records, black power, women's liberation, free love, stop the Vietnam War. And it seemed global – the May events in Paris, the Cultural Revolution in China. What an amazing time it was and so spontaneous. There was no Communist Party directing it or even influencing it. It was anarchism, and beautiful – a chrysanthemum in the barrel of your gun in Lisbon or a flower in your hair when you go to San Francisco.'

Sameh glowed with the recollection. 'To be young and in California at such a time was bliss. It raised a whole new agenda of hope.'

'I thought I'd lost him,' Yasmine interrupted suddenly. 'He was always a hopeless romantic. I was sure he would go off with one of those long-legged American dolls, high on pot, not caring who they did it with. But,' she squeezed his arm affectionately, 'he didn't.'

'Butrus was a teenager,' Sameh continued, 'just the right age to swallow it neat. He came back a complete anarchist. No one here could talk to him and he had to start all over again, learning to be an Egyptian.'

The first President after Nasser, Sadat had turned everything upside down. Now free markets, not nationalisation, was all the rage, the Russians were out, the Americans in and the regime allied with the Islamists to smash the left. But when the great revolt of 1977 swept the country, the younger members of the reconstructed communist parties (there were two of them then), with the Nasserists, did provide a leadership. Sadat and the Islamists denounced it as a 'revolt of the thieves and the Communists' and an attempt by the Russians to get back in. He used the opportunity to behead the Left once and for all. But then, when he broke with the Saudis and signed a peace treaty with Israel, he lost the Islamists – and they murdered him.'

'Yet I still can't get over how wrong we were,' Sameh said sadly. 'The nineteen-fifties have become a mystery to me. All that Third World stuff was such rubbish. Think of all those miles of posters – red-cheeked Albanian or North Korean girls, banners tossing over the Red Brigades, marching off into the sunrise to build another highway through the mountains.'

'It was a very modernist agenda,' Michael said with a smile, 'and I suppose Berkeley was the early warning of post-modernism: doing your own thing.'

Emile woke with a start, brushing the cigar ash off his jacket. 'What, are you still at it? You'll bore the poor man to death.'

'Not a bit,' Michael said. 'It's been a privileged education for me. But, I have shamelessly abused your hospitality, and eaten up most of the day on the excuse of lunch.'

To Michael's surprise, they all hugged him as they said goodbye.

As he stood at the doorstep, about to leave, there was a

peremptory knock. Sameh opened it to find a large armed guard standing to attention beside the door. The lift was rattling and groaning as it came up.

'Oh, Lord, I'd forgotten about Hosni. Can you stay a moment longer, Dr Michael, just to say hello?'

They returned to the apartment and sat waiting somewhat uncomfortably. The lift arrived, and with a clatter, a man looking like a more youthful Sameh, in a well-tailored three-piece suit seemed to bound out of the lift as the guard saluted, and entered the apartment at speed.

'Sorry to be so late and in such a hurry,' he mumbled as he hugged the family in turn.

'And you must be Dr Michael James,' he said turning to Michael. 'I've heard much about you from Sameh. The two of you,' he looked with a twinkle at Sameh, 'must have had a great time, turning over the past. I'm sorry I missed it. But I'm in such a hurry, I can hardly do more than shake your hand.'

And with that, he turned towards the door as if preparing to leave.

'But that's outrageous,' Sameh protested. 'We don't see you for weeks, and then you barely set foot in the door.'

'Can I offer you a lift, Dr James, as small compensation for my excessive discourtesy. And, Sameh, I am coming to you on Thursday – without fail.'

More embraces and shaking of hands, and to Michael's surprise, he was swept into the lift. More armed guards saluting, as they hurried to a large black limousine with smoked-glass windows. The guards opened the doors, and after letting them in, ran to the front to get in. Everything happened at great speed.

They sat in silence as the car moved smoothly away. Hosni was rummaging in an enormous briefcase. He found what he was looking for.

'I'm really sorry about this, but there is an emergency Cabinet meeting this afternoon, and I can't dodge it. Now where can I take you?'

Michael explained, and Hosni told the driver.

'So how did you find my oldest brother? Although I don't see him and Yasmine as often as I would like, he seems to have been moping in recent weeks and I hope your visit cheered him up.'

'He seemed fine,' Michael said, 'except when your nephew, Butrus, and his wife came to pay their respects.'

The face of the Minister darkened.

'Ah, you met them, did you? A dangerous couple – to themselves, to their parents, even to me. I could help Sameh and Yasmine if they got in trouble, but I can't help *them*. They threaten to bring the roof in on us all.

'Of course, one can't blame her,' he mused as if to himself. 'She was a waif. Butrus lifted her out of the gutter, invented her almost. But he should know better – he's educated and not at all stupid. He's flirting with all the worst in the world, and so close to the fire,' the Minister's voice hardened with menace.

'He's going to get burned. And it may not be long at all before that happens. We've put up with a great deal from people like Butrus, professionals who do very well in our society, but then use their position to mislead the innocent and ignorant. They're Pied Pipers. And no responsible government can put up with that for very long.'

There was another silence, and Michael, trying to steer the conversation away from these dangerous waters, asked:

'So Leila was born to a poor family, was she?'

'Not exactly, but through a series of appalling mistakes when she was young, she fell right to the bottom of Cairo society – and that is much lower than you can possibly conceive, Dr James. Only Butrus broke her fall.'

They arrived at Michael's apartment building, and as a guard from the front ran round to open the door, Hosni pressed his card into Michael's hand.

'If you need any help, don't hesitate to call me, and I hope we meet again soon.'

As Michael walked to the entrance, he was conscious of the porter looking on with admiration, as well as other bystanders, a couple of dogs, some lounging policemen, two men in grubby singlets and skirts, sitting on a string bed, and a wrinkled old man with a wheeled stall selling hot *baladi* bread. He was meanwhile regretting that he had not exploited the opportunity to cross-examine Hosni on his transition from being a Communist to supporting Nasser. He would probably not get another opportunity.

4

Letter 1

Mlle Natalie Kolakowski, London, to her brother, M. Jean Kolakowski, Geneva.

London, 13 Jan, 1872.

Dearest, dearest, darling Jeannot,

How wonderful, *wonderful* – at last! To be able to write to you without the censor reading everything. And how satisfying that you are *safe* in Switzerland, far from these wolves in Paris. Even if without your poor arm, – such a terrible loss, along with all our failed hopes for a future world.

But now, at last, my darling, I can write to you without Mme Grandier – do you remember that monster with the long solitary whisker who kept the Cambrai post office ? – passing my letters to the *gendarmerie* and the cockroaches of M. Favre at the Interior Ministry. She was a *terrible* Bonapartist, proclaiming that that disgusting little beetle was the greatest blessing of France, and, if we didn't agree, all of us Kolakowskis should be sent back to Poland or wherever we came from, if not worse! She must be so cast down now that Louis Napoleon is banished to Chislehurst (and what an insult that the wretched English who so roundly defeated his father should offer him refuge – to save him from the French!), the Empire is no more, and only the boring bourgeois Thiers – is left to reign, entirely without pomp or glory, absolutely none of the Emperor's gold braid, tassles and feathers.

It has been *so* long – years of unexpected turmoil and cruel defeats – since you proposed the arrangement for me to be here, as 'paying guest' in the Marx family to teach French conversation to the youngest Marx daughter. You must have forgotten all about it by now. Was it 1869? Three whole years ago? So long and so much has happened – can anyone *imagine* so many momentous occurrences in such a short time? All those heroic events make mockery of a little thing like learning a language! Now it looks as though I shall probably learn more German than English, especially how to *swear* like a Westphalian carter! Nor do I think the young Mademoiselle Eleanor Marx will learn much of conversational French, we are too busy babbling in our gibberish of German, English and French – with some Latin thrown in!

All the terrible things that have happened in these past three years made the old plan impossible. In any case, Eleanor now tells me that, in the meantime, M. Engels, M. Marx's old friend and closest collaborator, has reached a financial arrangement to allow M. Marx to complete his great work so that the family is not now so poor, and does not need the little money Papa contributes. Still, it was a kindly thought by Papa, and an act of great international solidarity by your *patron* in Paris, M. Besançon, to try to help the Marxes in their troubles then.

We little thought, when Papa reached the agreement with M. Marx, how different we would all be by the time it was accomplished. While I am here, you are exiled in Geneva, and, oh horror! without your poor arm, and the revolution which carried *so* many of our highest hopes *hideously* betrayed, and French soil soaked in the blood of our heroes, our finest. It makes me *so* angry to think of it. How dare they speak of the rule of law when so many of our *communards* – 20,000, 30,000? – were shot or sabred without charge or trial, thrown in unmarked graves? They care nothing for the law nor for their wretched religion – only that they shall remain in power and exploit us all. Their morality is only to pile the dead heroes so high, *no one* will ever again *dare* to challenge that *monster*, the *hateful* French Republic. They murdered Paris and the *finest* of a generation. Jean, please forgive me. I must stop since I get *too* emotional and cannot write – you see the tears on the page – the rage is insupportable.

A little later. You cannot imagine my apprehension when I came to London. This city's notorious fogs in January are one horror – and you know how I suffer from chilblains and colds. But then, imagine! I was coming to the house of *Prussians* after all the savagery that Prussia and that black monster Bismarck inflicted upon us – laying waste our lovely country and *stealing* Alsace and Lorraine. Papa who is *so* very good in these matters comforted me that M. Marx was *nothing* to do with Bismarck and the rulers of Prussia, but I was still not completely convinced that I should come. And one can see that others might share my suspicions – Eleanor tells me that some of her father's enemies maintain that *he* is an *agent* for Bismarck. My fears were completely *silly*. The Marx family gave me a most gratifying warm welcome.

Let me tell you something about them. They live in quite a large new and elegant house, Number 1, Maitland Park Road, standing on its own in a new leafy suburb of the city, quite high up, with a small flower garden in front and a large walled garden behind. You cannot imagine how *fierce* M. Marx looks. He has a massive square frame and a big woolly head, a strong nose and dark complexion (the family call him 'Moor' or 'Mohr'), ferocious black eyebrows and an iron grey beard.

He often wears an eyeglass, and seems always to be smoking cigarettes. He works all the time in his study consuming *oceans* of black coffee, up to midnight or later (except when he goes for long walks). Tussy (this is the pet family name for Eleanor, the youngest daughter and my special care) says she is afraid he will do himself some harm again if he continues to work so hard, especially as he eats little (and then only 'strong' foods – peppery or smoked). But he is almost *alone* in organising all the sections of 'the International,' which is what they call his great association of working men, as well as doing all his theoretical work. It seems he has written a book in German about 'capital' (I do not yet know what it means, only that it is *not* about capital cities) and it is now being published in French and Russian. He is so busy. Tussy has now been given charge of answering some of his correspondence and she is very honoured and *enthusiastic* in this.

I was quite *fearful* at meeting the great man, trembling that he would be so haughty before such a little worm as your sister, or that I would not understand his German English. But he gave me a *wonderful* welcome in *impeccable* French, saying how much he admired Papa and all he did in Poland in the 1848 revolution and afterwards for the great cause of Polish liberation; he said he had heard of your role in the Commune and its defence, and was grieved that you had received such a severe injury. He was full of admiration for our M. Blanqui and his leadership of the revolutionaries in Paris, a 'grand old revolutionary of the first rank,' he called him. He said he hoped I would read his report on the Commune (and give him my opinion!). So you see what a *grand* person your little sister has become, conversing with the mighty! I expect you will be quite overcome with *envy*!

Mme Marx is saintly and *very* kind; she made me tell her what happened to poor Mama, and then, with tears in her eyes, embraced me, saying she hoped that I would let her be a mother to me while I was in their home. Tussy – Eleanor – is exceedingly charming and so extremely energetic and full of life, I do not know how this poor little country mouse will ever keep up with her. I have not yet met the eldest daughter, Jenny, although she is here in London, but the third, Laura (M. Marx calls her 'Kakadou'!), is, as you know, married to Dr Paul Lafargue, and is at present abroad – in Portugal or Spain, I think. But the most wonderful member of this 'Prussian' family is Lenchen, the old housekeeper. She was a 'gift' from Mme. Marx's mother to her when she was twenty-five and has cared for the family ever since. She is so kind to everybody that they all adore her; but Tussy, the 'baby,' is her special favourite and can do no wrong.

The whole family is, like us, in *despair* at the defeat of the Commune. They are filled with awe at the bravery of the *communards* in defending themselves against the heavy weapons and artillery of the army, and rage at the *injustice* of so many being killed or driven to exile. Especially Jenny, Tussy tells me, who is cast into *great* gloom and thinks the revolution is now postponed for a generation. Everybody is spending much time trying to raise money for the *communards* (all your old friends in the Commune!) who are refugees here in London, to find them places to live and work. Many are *desperate*, wretched and starving, sleeping on the streets in this awful winter. The English trade unions have done much to help, they say.

Did you hear that those monsters, Thiers and Favre and their 'French Republic' have demanded the 'extradition'of the *communards* from London to France – as *felons(!)*? The English are still considering it, but they say the Swiss might agree to return their refugees – can it be true? Oh, how I *fear* for you, that you might once again have to flee, and perhaps this time go all that way to the Americas. Tussy says there will be big demonstrations to stop extradition happening. I *dearly* long that it should be so. At least in Geneva you are not so far from Papa and me – but in America, I fear you would be lost *forever*.

The household is *chaotic*, and so untidy, nothing can be found. It is so different to my quiet peaceful life at Cambrai. Everybody is always so *busy*, and there are endless callers from everywhere and meetings and comings and goings from all the world. It is *impossible* to know what is happening. Even catching the names is difficult though Tussy tries hard to keep me abreast. She confessed yesterday that she was glad I knew so little about her father's *terrible* scorn for our M. Proudhon. There are so many people, it seems, M. Marx scorns. I will have to work hard to catch up.

There seem to be so many attacks on M. Marx – a Mr Bradlaugh has attacked him for being a Bonapartist! Somebody else thinks he is an agent for the other side, the Prussians! M. Marx is also, it seems, *very angry* with something called the 'Alliance' (and a M. Bakunin), which Tussy says is *secretly* conspiring to destroy the International. I hope I will be able to understand all this in time. At present I am all in a great muddle and not to be helped.

Dear, dear, Jean I have written too much. Do not expect to have so much sisterly chatter in future. But they are calling me to Sunday lunch. This is a *grand* English meal, it seems, with roast beef prepared by Lenchen, and all the family and friends gather, so I mayn't delay.

I dearly hope you are well and that the cough is now abated. I *long* to hear news of you. I expect, like me, you are a little homesick. I long for my little room in Cambrai, with flowers along the window-sill, far away from here, which seems perpetually in the eye of a *great* storm. But then you had storms enough in Paris for all those great days, so Geneva might now seem quiet and dull for you. I worry for poor dear Papa, alone now that we are both away. I treasure the memory of dear Mama, but I would feel much more composed in my mind if father were to marry again and have a little loving care. Do you not agree?

Forever your loving sister,

Natalie.

5

Letter 2

My dearest Jeannot,

What a *joy* it was to receive your letter and hear that you are well – or as well as can be expected given all your trials – and so busy working with so many *communard* exiles in Geneva. It is *good* to hear so many of your friends were saved, and you are not *completely* alone and cast down.

You can imagine my *astonishment*, however, to hear that you have actually met the great *monster*, M. Bakunin, who is destroying M. Marx's International. I had no idea when I mentioned the great hostility towards him in the Marx household that he was in Geneva, nor that he is both a *grand* Russian prince and a wonderful old revolutionary. I dare not breathe a word of this in this house or they will throw me out as a spy! Your meeting with him sounds very inspiring, even if his French is very Russian. (Do not all the Russians speak French like the Poles?) M. Bakunin's advanced views are most interesting, especially his belief that we would *all* live in peace and harmony if *only* the *violent* State could be ended. How true that is of our poor France! But I am sad to think he holds M. Marx responsible for the defeat of the Commune because he would not insist immediately that the *communards* abolish the French State. However, Tussy tells me that her father and the General Council (the leadership of the International) had *no* role at all in the Commune, so, she says, the charge is false. You know this better than me but she says the leadership of the Commune were either followers of M. Proudhon (who agrees with M. Bakunin) or our own dear Blanqui. Incidentally, is there news of him, Blanqui, 'the Old One'? I *fear* for his health now that he is back in prison – 33 of his 67 years, and those the best years, have been behind bars!

The *scandalous* stories about the Commune are *endless* – some reactionary newspapers said M. Marx, a Prussian, and his International, organised and financed the Commune to help the Prussian invasion! But you know all this, and probably saw the *Figaro* story that Marx, to the contrary, supported the anti-Prussian side and was really a Bonapartist! How he could be both working for Bismarck and Prussia, *and* for their enemies, Buonaparte and the French Empire, is quite beyond me – and with no money at all to pay for such ambitions, let alone for his dinner!

We celebrated Tussy's 17th birthday on the 16th, and so I met not only Jenny, the eldest sister – *very* serious – but also M. Engels, Marx's main collaborator. Tussy is a dear, but *so* active and energetic, I cannot keep up. Her favourites are Shakespeare (her room is decked out as a Shakespeare museum!) and Garibaldi – and she *hates* cold mutton! She has lots of pets that she loves madly, and she is such *great* fun, bubbling and gay (if I cannot always follow her English, let alone her German), but, I fear, far too bold and forthright for most suitors (more of this later).

The *obsessions* of her life, if not the *communards*, are the Irish struggles, and most recently, the imprisoning of many leaders of the movement for Irish independence. They are called 'Fenians'. Her Irish concern seems to come from her great attachment to a friend in Manchester, Lizzie Burns, a great friend of M. Engels, M. Marx's friend who resides in that city. Tussy is *much* mocked as 'the Poor Neglected Nation' (Ireland) because she uses the phrase so often. Two years ago, she says, she dragged her mama and papa to a great demonstration in Hyde Park in support of the Fenians – it was, she says, a glorious sea of red, green and white banners (the colours of the Irish movement) and of red Jacobin caps! Last November, one of the Fenian prisoners, a Jeremiah O'Donovan Russa, was elected to the House of Commons. Tussy says she was *mad* with excitement.

Tussy has also travelled. She went to Paris two years ago and loved it. How *envious* of her I am! Living so much closer, in Cambrai, but *never* going to Paris in my whole life! More seriously, last year she went with her sister, Jenny, to stay with the Lafargues, but they had to flee to Spain to escape the hunt for *communards*. After Tussy and Jenny had been to Spain, they were arrested on the border, as they returned to France, by our people and interrogated, Tussy says, by 'some reactionary count' from Paris. Are the French police not despicable? Anyway, they were finally released. Tussy tosses her curls in derision at this 'Great Adventure' and giggles at the count, but they were *indeed* fortunate to escape without worse happening.

She has *lots* of lovers, especially now with so many of our countrymen here (with nothing to do but imagine delicious liaisons!), and she loves to flirt in the most charming ways. You must know some of her beaux – Leo Frankel, a Hungarian and something important in the Commune? And then there is M. Lissagary who, as you probably know, is said to have been the last fighter to withdraw from the last barricade. He is *very* handsome and debonair. He has written something on the history of the Commune and loves to read it to Tussy when they can escape the crowd. I think she favours him. But I fear her mama *disapproves* of all this and does not want a second French son-in-law.

All the family is *so* worried about the International. It seems your M. Bakunin is seen as the main enemy. Tussy says he has stolen the Italian youth away from Mazzini for his 'anarchism,' and also the Spanish; there is, she says, trouble with the Belgians who say the General Council and M. Marx are *over-mighty*. And the English trade unions who were always the bedrock of the International are growing cool. Many disapprove of the support the General Council gives to the 'Fenians' and to their 'terrorism,' and some resigned in protest when the Council – under M. Marx's goading – championed the Commune. Tussy says the English are becoming frightfully *respectable* and now they have won Parliamentary recognition, want *nothing* to do with all these wretched squabbling foreigners and their violence; they just want to be favoured by the Liberals (now in the government under Mr Gladstone). So you see why the family is afraid. The International is going in many different directions and the revolutionaries are quarrelling bitterly

And all this is happening at a time when the powers that be think the International is the *greatest* monster in the whole wide world, behind *everything* that happens anywhere! The General Council is even supposed to have been behind the great fires in Chicago last October! You must have heard that Thiers and Favre are trying to create a *grand coalition of powers*, led by France, that will intervene in *any* country to put down revolutionary agitation. The British are cool but Bismarck and Prussia may favour the idea, and could unite with Austria and Russia as they did in 1848 to crush all progressive

46

movements. M. Marx is unperturbed; he says that, if the workers are united, all their grand coalitions of rulers cannot change much.

By the by, M. Marx held forth at some length at lunch yesterday on why he disagreed with M. Bakunin. He says MB does not understand that Europe is now becoming dominated by *manufacturing*. This creates for the first time a 'mass industrial working class' with the size, discipline and culture to liberate itself and come to power to create socialism. It does not need the old revolutionary conspiracies and sects and acts of terrorism that led our revolutions in France. MB, he says, is part of the old tradition of small secret societies, conspiracies of what he calls 'petty bourgeois elements' (I think he means middle class and professional people like us). They commit acts of terror to incite the mass of the poor to revolt. That can only work, he says, where there is no 'industrial working class' as in Russia or Italy or Spain. As an innocent, I thought what he was saying about MB sounded very like our M. Blanqui. But Tussy explained that MB wants to *abolish* the State as the *first* step in the revolution. Tussy says that abolishing the State means the workers will have no power to defend themselves and so will make *inevitable* a counter-revolution of the old order. M. Marx, however, agrees with M. Blanqui that the workers must remain armed and keep a strong State – in M.Blanqui's phrase, 'a dictatorship of the proletariat.' For your little dunce of a sister, it all seems fairly *silly* to fall out over such things, but M. Marx is *very* fierce on the question.

How delighted I was to hear from you that the Swiss may reject the French request to extradite the *communards*. That is *wonderful* news and you are, at least for the moment, safe, and not making that *dreadful* journey to New York. Here, M. Marx published the news about the Favre request for extradition of the *communards* as felons to France – and it made a great to-do; M. Marx believes that this 'forced the hand' of Mr Gladstone· so he was obliged to reject the request. There was *much* rejoicing among all your friends! But M. Marx says Mr Gladstone is still helping Thiers – his letters to Europe, which are all carefully routed through Ostend, are redirected by the British through Calais so M. Favre can snoop on them!

My only other news, already mentioned, is that I met M. Engels. He is a tall bony man with sharp features, long sandy whiskers and a ruddy complexion. He is very talkative, merry and sparkling, and I understand why Tussy adores him (as he adores her). It seems he is a *great* authority on military matters – the family call him 'the

General.' He told me about the terrible conditions the Irish face in Ireland and in his last home, Manchester.

Finally, darling Jeannot, I have heard from dear Papa and he is well if a little grieving that we are all away and he has only work to console him. Do write to him when you can since he *longs* to hear news of you. And, *very important*, let me hear from you soon.

Always your loving sister,

Natalie.

6

Leila I

When he next saw Leila, she had been panic-stricken. It was a bizarre coincidence. He was on al-Nil in Dokki. He had been tramping the west bank of the Nile under the pretext of searching for a shop there that sold rough recycled glassware. But in reality he was just exploring. It was dusk and the road was packed with cars racing in serried ranks, horns blaring as they went. He glimpsed dimly on the other side what he took to be a frieze on an apartment block. He crossed the road to see it, threading his way by stages through the speeding traffic. Cairo cars were remarkable for missing pedestrians, provided they walked calmly and predictably.

The apartment building had a grand marble portico and mahogany double doors. He could not read the Arabic name-plate in ornate brass. Nor, in the now gathering dark, could he make out the detail of the frieze.

As he stood to one side, peering upwards, one of the doors opened and a large man, in black with close cropped white hair and beard, appeared at the top of the stairs. He stood for a moment, looking about – his eye swept briefly over Michael – and then beckoned to a long car with smoked-glass windows parked at the side. It slid out of the side road quietly and drew up in front of the steps, the back door opening automatically. The man made a gesture to someone inside the building. A woman emerged hurriedly, dressed in a voluminous black gown, her head also covered in black. Gulf Arabs, Michael thought absently, on holiday in the Cairo fleshpots. But it wasn't.

He noticed in quick succession that the man was wearing a prominent gold cross round his neck, and his fingers were covered in rings. He carried himself as people do who are accustomed to exercise authority. The woman hurried down the steps to the car,

49

but there was time for Michael to note that her face was not fully covered, and then, that she was almost certainly Leila. He couldn't be absolutely sure in the gathering dusk, until she turned, looking about her and suddenly caught his eye. In an instant she recognised him and knew she had been seen. Dark though it was, he thought she cringed in horror before she was swallowed in the car. The man gestured impatiently and the car swung smoothly away from the pavement into the stream of traffic.

Michael was certain she had seen him, and it was not long before it became clear. The following day, he was in his office on the Greek campus. There was a light tap at his door.

To his astonishment, it was Leila, again dressed from head to toe in black. He wondered idly whether it was permitted for a pious Muslim woman to be alone with a man who was not related and wondered whether it was not dangerous for them both. She was breathless and ill-at-ease. But this time, she did not lower her gaze but stared at him with a steady gaze. This time, also, she offered her hand to shake.

He welcomed her, gesturing to a chair. She sat on the edge, her hands tightly clasped together. The black *hijab* seemed only to exaggerate the wonderful symmetry of her face, to highlight the brilliant green of her eyes.

'Dr James,' she said at last, and once started, became brisk and professional. 'I am sorry to trouble you. I don't know whether you remember me? We met briefly a few weeks ago in the house of my father-in-law, Dr Cyprian.'

She paused, and then in a rush, 'I have a rather embarrassing request to make to you.' She paused again, as if uncertain how to proceed. Michael murmured that of course, he remembered her, and would be delighted to be of service.

'You saw me yesterday, leaving a building in Dokki?' she said, staring at him intently.

'Yes, I thought it might be you, but it was too dark to be sure.'

'The man there, showing me out, is an official of the Coptic Church. He knows my father well. My father is a Coptic priest, but we do not see each other now. I go to the official occasionally to get news of my father who is now rather ill. However, I hope you can understand that it is rather dangerous – with my present commitments – for me to have any contact with the Coptic establishment, so we try to keep these short meetings secret.

50

Normally we are able to be more discreet, but this was an emergency...'

She paused again, staring at him as if to test whether this story carried any conviction. 'In addition,' she went on, 'a long time ago, before I was married, my husband Khaled, wrongly suspected I might have some special relationship with that man. Khaled was, I fear, rather jealous and forbade me to see him. But he is my only link to my father.'

Michael thought he heard a catch in her throat, as if she might weep. But she remained dry-eyed.

'For this reason,' she continued, 'I would be grateful if you would not tell my husband that you saw me. I know it is wrong of me, a perfect stranger, to ask such a thing, but it is important for me.'

Michael doubted that the story was true – two reasons for the same thing encouraged scepticism. But he had to admit that he enjoyed the bond of complicity with this beautiful woman, a secret between them that excluded her husband. He was, he reflected, not too old to be foolish.

'I won't say a word,' he said. 'And I hope your father recovers soon.'

'He is now very old,' she went on, 'and the worst can happen. But thank you for agreeing – you cannot know what a relief it is to me.'

She rose from the chair abruptly. 'I'm sorry but I have a class just about to begin, so I'd better go or I shall be late.'

Michael stood to shake her hand. 'Do you teach here?' he said with surprise.

'Yes, part-time on Tuesday mornings, and just for this academic year: a junior course on the Egyptian public health system.'

She had not lowered her eyes once while she had been in his office, scrutinising him closely to detect whether his promise had any value.

'Maybe we could meet for a coffee sometime when you are here?' Michael said, alarmed at his audacity. She stared at him in surprise.

'Perhaps,' she said doubtfully. 'But I must go.'

This time she again shook his hand without equivocation, the firm warm grasp of a strong and confident person.

And she was gone, the rustling black tent, scudding out of his office. Michael lay back in his chair, tilting on two legs, with his hands behind his head. He reflected that he would probably never know the true story.

7

Letter 3

London, 10 Feb, 1872.

My dearest Jeannot,

London is *woeful*. When it is not invisible in those famous fogs – that clog the throat, the eyes, the lungs, all, then it is *drenched* with cold rain, the 'drizzle' (a complete misery). And the days seem so short and dull because it is often *so* dark and gloomy. How can a people bear such a dreadful climate? They are all grey now – grey skins and hair and clothes and everything. And they all wear black, so there is no colour at all. No wonder they flee their island to make an empire in all those parts of the world where there is colour and light and warmth!

There, you see, dear Jean, how *dreadfully* gloomy we all are, and how I long for us three to be together again in my beautiful Cambrai, and even more, to be there in the spring with the hawthorn in bloom and all the new greens so bright and cheerful and charming. Out with the old and the grey – in with youth and laughter and colour! It seems here the gloom will never lift. We all have dreadful colds, and weep and stream all the time. M. Marx has inflammation in his right eye from overwork at his desk. Mrs Anderson, the physician, is ever in and out of the house, treating our sickrooms one by one as if it were a hospital! Only Lenchen keeps the ship on course, singing the live-long day in the kitchen, the only warm place in the house.

The family is also very cast down, for, it seems, little Schnappy is most poorly. You remember he is M. Marx's only grandson (two others, born earlier, have most wretchedly expired), child of the middle daughter, Laura, and Paul Lafargue whom you know. It seems he never properly recovered from cholera last August, and now, with the crushing of the Commune, the family has had to flee from France to Spain and he has no rest. What a poor waif, all his life in flight. I pray he may make some recovery – poor Tussy worries all the time.

Now, dear Jean, to your letter. I should speak to you most *seriously* although I am younger than you, but since we both lack a mother, I must be given a *little* indulgence in one as close as you. I do *worry* about all these wild-eyed fiery Russians with whom you now seem to consort, and all the talk of retribution against the criminals in power, a reign of terror. I know that when our rulers are *so* cruel, so lawless and wicked – as Thiers and his gang of ruffians have been in murdering France's finest – that it seems nothing but the most cruel vengeance is demanded to scourge the villains. Our terror to match theirs, and, once more, a Jacobin guillotine on each street corner as in 1792 to punish the rogues. But this is *fantasy*, a dream, which cannot be, for we have been *defeated* and most cruelly so. Indeed, does individual assassination of the mighty ever do any good? Do the accused ever *learn* or change the way they use their power? Does not the overwhelming arrogance of the State always conquer whatever government there is, returning it to terror as soon as, with false grief, they have buried the dead?

Tussy says terror may work in places like Russia where the *monstrous* tyranny of the tsars allows no room at all for any *critical* opposition, and the mass of the people are so hopelessly oppressed and wretched. But in England, this is not so. The new 'working class', she says, will advance steadily on power, without individual acts of terror. She passionately supports the struggle of the Fenians (you remember, those who struggle for the liberation of the Irish nation), and admits that acts of terror may be inevitable there. But such action by hotheads only serves to *lessen* the enthusiasm of the workers. In democracies, do we not have the vote, can we not turn out governments without murder? England now has mighty unions of workers and can they not discipline the rulers? In Ireland – like Russia – the ruling power has been so cruel for so long (and the 'potato famine' is surely one of the cruellest acts of any regime – I will tell you of it later), directly attacking the English chiefs is understandable in raising the mass of the peasants. But acts of Fenian violence in England only serve to *demoralise* the English workers and drive them into *hatred* of the Irish and into the arms of their rulers. She says Irish and English workers must *unite* if they are to destroy 'capitalism'. For that, *all* the politics must be *public* so that the workers can read a free press and know what is happening, but terrorism requires the utmost secrecy. In these matters, France is more like England than Russia, and wreaking retribution may *drive* the people into the arms of Thiers!

However, all this is less important than that the enemy agents are everywhere, waiting only to pounce. In your cafés and taverns, you cannot speak of these things since all the walls and alcoves have eyes and ears. In their drink, these exiles give everything away. The *communard* groups in Geneva, like those in London, are full of the spies of Thiers. Wild talk of retribution can lead to the most *dire* results, and in the police dungeons, who will say who was guilty and who not. You must be more careful, Jean, and think of Papa and me who rest so many hopes in you.

Later. I was dragged away by Tussy who wanted to show me the new tricks she has taught Whiskey (her much over-loved dog). But then I thought again about all these wretched Russians. The basic question, Jean, my dear, is your honour, or rather, our honour as a family. *We cannot seem to approve of murder, to allow ourselves, no matter how unwittingly, to be thought to approve of death by violence – unless we are absolutely clear, that there is no other way.* And I dearly hope you will never have to make such a choice, for it is indeed a momentous matter. Very well: I shall stop this solemn sermonising!

I hear much talk here of the Cercle d'Etudes Sociales. It is the club of the *communards* in London. The discussions sound most *lively* and interesting and they have visiting speakers. I long to go even though I am not a revolutionary in exile, but I would love to hear talk of our beloved France. Is all now lost? We destroyed the Empire of Louis Napoleon but did not create the socialism of our dreams. However, as you well know, it is not at all *dignified* for a respectable woman to attend such a meeting of men, even we who claim descent from the heroic women of Jacobin Paris. What a *tedium* it is, this wretched business of being the wrong sex! However, I have met one or two members, and talk much when I can with the charming M. Hyppolyte Lissagaray, whom I mentioned in my earlier letter. He is quite a beau of Tussy's (I think she thinks they are 'engaged', for pledges have been exchanged!). He is a bold and brave fellow who, as you know, is supposed to have stormed the Palais Bourbon in Paris as well as organised the army of the Commune – let alone being the last man on the last barricade! But sadly, in the Marx family, no one seems to like him. Tussy says her father regards him as *hot-headed* and undisciplined, even if he has much courage. I think also he does not approve of M. Marx's idea of a *workers'* political party. I fear the path to happiness for Tussy will not be smooth!

I have also now heard at length from M. Engels, M. Marx's collaborator, and he is a splendid fellow, *most* interesting. He spoke much of the *terrible* conditions in Manchester where he lived for long and how always the worst conditions are suffered by the Irish. This is the second city of the country, like Lyons in France. It seems when the great manufacturing industries developed there, the mills, the hungry Irish flocked to the city for work. But much as they worked, they were driven in to the most dreadful slums behind the grand main streets. Slip away from the great thoroughfares only for a moment, and you will see, he says, the blackest slums of Europe. Here in this great empire, so full of pride, prison conditions for the majority exist, except that prisoners usually have water and a dry place to lay their head, but here thousands of children and mothers are cast into the gutters with the rats. He says that generally people only live for 30 years. One day there will be such rage at this tyranny, whether in Ireland or here in the 'motherland.' M. Engels promised to lend me the book he has written on the subject.

So, *dear* Jean, loving greetings from a London sunk deep in despair and gloom. Please forgive me if my *lecture* is too hard. You know it comes from a loving heart that cares only for your happiness in these *most* troubled times.

Your ever loving sister,

Natalie.

8

Letter 4

London, 24 Feb, 1872.

Dearest Jean,

So much ado here with the coming and going of people to see the Bonaparte himself. You know he fled here after his great defeat by the Prussians and the British gave him sanctuary – as with the *communards* after him. He made his lair in Chislehurst, a place not far from London, and though, I suppose, it is not at all as grand as Versailles, he manages to lead a quiet and comfortable life. The dear Empress, Eugénie, does needlework and takes tea with the local dignatories who remember the days when France was glorious and great. M. Crémieux is come from Paris with an army captain to see him. Do you think they have *any* hope to restore the monster – a creature so hated, even Thiers seems a lesser shade of black! Two others that Tussy says are old followers of your Mr Bakunin and his 'Alliance', Albert Richard and Gaspard Blanc, are also said to have declared for Bonaparte and a restoration of the Empire! Imagine such a bizarre project? France has, I hope, now had enough of the wretched Bonapartes and their pretensions of glory – let them return to Corsica and there lead modest and industrious lives!

Meanwhile, I hear that 'the Old One', our dear M. Blanqui, is at last brought to trial again after his court martial at Versailles two years ago. I earnestly *grieve* for his health now he is come to such an age. He is the only true patriot and yet they scorn him! Since the Great Revolution, he alone kept faith, a giant in his native land whose whole life has been dedicated to cleansing France of all that is backward, and yet he will die in an unmarked grave.

I fear your M. Bakunin is now a *great* enemy here. Not one good word can be said of him, although Tussy tells me that her father once thought highly of him. They say that on the barricades of Dresden in

1848, he was most noble and his companion, the German composer, Wagner, was so inspired he has now written many works of opera with Bakunin as the hero. But here in London all talk is of his conspiracy to destroy the International, to help Bismarck and Thiers in their evil work to enslave Europe.

I agree with what you say in your letter that it is strange why M. Marx wishes to restrict the revolution only to industrial workers, what he calls 'proletariat' (Blanqui, I believe, calls all labouring people 'proletariat'). I hesitate to think, as Mr Bakunin seems to do, that we may expect all to respond to the call for revolution – from the nobility, the army to the brigands, the beggars and the great legions of ruined peasants. Perhaps in Russia all these things are different – and after all M. Bakunin is himself from the nobility and responded to the call. Students everywhere seem to be the *noblest* creatures, willing to sacrifice everything of their young lives to liberate the people. However, in England, the students do not at all seem to want to sacrifice themselves. The great lords, the mighty managers of railways, factories, mines and ports, let alone the polite ladies in their homes, think nothing of revolution.

Tussy tells me that all this – as in Russia – was in the past before 'capitalism' made such great cities, such great concentrations of factory workers. Once the workers realise their power to hold the country to ransom, nothing can stop them. And there is no need of students and the rest (all those whom, it seems, M. Marx insists on calling 'petty bourgeois'). But there must be some truth in what M. Bakunin says: that once the factory workers become better off, they will become bourgeois themselves. The great working men of London live in very neat houses with curtains and gardens, with lots of books and even *pianos* about them. Can they be for revolution? It is *very* confusing! I am also puzzled that we must *await* the right conditions in the development of the industrial working class before attempting revolution. How will we ever know if we do not try? It could take years of waiting; and meanwhile, the ardent heroes, eager for action, will grow cold, old and weary. I am interested that M.Bakunin agrees with me in this, that one can *never* know when the time is ripe unless one tries to act *now*. Could Brutus know that Rome would not rise if he did not act to slay the tyrant now? Surely the *deed* is needed to inspire the masses? The misery of the people is *so* great, they will all respond, I know, if someone has the courage to try, if they be noble in intention and action.

I am so glad that you are able to apply yourself so earnestly to your studies, but I still fear the magic potions of M. Bakunin may turn your brain! We have still to remake France, and Russia must wait a while!

Shall you resume your architectural studies again? You had nearly qualified with M. Besançon before the Commune. It would be so grand if you might once again be able to work. Are you able to draw now? Of course, it will be most difficult with your poor arm, but perhaps you can teach yourself once more. You had such talent there, it must not be allowed to waste.

I am sad that you have dreams of dear Mama, which are so melancholy. In my case, I am sad because my memories of her grow dim, no matter how much I try to keep them green. All I recall properly now is Papa's sad face, the tears in his eyes. But I can no longer hear Mama's voice as I used to, hear her lullabies, and catch her scent. A sad note to end on!

Today is one of the rare ones with a little sad watery sunlight, so we are all to go on a great expedition to Hampstead Heath, a vast park to the north of which the Marxes live, and I am called. So this short note must suffice for the moment.

Your loving sister,

Natalie.

9

Khaled I

Michael met Khaled a second time by accident. He had agreed to give a public lecture: 'Trends in modern terrorism'. There was a good crowd in the Oriental Room in the main campus. He recognised Khaled Cyprian almost immediately, sitting at the back. He was sitting next to a small thin man in jeans, almost completely bald; they were chatting animatedly. Michael noticed him because he was wearing dark glasses even though the room was quite dark.

After the lecture and the discussion, the audience streamed out to the foyer for refreshments. Michael spoke to several people as he searched for Khaled, finally finding him, standing alone beside one of the pillars.

'How kind of you to come,' Michael said.

'No, it was my pleasure – and an education. Though I don't think you can use the word "terrorism" about those who fight vicious governments, unless you use the same word about the vicious governments themselves.'

'I agree,' Michael said. 'But in one lecture, there isn't time to change the language. I use the word as the audience does, even if it involves a political judgement.'

'What you had to say about the continuities,' Khaled went on, 'between guerrilla warfare in the sixties and seventies – or political assassinations in the nineteenth century, and Islamism today, was interesting, even if I have some disagreement. After all, Islam is not just a surface decoration of what is basically the same thing even when it is undertaken by atheists. I'd love a chance to talk more about it. Are you free afterwards? Can I offer you a drink, or will you be too tired?'

Michael was again surprised. Khaled could neither drink nor be seen publicly talking to a foreigner. But Michael could not miss the

59

opportunity. They arranged to meet after the meeting broke up.

The main gate was in darkness as Michael came out. The guard, recognising him, nodded and, a mark of privilege, refrained from searching his briefcase. Michael could not see Khaled. He seemed to be hiding in the shadow, but he stepped out as he saw Michael.

They walked through the dark streets to the Estoril, a Lebanese restaurant, which Khaled knew. It was almost empty at this hour, and it was easy to find a table. Michael ordered a Stella beer. Khaled had tea.

Khaled was unusually animated, almost excited, unlike the sullen person he had been in his father's sitting-room.

'I confess,' he said, 'it was a pleasure to listen to your English, apart from what you were saying. It's a long time since I was in Cambridge. I loved it though I also felt guilty – the peace and ease seemed immoral compared to Cairo. I also enjoyed what you had to say – and your empathy with the rebels. In my line of work, I rarely hear a first rate lecture on a topic like this, and never one that shows anything but horror about militant Islamists.'

They must have talked for an hour or more. Snacks came and went, and more beer and tea. The waiter seemed to know Khaled. Michael allowed himself to be cross-examined, to have his brains picked, carried along in the hope of learning something about Khaled and his bizarre transition from Marxism to the Brotherhood (if that was in fact his affiliation). But he learned little. Khaled was too eager to get Michael to talk, and they hardly noticed how swiftly the time passed.

'Perhaps we could meet again?' Michael ventured tentatively. 'Since I want to know more about the Islamists and how you came to be part of that movement. Don't you do some teaching at the AUC? Maybe we could meet then?'

Khaled looked doubtful. 'I would love to,' he said, 'but politically it is quite difficult for someone in my position, as you must know. 'My friends could well misunderstand what it was about, and the security services would want no encouragement to put the worst interpretation on it and use it to try and destroy what we are trying to do. Knowing a foreigner can be tricky in Egypt – on any excuse, they will accuse you of spying, of treason.'

'What a pity,' Michael said. 'Couldn't you see it as a cover? Consorting with a foreigner is a kind of alibi with the government that you are doing something the Islamists could not tolerate. On the other hand, you could tell your friends that this is a tactic to mislead the government.'

'That is too clever – the government would not waste time on it for a moment if they wanted to destroy me. But, I am tempted. It would be great just to talk freely like we used to do in Cambridge. And I'd like to test out on you ideas I have about Egypt today.'

Then, as if on an impulse, Khaled decided. 'Let's try. We can't spend all our lives hiding, and the government doesn't need the pretext of me having lunch with you to kill us all. I'm here on Thursdays, late morning, so we could meet for lunch.'

'Great,' Michael said. 'Provided we eat good Egyptian food and not the awful stuff they serve in the faculty dining-room.'

'I promise,' Khaled laughed.

Michael noticed for the first time what an attractive personality he had. He had his mother's fine beauty, but he was also his father's son: impulsive, talkative, frank to the point of rashness.

Or at least that is what he thought at the time. Later, he went over this first proper meeting with closer attention. Had Khaled in fact been leading him on, weaving him into some unknown plot, and the appearance of impetuousness was all part of the plan to mislead?

They agreed to meet the following Thursday. But on Monday, Khaled rang and apologised, saying he could not make it.

10

Letter 5

My dearest Jeannot,

Thousands of thanks for your letter – it is so *wonderful* to hear from you. I am delighted that you have been able to resume hiking, your great passion, after so long. The mountains round Lake Geneva must be very *inspiring* though I cannot think how, at this time of year, you bear the cold. It is also most gratifying that dear Papa has been able to arrange a small allowance so you can pay off some of your debts. Shall you now be able to get back to architecture?

Our big news concerns Jenny Marx, the eldest daughter. I mentioned her in an earlier letter to you. You may not be able to believe it but she has been so *busy* while I have been here that, even though we share the same house, I have scarcely seen her. She is *completely* taken up with organising relief for the *communards* and helping her much loved Fenians. She seems to leave home before we rise and come back after we have gone to rest! Tussy, in an unguarded moment, let something slip the other day, perhaps a little shamefaced, that Jenny was *working* – or had worked (I could not quite understand) – as a governess in the home of a neighbour, Dr Monroe. It shows just how difficult it has been for the family to secure enough to live. Everyone is a little ashamed that Jenny was obliged to do this and does not like to mention it. So perhaps my not seeing Jenny is because of this excessive burden of work. It is so difficult for a respectable family when there are only daughters, but I hope that now, with M. Engels' help, the problems will not arise again.

Of course, on Sundays she usually attends the big family dinners, and chooses the wines, for she is a *great* connoisseur and commands the Marx cellar. But she is so *serious*, I find her a little frightening!

But she has not been so busy with work as to exclude *all* other matters. For Mrs Marx has just announced that her daughter is to marry in July! Of course, it has long been obvious who is her favourite – do you know him? M. Charles Longuet. He is a journalist from Caen and tells me that he was on the Labour Committee of the Commune (and editor of its journal). You must know him. He seems very pleasant although also very serious! I do not know when he and Jenny were ever able to get time to make love.

So you see, we French are *taking over* the Marx family! Mrs Marx is, I think, a little alarmed by this narrow nationalism. If Tussy marries her M. Lissagaray, the picture will be complete. In the future, we will say that although the *communards* could not conquer France, they could conquer the Marxes!

Tussy and I slipped away to see the grand procession to celebrate the recovery of the Prince of Wales (the *dauphin*) from sickness. We took Tussy's dog, Whiskey, but the poor dear was so *frightened*, we had to carry him all the way. We felt very *wicked* to be going to such an event, but Tussy said it was to show me the enemy in all his glory! The crowds were *enormous*, so many people packed in all the streets, hanging from lampposts and balconies, cheering and waving a sea of flags. The streets were decorated, and it was most merry. So many loyalists, how could we ever change the world when so many are pledged to keep it as it is? The procession was very grand, but so long it grew quite wearisome and we slipped away to buy roasted chestnuts from an old Italian on a side street – they were delicious.

The crowds were so *big*, it was impossible for the General Council to hold their weekly meeting, which was perhaps a good thing for M. Marx who is still *suffering* from his inflamed eye. So all stayed home to avoid the great crowds.

There was also more news from your M. Bakunin in Geneva – have you heard it? He tried to convene a great congress of his International – did you go? They say it was to resolve that the General Council of our International here has far *too much* power and is *bullying* all the sections to get its way (or, M. Marx's way!). Tussy says that M. Bakunin and his followers say that the International should be an 'embryo' of the new society, and therefore *without coercion* at all, without anybody having the power to discipline the federated sections – is this true? There must be no tyrants within the International , but all must give their support (or not) freely. But they say, this is not so, and M. Marx and M. Engels bully all the sections to do what the Germans want. Tussy says it would be disaster if the General Council were weakened because it would not then be able to use the stronger sections to help the weaker and those under attack. I get so *confused* with these arguments – and everyone is so *fierce*! My head goes into a *whirl* and I cannot think what I should decide. I need my brother's counsel!

I have left to the end your news about all these young Slavs. I cannot help but feel that these new friends are *dangerous*, so *wild* and *impetuous*, and so obsessed with universal destruction. Why are they so sure a mighty uprising is coming in Russia just because there has been a peasant revolt in the same year in each century? One does not have to be a follower of M. Marx to see that it is not the accident of the year, and once a century, which makes a revolution. I fear this group of Serbians – or are they Bulgarians? I get so confused – will drag you into something most dangerous. And their vodka does not help – where do they get the money to drink and carouse? I fear they do not *study* enough, and there is altogether too much idleness. As for this M. 'Stephan Grazdanov' (have I spelt his name correctly?) who seems to have *impressed* you so with his zeal and devotion, he positively sounds the *worst* and most dishonourable. Perhaps he was very successful in creating his secret organisation to overthrow the Tsar. But it is now all crushed with *hundreds* arrested and executed or banished. And what foolishness is this to wear dark glasses and keep his hand in his jacket like a toy Napoleon! I think it is not at all right to be so *ice-cold* and fanatical, to sacrifice all human feelings to the pursuit of revolution. He must *feel* for the People if he is to be true to the cause – he must *love* them. *Do not fall under his spell* for I am sure he is evil! I worry so much that you do not have there wise and calm counsellors who can advise you of the pitfalls along the way, only mad caps. I thank goodness that his French is not good enough to make you captive!

Enough sermonising, dear Jean, I hope you will forgive me, but it is only for your care that I write so. Thiers and the Republic have long arms and I fear that they may be able to reach to Geneva and pluck you out – then you might go forever, like so many others, into exile in the South Pacific, in New Caledonia, and we shall never see you again until you are old and broken. We have had too many disasters on our heads to risk more!

Your loving sister,

Natalie

11

Letter 6

London, 25 March, 1872.

Dear dear Jean,

At last, a little of blessed spring has arrived. The light grows stronger and *sometimes* the air even a little warmer; the trees are once more finding their new leaves, the delicious pale green of young shoots, and brilliant daffodils are in the parks. The birds have returned and sing so prettily in the trees all around. The family has a conservatory and it is crowded with potted plants, now becoming gay and fantastic with the call of the sun. I wish you could see it, it is so *uplifting*. Tussy has pet names for all her favourite plants and coos to them and strokes them, which makes her mother laugh out loud. Soon, I hope, we may go to Ramsgate to take the sea air; it is a town on the sea that all the Marxes love.

Last Sunday was a *grand* affair. M. Longuet, Jenny's betrothed, displaced Lenchen in the kitchen and once more tried his hand at cooking our dinner – *sole á la normande,* his 'national dish' as everyone called it. By general agreement, it was pronounced rather good, and a great improvement on his last effort (*boeuf á la mode*). We were quite a crowd and very gay. Mr Engels and his lady, Mrs Lydia Burns (I know not why she is not Mrs Engels but dared not ask lest everyone think me foolish), were there, and Jenny chose excellent wines. Mr Engels has an *immense* fund of jokes and stories and kept us in *hoots* of laughter until we cried. We were so merry, you could not think the world is so hard. Even Mr Marx who still suffers with his eye and is quite often so *gloomy*, raised quite a few smiles, which greatly pleased everyone, especially Mrs Marx who worries *so much* over his health. But, most sadly, there is no better news from Spain of their little grandson.

We all set out for a grand meeting to mark the Paris Commune on the 19th. But when we arrived, we found that the landlord of the premises had *cancelled* the booking! He declared, it is said, that the French *communards* should not be allowed to meet in London. There was *great* indignation among the several hundred English and French who had gathered there, and *rage* that Mr Gladstone (the British Prime Minister) should be so servile as to do the bidding of that wolf, Thiers (for everyone assumed the government had obliged the landlord to behave in such a scandalous fashion). We all protested that this was not England where all have the right to freedom, but we could not persuade him to change. After a time, a hundred or so were nominated to go to the Cercle d'Etudes Sociales, the *communard* club in London, to mark the occasion. Tussy and I came sadly home. Did you also mark the time? I hope the Swiss were not so foolish.

Did you hear? Our M. Blanqui was sentenced to life imprisonment! T. and I were *much* cast down. He may never see the light again! And it is *so unjust* when, of all, he was the greatest patriot to stand against the Prussian bayonets at the moment of greatest challenge, while Thiers and his crew were busy betraying France to Bismarck.

I am very pleased that you will enquire – about Mr Grazdanov – from Mr Bakunin when he next visits Geneva. He is *sure* to know what is happening in Russia and whether Mr G. really did nearly raise a revolution as he boasts. The rumour that he was mixed up in some kind of murder is most shocking, and the murder of one of his own followers, a member of his own organisation – how can it be that he is so ruthless? Let us hope that is only the idle boasting of the young and foolish, and without substance. How can he even speak of such things, and so boastfully when *all* the walls around him have ears. I do not like your Serbs, dear Jean, and fear they may drag you into all sorts of infamy.

I hope also you will not allow yourself to be influenced by Mr Bakunin's denunciation of science and learning. There at least I am with Mr Marx on the importance of study. It is all very well to say that learning *corrupts* the revolutionary spirit and *shrivels* the vigour of real life, but we *cannot* advance without seeking to understand and *master* the world of nature and ourselves. How can we raise houses that will stand without architects. And it is most unfair to say Mr Marx only studies in order to control people, to frighten them with his great science.

However, I am very glad that you are meeting so many new people and hearing many new ideas. Exile may not be as terrible if you can find so many friends. The workers' meeting with M. Guillaume was very exciting. If all those real workers have as much revolutionary spirit as seems in that meeting, the International is *sure* to triumph! I pray that it will, not least because that will divert your thoughts away from that longing to go to America!

Your ever loving sister,

N.

12

Khaled II

Michael did meet Khaled again. It was a Tuesday, he recalled, and he carefully timed his visit to the library so that it might coincide with the end of Leila's class. As usual, at that time of day on the Greek campus, the raised quadrangle, the high steps leading up to it and the garden below were littered with students, draped over the steps, the chairs, the balconies and grass with the languid grace of youth. They were dressed for modern marriage, in jeans and T-shirts or sweaters, and now, at this chillier time of year, with some black leather jackets and coats. The legs were absurdly long, the breasts absurdly prominent; the fashion in lips, it seemed to Michael's untutored eye, was pale pink close to the mouth, darkening to crimson towards the outer rim. It was a long way from Islam, closer to Minneapolis, the ball game and the high school dance. Everyone seemed to smoke; it was part of the designer culture.

The litter of bodies was everywhere, so crossing the campus involved finding stepping stones between recumbent bodies. The noise was continuous – the babble of voices, hoots, screams, shouts, giggles, like the cawing of a multitude of rooks in a copse. Islamic dress was rare here. These rich boys and girls flaunted their cosmopolitan secularism, their Americanism. Not wearing Islamic dress was a loud statement of wealth, of class arrogance, of contempt for the other Egypt, of the Cairo lower-middle class, let alone of the villages.

As Michael crossed the quadrangle on his way to the library, turning a corner, he almost bumped into Khaled.

'How good to see you!' Michael said, smiling as much as he dared. Khaled was startled, flustered. He was dressed in a well cut three-piece dark suit, the uniform of the medical profession. He said, stuttering slightly, that he was waiting for Leila to finish her class. So

68

Michael, to his surprise, invited him for coffee, and after a moment's hesitation, Khaled accepted.

They made their way to the refectory corner, threading between the crowds, and arrived as one lot of people were leaving. They sat out in the open at a wicker table, where Khaled could see Leila pass. Michael was about to go inside to get the coffees when Leila appeared. Khaled rose to call her softly.

The billowing black tent looked bizarre among the tight jeans and bright sweaters. She looked like a giant crow, hooded and sinister. It made a special sensation to be all in black and hooded, an almost arrogant statement of difference in such a crowd.

She changed direction and walked towards them. Then, as she saw Michael beyond him, her face darkened and she almost scowled. By the time she reached them, she had recovered herself. She managed a perfunctory greeting and even a half smile. But she did not shake hands, and she accepted their invitation to sit with ill-grace. The body language was hostile. She finally agreed to have a coffee, and Michael made off to the refectory to fetch the cups.

When he returned with tray and plastic cups of coffee, the couple seemed to be having a repressed row, whispering and scowling. Even so, Michael noted how Leila's flashing eyes looked splendid. Black hood or not, torments of this kind could not be concealed.

'And how do you find the AUC, Dr James, now you have had time to settle in?' Khaled was making some effort to behave normally, while Leila stared away in sullen silence. Michael put down the tray and passed a cup to each.

'It's great,' Michael said, as he sat down in the wicker chair opposite. 'The students are a lively bunch and many work hard. The only misery is learning Arabic. I have left it far too late in life – my ancient brain is too addled to absorb it. I drive my Arabic teacher to distraction.'

He laughed shortly, hoping to extract a smile from them, but Leila stared away in stony silence. 'And the library is great,' he added lamely.

'Yes, the library is good – a pleasant place to work when it's not too crowded,' Khaled said. 'We use it when we can although there are no medical studies here so no medical section. It's sometimes difficult getting recent books in our fields. But that's the third world so I suppose we must put up with it.'

'What sort of books do you lack?' Michael asked.

69

'Oh, you know, you read a review of a serious work of medical research in one of the journals from Europe or America, absolutely in your specialism, and you know it won't be around in Cairo for another five years – or long after you need it.'

'Surely, we can do something about that?' Michael said slowly, and then impulsively, 'I go to London once a month to lecture. If it isn't too much trouble, I could try and pick something up.'

Khaled looked up. 'I couldn't put you to the trouble – my books are only available in obscure specialist bookshops.'

'Let me try – and do something for Egyptian health. As it happens, I'm on one of my regular trips tomorrow.'

Khaled finally gave in, and groped in his briefcase for paper to write the details on.

'Just in case you have time and happen to be near a medical bookshop. The BMA might be easiest – Woburn Square.'

Leila continued to stare impassively to one side.

Khaled handed him the paper. And then, abruptly, stood up. 'You have been so kind,' he said, 'but I fear we must go. I've just remembered an appointment I fixed and I'm going to be late.'

'But you haven't finished your coffee,' Michael protested.

'Yes, sadly. But I'll call you. When will you be back from London?'

'I'll be in the office on Sunday,' Michael said.

'Good. I'll ring you then and we may finally get to fix a date for lunch.'

Leila stood, her eyes lowered submissively. Michael knew he was the reason for the sudden departure, and not some invented appointment. He rose and Khaled shook hands, Leila did not.

As they left, Michael sat back in his chair, watching this ill-matched couple thread their way through the crowd – the slim three piece-suit, limping, and the small billowing black tent trotting beside it. Their body language breathed resentment. Of course, the pious could not walk arm in arm, much less holding hands, but this couple walked with a frosty distance between them. Was Leila hostile to him, Michael, he wondered? He was of no significance in her life. Perhaps she did indeed hate foreigners?

Michael's trip to London was uneventful, marred only by persistent rain. But he did find the book. He was rather pleased with himself. He now had Khaled under some sort of obligation.

* * *

When he returned, Khaled rang him and he was proud to announce his success. They arranged to meet for lunch on Thursday.

When they met, Khaled apologised for leaving the refectory abruptly. Leila had been upset, he said; military units had shut down some of their slum health centres and roughed up the staff. He feared it might be the start of yet another wave of repression.

That is how it began. One lunch somehow led to another until it became, if not a weekly fixture, at least a regular occasion. Perhaps they met a dozen or more times during the year, exploring the restaurants and little cafés clustered in the downtown area in the narrow back streets, around the AUC.

Michael often wondered why this curious relationship developed and lasted. He knew that he was lonely and eager to learn about Egypt and Islamism. But what was Khaled's interest? Given the risks of such an association for him – from the Islamists as much as the thugs of the Ministry of Interior – it seemed bizarre.

Michael remembered well that first occasion. They were to eat brains in batter, a speciality of the dark open-fronted café, with its clean marble-topped tables and iron chairs. The place was empty of other customers, which was reassuring. The patron in his grubby white apron knew Khaled and chatted with him. Outside, the midday sun, weaker though it was at this time of year, still beat down relentlessly on the passing lunchtime crowds. Horns blaring, dense traffic clogged the road, children dodging between the vehicles. A donkey wandered forlorn between the cars. Young women in coloured gowns and veils giggled to each other as they passed, glancing boldly at a passing boy.

Khaled was nervous. Michael noticed his anxious habit of pulling down the eyepatch to cover the cavity of his eye more closely – much as Leila pulled her veil down – as if to hide his vulnerability. Yet, as so often happened, the talk seemed to give him confidence, to elate him, as if having an attentive audience lifted his spirits. They had hardly ordered the food and a Sprite to drink before he began.

He rarely got a chance to talk, he said impetuously, even though talking always helped get issues clear, especially in a foreign language – it seemed to distance matters. There was no time for doctors to talk – the hospital, clinics in poor areas, teaching, masses of additional consultations, and, in theory, research and writing articles in medical journals. It was probably why doctors smoked so much.

Michael tried to remember when it was he finally mustered the courage to ask his key question: What had turned Khaled from Marxism to Islam?

And slowly, the story unpeeled, layer on layer, though which revelation came when he could now no longer recall. But it began then, and he could still hear Khaled's voice telling the story, slowly and patiently.

There were many reasons for his change, he said. He was in prison for a time, in the headquarters of the State Security Investigation Department at Lazoghly – 'our Peter and Paul Fortress'- he said with a grin, knowing Michael would know the notorious St Petersburg prison.

He had been a Marxist in those days, and it earned him his lost eye and smashed leg. But prison also gave him time to start thinking about why the Marxists, despite all their knowledge, not only failed, but were largely irrelevant to events. They were by-standers. Irritating for the regime, perhaps, but no threat since they were barely embedded in Egypt at all, but in a foreign fantasy world of their own invention, the great struggle of proletarian good and bourgeois evil. Then he met some Islamists, fierce and dedicated idealists with an apparently infinite capacity for self-sacrifice. But unlike the Marxists, they were rooted – in the cities, the villages, wherever anyone rolled out their prayer-mat or put their hands to their eyes. Everyone in Egypt went to the mosque and so did the Islamists. They didn't have to stand on street corners or outside the factories giving out leaflets when the workers couldn't even read.

Then his father did for him what Uncle Hosni had done for his father when he got him sent off to Berkeley to keep him out of mischief. But in Khaled's case, he went to Cambridge.

Cambridge was, he said, weird, a world on its own – on the one hand, a wonderful experience, intellectually stimulating, beautiful (he was there in the summer); on the other, it crystallized his growing doubts about Marxism.

Leila and he had had, he said, a rough patch in Cambridge, and out of it, she became much more aware of 'Arabness'. She began evolving in a similar way. And in London, Khaled met so many fine heroes, fighting all round the world – Chechens, Algerians, Somalis, Acehians from Sumatra, Mindanao in the Philippines, Kashmiris, Palestinians, Bosnians. Londistan was the centre for the global movement of one nation. Until then, he had had no idea how far Islam stretched. Islam as a world movement was the only serious force fighting against the terrible prison of separate nations that the West had imposed on everybody. It was ahead of the world because it was already a global nation.

Furthermore, it wasn't little groups of intellectuals, chattering Marx in café corners with nobody listening – and if they did, no one understanding. The Marxists in Egypt were always foreigners. To be an Egyptian and a Marxist, you had to become a foreigner – to learn an arcane language and be obsessed with France or England or Germany in the last half of the nineteenth century. How could any real Egyptian relate to it? Marxist internationalism meant you belonged nowhere; Islam meant you belonged everywhere.

He realised that Marxism was a form of cultural imperialism – it cut people off from the real Egypt, made them politically impotent. They couldn't speak to people in a language they understood or about issues of real concern. And it was worse. Marxism was all upside down – revolutions were not made in developed countries by mass industrial working classes; they were made in the Third World, where the whole social structure was rotten. And they were made by the mass of the alienated, whatever class they were in, by people like Mohammed Atef who blew up the American embassies in Kenya and Tanzania, an ex-Egyptian police chief; or Zawahri, Bin Laden's second in command, an ex-Cairo surgeon.

He paused, his face flushed with excitement as the ideas tumbled out, and then slightly embarrassed at his talkativeness, lapsed into silence.

'Have some more to eat,' he said eventually, 'the food is delicious.'

'So Cambridge gave you and Leila the reasons why Marxism was not the answer in Egypt?' Michael asked, to get Khaled to continue.

In Berkeley, as a young teenager with his parents, he became interested in anarchism: Bakunin, Kropotkin and so on. The American movement was all that – faraway from the old Marxists. In Cambridge, he went back to look at them again, more carefully, and at the same time, he was getting an education in Islam. The anarchist attack on the Marxists clicked: the Marxists were an alienated intelligentsia, trying to exploit the workers to come to power in order to impose a dictatorship on them. What happened in Russia, Stalinism, was not a betrayal – it was exactly what Marxism was designed to achieve. And Bakunin was the one who saw why it would inevitably happen in backward Russia, not economically advanced Britain.

This took him back into the history of the Russian movement, and he realised that Lenin, like Mao, was really an anarchist – he made a revolution in a backward country, with whoever would join him. The nineteenth-century anarchists in Russia raised the people through acts of great heroism to overthrow the Tsar, and despite all the lies about 1917, that's exactly what happened. It was the will, not economics that produced such heroism, such self-sacrifice.

One of those Russian anarchists, in particular, took Leila's fancy. Khaled had forgotten the name but he remembered that he had written a book with the word Catechism in the title.

'Sergei Nechaev: *Catechism of a Revolutionary*,' Michael said helpfully. 'I've just finished editing a collection of letters about him. What specially attracted Leila to him?'

'I don't know but perhaps it was his complete single-mindedness, a sort of ruthless dedication to the cause, and a lack of any doubt.'

'But those Russians were all militant atheists – how can they be relevant to you?' Michael asked.

'They had had to be atheists because Christianity was a weapon of the State. If you rejected their State, you had to reject their religion.'

'Would you be willing to do anything – cheat, lie, murder – for the sake of your revolution?' Michael asked, musing on the paradox of Khaled's neat suit and tie.

Khaled paused, thinking, and then said slowly and deliberately: 'They kill us, torture us, gaol us, and the only check we have is to strike where we can. We try to create a balance of terror – that's what we learned from the Cold War. Now the balance of terror is between us and America – and we will carry our attack into America itself.'

Michael, with difficulty, controlled his shock and the temptation to anger at this absurdity.

'But the State is the supreme instrument of violence, of terror. You provoke it at the risk of massive retaliation, laying waste the land and slaughtering everyone – look at Vietnam, at Chechnya, at Kashmir.'

'They will crack before us,' Khaled said quietly. 'Look what happened to the Shah's army – it disintegrated and the grand Emperor had to flee.'

He paused, checked by his own torrent of talk and embarrassed to have betrayed so much of himself. And, then, as if to himself, he mused quietly:

'If you took the old revolutionary agenda – liberty, equality, fraternity from the French, universalism and solidarity from the Russians – where else would you find them today but in the Koran and the Islamic community? It is not

the Communist International that sends its fighters round the world to battle for universal liberation but the warriors of Islam. Afghanistan's war is the equivalent of the Spanish Republican war, except that we won against the Soviets and the Spaniards lost. One day Al-Qaeda will rank with the International Brigade as freedom fighters against imperialism.

'And then they will reclaim Christianity. Muslims accepted Christ as one of their prophets and shared exactly the same agenda in terms of helping the poor, social justice and equality. But the Romans turned Christianity into a State religion – one of its truncheons. Islam will save the Christians and show the way in good works – running hospitals and clinics, schools, slum upgrading, sports centres – all the old social democratic agenda. Muslims do not need the State to care for the poor – the faithful will do it all. In Upper Egypt and slum Cairo, they have already created Islamic republics under their own emirs.

'And now immigrants are making even Europe part of Islam – at last, the world might be united once again after the dark night of the nation States and perpetual war between them.'

Michael stared at Khaled dumbfounded. 'This is as completely utopian as the old idea of world socialism,' he said.

'Or its final fulfilment,' Khaled responded.

Khaled stopped, as if embarrassed at his confession. 'Amazing,' he said. 'I haven't talked like this for years – and I'm doing it with more English than I thought I possessed. You must think I'm mad. But it is your fault since you are such a good listener.'

The food was finished, and they moved on to a coffee shop. Michael was induced to try his first water pipe, a *hookah* (or a *shisha* in Cairo). There were too many people to risk more talk.

* * *

Had he really heard all that? Had he misunderstood or muddled many conversations? In the Felfela, a tourist trap – 'but you have to have tried it, and it has Stella beer'- or in the numerous *kusri* shops in the centre of town, or in a grubby lean-to in old Fatimid Cairo over stuffed pigeon, or in a sleazy stall with only three tables in the market, or even squatting on the pavement over a plate of pasta. What an immensity of talk there had been, as if Khaled were telling his autobiography.

Then there had been the time when Khaled told the story of his political experience after California.

He had come back from Berkeley as an anarchist. He 'addled his brains' reading Das Capital in the small hours, wondering whether to throw over medicine and take a job as a labourer in Helwan steel plant. Would any employer have looked at him and his soft hands; would any worker have trusted the spy from the upper classes? He had joined a communist group but it was hopeless and they split – and split. They had flirted with Maoism, dreaming of starting a remote base for guerilla warfare, a Yenan in Siwa in the western desert. He gave a derisive laugh.

Then they had created a little Trotskyist group, which was more comfortable but no more effective. He had spent all his spare time scribbling articles, commentaries, internal papers, and even a small booklet on Egyptian capitalism. They used a lot of paper, but they didn't move the world one jot. Then the police had sniffed them out and knocked them to pieces, just to keep themselves from boredom. He went to gaol as a military threat to the State.

'Was Leila with you then?' Michael asked.

She had been much more successful. While Khaled was practising as a doctor, she was a student leader at Cairo University. A real firebrand, absolutely fearless. She was so fierce at student meetings, people just caught light when she spoke. She seemed to be able to lead them anywhere. She had been accused of setting fire to the university administration building, but that had been a police frame-up.

* * *

When had they talked about terrorism? Michael had been reading about Peru's Shining Path, the Senderistas, and their horrifying exaltation of slaughter. Guzmán, the leader, said the cadres had to meet a 'blood quota' to show their true mettle, to ford a 'river of blood': 'the triumph of the revolution will cost a million deaths.' And killing was done with such pitiless cruelty just to save ammunition:

> 'As if slaughtering a hog, the cadres made the victim kneel and proceeded to cut the throat, allow the blood to run, and sometimes crush the victim's head with a stone. In *senderista* language, the point was "to smash with a stone as if destroying a frog."'

76

The Peruvian army, they say, was even worse. Michael reflected that some American fundamentalist Christians also rejoiced in such a fate for unbelievers at the Day of Judgement.

Could anything ever justify such horror? Nechaev would have known where he was in Guzmán's Peru or in Pol Pot's Cambodia. Did Khaled?

It was in the Estoril again, this time in the early evening for reasons Michael could no longer remember. But the early hour meant there was no one else there. It was chilly, and they were eating snacks. Michael had a Stella, Khaled a soda water.

'Let's go back to the Narodniks in nineteenth-century Russia,' Michael opened. 'They only assassinated those they regarded as guilty – the head of the secret police, a king, president, an unjust judge. How can you justify killing those who are not directly guilty – as happened to those poor Germans at Luxor in 1997 or outside the Cairo Museum?'

Khaled considered the issue slowly. *It was, he said, a sad lesson of the modern State. Just as the Nazis blitzed London, the British bombed Dresden and Hamburg as the Second World War was nearly over – to maximize the number of casualties. Though 45,000 here, unlike the 58 at Luxor. And the Americans killed even more in firebombing Tokyo, and then dropping nuclear bombs on Hiroshima and Nagasaki. Even Mubbarak when he laid waste whole villages because some peasant threw a stone, looks small beer beside that. It was governments who were the biggest terrorists – and the mortuaries were full of 'innocent bystanders'.*

Michael, despite himself, was shocked. Khaled was trying to justify the horror. He controlled himself.

Khaled continued that one crime did not justify another, and a gigantic crime did not justify the sort of little ones of which so-called terrorists were usually capable. One innocent death was bad enough – the numbers did not make it worse. They said 60,000 had been killed in Sri Lanka in the war with the Tamil Tigers. Luxor was insane and politically catastrophic, but he understood the logic. The real issue was: given the grotesque imbalance between the powers of destruction of the State and the terrorist, was it ever right to risk rousing the State, which would then kill thousands of innocent people? Should you ever wake the beast?

Michael stared at Khaled to detect his meaning, Khaled in turn gazing off somewhere to the left, to a picture on the wall.

'I spent a lifetime not making up my mind on that,' Michael said

77

quietly. 'But now, in my old age, I think it can never be right to kill someone, whatever the cause. Humanity has spent thousands of years trying to embed in our heads a ban on killing, and, despite professional soldiers, it is a fearful thing to break it down. We spent the last century wading through blood to reach a world where no one wades through blood, and we still haven't arrived. Despite the unspeakable cruelty of governments, civil war is worse – look at Algeria or Colombia. Look at Egypt – killing Sadat only led to worse savagery.'

Yet, for Khaled, there were cases where you had no choice. What would Michael do as a Jew in Nazi Germany – wouldn't he rather be a suicide-bomber and kill some of the bastards if he knew he was heading for Auschwitz anyway? And who condemned Stauffenberg, the man who tried to murder Hitler, as a terrorist, as a suicide-bomber? What would Michael do as a Palestinian, knowing that, day in, day out, the Israelis were stealing his land and nothing at all frightened them except a suicide bomber?

'But look at what is happening,' Michael said. 'The Israelis are even more brutal, pitiless.'

'The story is not over yet,' Khaled said quickly.

'Unfortunately, it never is, and meanwhile the innocent are slaughtered.'

*　*　*

Then there had been a discussion that began with politics as a gamble, a giant speculation on what people wanted, and one that, if it was wrong, destroyed the gambler. The place was out in the open. It was evening. They were eating hunks of roasted lamb and hot flat bread under a brilliant night sky, with swathes of smoke from the barbecue grills. The moon was very clear, making the dark like day. There was a scatter of scrubbed wooden tables in the road, wobbling on the uneven surface, outside where the old abattoir had been converted into a lorry park.

'So you could say,' Khaled continued, with a wide smile, 'Islam is my gamble, a great bet on where the world is going and who will come to power to shape a new world.'

'You mean you are just exploiting Islam to come to power, just as you say the Marxists exploited the working class to seize the State?'

Michael softened the accusation with a smile.

Khaled laughed.

Becoming a Muslim had been his baptism as an Arab and an Egyptian. More, he had accepted that the modernist agenda – Nasser and Arab socialism – could not succeed when they were so remote from the daily life of the people. In trying, Nasser nearly wrecked the country.

The failure of Nasser left a horrible vacuum. The fellahim, *the peasants, had been torn out of the countryside and plunged into hideous city slums. The student and professional classes had been vastly expanded, educated and ambitious but without jobs. When the nationalist agenda failed, their lives had no higher meaning. Women were increasingly educated and moving into work but still chained to the old roles. The only thing that kept them sane in this chaos was the faith of their ancestors. It was the technical intelligentsia – the engineers, the doctors, the lawyers, the architects – who were hit hardest by the disintegration of Nasserism. They had put all their faith in secular progress, in nationalism, and it failed.*

Then there were the urban poor, betrayed by all Nasser's unfulfilled promises. The government privatised everything, so now they were completely excluded. The only people supplying medical services and schooling were the Islamists. In some poorer parts of the city there was almost a permanent civil war with the regime. Police did not travel singly or at night.

The country was drifting, rotting, decomposing. And the only people who knew what to do – and had the trust of the people – were the Islamists.

Khaled seemed in the darkness to glow with excitement, his eyes flashing, only just able to keep his voice low. He broke off, suddenly aware of where he was, of Michael and the scatter of tables, the smell of roasting meat and smoke, the clatter of dishes and low mumble of voices, the great dark beasts of the trucks parked behind them. The other diners were spread out across the road so no one could hear his whispered declamation.

Michael had so many questions, he did not know where to start. He limited himself to one:

'But Islam is many things. How will you make sure your revolution leads to what you think is needed? After all, Iran did not turn out to be very progressive.'

'Ah, that's a different discussion. In essence, here we have a progressive Islam, and we have infiltrated the State and all its agencies … There are no Ayatollahs here. Minds change themselves through the struggle, and that is what we are doing.'

It was not a convincing argument. It was an act of faith, a gamble. Through the talk Khaled had filled Michael with one story, one dimension of Egypt and Islam, reshaping his perceptions to this peculiar and unlikely view of the world. As an atheist, Michael had to suspend disbelief, to allow himself to be carried along on this fierce tide.

* * *

Meanwhile, the weeks turned to months and the winter ended. The air of Cairo grew warm, moist with Nile humidity. The wind of the desert, heavy with unseen sand, cut exposed flesh as he walked across the Nile bridges. Faraway on the horizon, the citadel gazed down on the city, beside the minarets of Mehmet Ali's Ottoman mosque, quivering in the haze; and beyond, barely visible, the Muqattam hills. He walked further and further, through the narrow streets of Bulaq, full of animals and chickens, bands of merry urchins scrambling over the garbage; even as far as the half-built unplastered brick structures of Imbaba, where barefoot children with runny noses in dirty shifts stood in the earth roads and stared at the foreigner.

His exploration of Cairo gave way to visiting the country. He made trips to the Delta to luxuriate in greenery, and see the tumble of village cottages, the great white mud castles of pigeon cots, the quiet middle-class farms. He went to Alexandria a couple of times and along the Mediterranean coast, marvelling at the miles of high rise apartments, cheek by jowl. He travelled across the desert to Ismailia and down the Red Sea to a group of ancient Coptic monasteries, fed by one spring in the gaunt dry mountain; and once across the Sinai desert to the Gulf of Aqaba. Later he went to Upper Egypt, to Assiut and Minya, strongholds of the Islamists and now armed encampments of the government, crawling with military and police on the frontier of Islamism. In the Assiut Hotel, he met some merry Mexican cement engineers on a consultancy to Assiut Cement, and they discussed the revolt in Chiapas.

The real world of Egypt, was only dimly pictured through the opaque censored English-language press. There was shooting in Imbaba, rumours of new clashes between Islamists and Copts in Assiut. There was talk of some kind of riot in prison in protest at the murder of a prisoner by the staff. The government released no information so it was all gossip. Journalists were mysteriously roughed up; others disappeared. A businessman in Alexandria in his speedboat ran down and killed a swimmer, but was not arrested –

or so people said. In the student elections at the end of the year at Cairo's three public universities, the Minister of the Interior intervened to cut from the lists of 12,000 nominations, 3,000 banned names. There were protest demonstrations and, as usual, the police laid about them, cracking heads and making arrests. The leadership of a professional association was purged and the Minister appointed his own creatures in their place.

Then there was the incident outside the AUC Greek campus. Michael walked there for his midday Arabic class. A crowd of several hundred students stood in the street outside the gate, shouting and waving rough placards. He stopped at the faculty office to ask what it was about.

'Haven't you heard,' the secretary said. 'The Americans are bombing Baghdad again. That's why all the streets round the university have been cleared of parked cars for the last three days. The students want to have a protest march to the US Embassy.'

Michael went back to the street, and was just in time to see the arrival of truckloads of paramilitary police with shields, helmets and long truncheons. Behind them were ranks of armed men. There was no warning. The police waded into the students, laying about them as viciously as possible on any head they could reach. He saw a group of girls, weeping and bloody, hanging on to each other in terror, hemmed in by the crowd.

A flash from above drew his eye to a balcony on the first floor where a short slim man with a crew-cut in T-shirt and jeans was taking pictures. Beyond him in the room, Michael glimpsed a woman of considerable size in flowered dress and *hijab*. She was craning her neck to see the crowd.

This is how terrorists were made, thought Michael, as the crowd surged around him – by rage at the blatant injustice of governments and without any means of reply. This was the unlovely Egyptian State.

The press reported nothing.

*   *   *

There was an issue concerning Khaled that Michael knew he avoided thinking about. It began with his success in finding the medical textbook for Khaled on his first trip to London. The next time he went, Khaled asked him if he would mind posting some letters in London – the normal mail took so long. He even had the

British stamps to send the letters. Michael looked them over on the plane, one to a bank in Cambridge, another to a woman with an English name in Cambridge, to a medical publisher and a medical journal. It seemed harmless.

On other trips, there were other letters, and even a small package. Over the months, the list of recipients grew longer. He made a note of the names on his digital organiser in an encrypted file – the first time he had ever done such a thing – and left the file in London so that the Egptian security at Cairo airport would not find it. The names were Islamic: to Yasser al-Sirri of the Islamic Observation Centre in west London; to Abu Hamza at a mosque in Finsbury Park; to Sheikh Omar Bakri Mohammed in Tottenham; to Abu Qatada at the Islamic Centre in Acton; to Baghdad Meziane at an address in Leicester; to Sheikh Abdul Qadeem Zakloom (Hizb-ut-Tahrir) in London; even one to an Imam Abu Emad in the Islamic Cultural Centre in Milan.

The names meant nothing to Michael; only long afterwards did they acquire a notoriety. Khaled had a surprisingly wide variety of contacts in Europe. He wondered whether he should open one, but of course, it would be in Arabic, and if concerning anything clandestine, in code as well. It probably meant nothing.

Yet he could not suppress all qualms at the airline counter when, fixing him with an absurdly solemn expression, the official asked: 'Did you pack your baggage yourself? Are you carrying anything for someone else? Has anyone given you something which is in your baggage?' And with equal solemnity, he had lied.

To be a courier is one thing, he reflected, but to be a courier by accident, without being asked, is stupidity. Had he, at some level, knowingly collaborated, hoping to exchange this service for access to knowledge of the terrorists? But had Khaled and his friends simply been playing him along, the foolish Englishman, the toy Faust, making his contract with the devil?

13

Letter 7

Dearest Jeannot,

What incredible news in your letter! I am still suffering from shock – and relief. It shows how careful one must be, especially among political exiles. It is one thing for your Mr Grazdanov to travel under an assumed name to protect himself from the *unwanted attentions* of the Tsar's police, but quite another, that he himself should be the *notorious* 'Sergei Nechaev,' a murderer. On Mr Bakunin's account, he seems to be a *complete* scoundrel – or a madman – who lies, cheats and now even *murders*, all supposedly to speed the revolution! How could he steal M. Bakunin's papers in order to blackmail him when he had been treated so generously? How is it possible to pursue the great aims of universal liberation through such *contemptible* means? Should means and ends not be equally noble? Must one not always be honorable, never stooping to the despicable, for such high purposes? To execute a notorious evil doer is one thing, but Nechaev seems to have murdered his *comrade*, and to propose the murder of *all who stand in his way.* Can it be true – or is it just some student boasting? As to having a list of all those to be executed when he comes to power, God forbid such a universal massacre, without charge or trial or judgement, all in the name of liberating the people. Are you sure he is not a secret policeman, an agent provocateur?

However, I wondered why Mr Bakunin declared that N. – like Mr Marx – is a Jacobin. Is it because both, like Mr Blanqui, intend to *immensely* strengthen the power of the State after the revolution, whereas Mr Bakunin intends to abolish it as the *primary* means by which people are oppressed? I fear I become *confused* at this point. I

83

am restored only by a sense of relief that you escape this dreadful Mr Grazdanov. How little he has to do with the noble purpose of *freeing all mankind.* Of course, I long to tell it all to Tussy so that she may share my horror and indignation, but I cannot reveal to her what I know, for the whole family is united in their *deep detestation* of M. Bakunin and all his works. That hatred would only grow worse if they learned of M. Grazdanov!

What else has passed? A Mr Edouard Vaillant came to dinner. Do you know him? He seems a fine upstanding young man, a doctor like dear Papa, and of course, a follower of our own Mr Blanqui. He is on the General Council of the International, and I think is being encouraged to consider the revision of the rules. He was good enough to engage me in conversation. Mr Marx said I was lonely, not speaking my own tongue, or only with barbarians with awful German accents! Mr V. was most gracious, but seemed somewhat amused that a poor little provincial mouse like me should be lodged in this great lion's den!

Tussy is *very proud* that now her father's great work, *Das Kapital* – 'to give a fully scientific basis to the struggle of the industrial working class to free itself and mankind,' as she most solemnly intones its dedication – is now appearing in several languages. The Russian edition has appeared. Evidently the tsarist censor allowed it to be published on the grounds that it was *quite unreadable* and therefore no threat to His Imperial Majesty! But the 3,000 copies printed have sold very well. I wonder what the Russians make of it since, according to your Mr Bakunin, there is no working class in that poor wretched country, so they have no use for the book to make a revolution! According to Mr Marx, they cannot make a socialist revolution without a working class!

The French edition is being produced and will appear in instalments. There is a *great excitement* at the first instalment because – what a sensation! It has a *picture* of Mr Marx in the front!

Dearest Jean, I cannot tell you how great is my relief that you have discovered the truth about 'you know who' (I cannot bring myself to repeat his name, so great is my horror and detestation). I pray now that you will be careful in choosing your friends!

With much love,

Natalie.

14

Letter 8

London, 22 April, 1872.

Dearest Jeannot,

The weather now is quite lovely, though they say endless rain will soon drown us! But we are all plunged in *deepest* gloom, since it seems the International is *besieged* with attacks both from within and without. Mr Marx and Mr Engels seem not to know which way to turn to defend their great and noble purpose. Both work *so* hard every day, and we all watch anxiously as they try to ward off yet another heavy blow. What will become of it all?

The most recent attack was public, made by a Member of Parliament in the House of Commons (this is the lower house of the Assembly here). This person, a Mr Cochrane, seems to have said the International was a great secret *conspiracy* to *destroy* civilisation. Evidently, he said there were 180,000 members in England alone and that the General Council had organised and financed the Paris Commune and ordered the murder of the Archbishop. Can it be the same organisation that is such a terrible threat to everyone yet does not even have someone to answer letters? Mr Marx is drafting answers to all the charges, but we are most *fearful* lest the Marxes lose their place here and are forced into exile. Where would they go? To Berlin and into the arms of Bismarck? However, on the good side is the news that the Gladstone government has definitely refused the request from Paris to extradite the *communards* as common felons – that is a mighty relief! You can imagine the rejoicing among the *communards* that now they are safe. Tussy and I were also much rejoiced at this mercy.

Then again, *within* the International, there is *so much* disunity, *so much* quarrelling, *so many* bitter divisions. It seems a whole mass of disaffected refugees here: *communards,* Germans (what Tussy calls 'Lassalleans' though I have no idea what they are; 'Bismarck agents' Tussy mutters darkly!) and some English have formed an 'alternative International,' called the Universal Federalist Council. Then there are the great and insoluble divisions among our countrymen. Mr Engels says that much of it is fomented by the *mouchards,* spies of Thiers; indeed, he says, sometimes there are more *mouchards* than *communards!*

More bad news from Germany. Two great friends of Mr Marx, a Mr Liebknecht and Mr Bebel, have been put on trial for treason. According to Tussy (who is great friends with Alice, Mr Liebknecht's daughter), the two are deputies in the Reichstag, the German Parliament, and, in 1870, *dared to oppose* the vote in support of Bismarck and his war on us. They were arrested and tried for treason. Mr Marx thought Bismarck would not have the impudence to sentence them, but it seems they have received two years' imprisonment (which for the charge of treason is not as bad as it might be). But it was all a revelation to me – that there were Prussians who did such things – to publicly *oppose* their Emperor, the Kaiser, in the name of international solidarity with the French working class! How fine that is! It quite restores my confidence in the very purpose and nobility of the International!

And, as if all these troubles were not enough to worry us, Schnappy, the poor tiny grandson, remains very ill. Madrid has not restored him at all. Tussy adores her little nephew, the only one, and cannot help but fear for the little soul. All the family will be *so* cast down if the worst happens.

Yours with much love,

N.

15

Leila II

It was sometime in late November or early December that Michael saw Leila next. There was the usual crowd milling about the refectory, but clad now in sweaters and leather jackets against the season's chill.

He caught sight of Leila, as usual all in black, wending her way distastefully between the bodies, as if crossing a battlefield of corpses. Her gown billowed, an inflated black column. He quickened his step to intercept her.

'Dr Leila,' he called softly, aware of the student eyes all round watching. She stopped and turned. He expected the scowl or at least a touch of resentment that he dared address her, even a gesture of repugnance. But, to his surprise, she made no sign of hostility.

'Dr James, how nice to see you again.' She paused, smiling. 'And how are you getting along at the AUC?'

'Fine,' he replied, confused by the warmth of her greeting. 'Can I offer you a coffee, if you have a moment?'

Leila looked alarmed, a little frightened, and glanced about her as if to see who might be watching her flirtation with disaster. But the students all around had lost interest in them and were busy with their own talk. But then, as if giving way to an impulse of bravado – rather like her husband – slightly defiantly, she agreed.

They sat at almost the same table as before, and he went off to get the coffee. He reflected that she spoke now with such confidence, it was difficult to believe she was the same person. Her resentment before could not have been provoked by him.

Leila settled herself demurely in her chair as he returned with the cups, ignoring the frank stares of appraisal of some of the men sitting at nearby tables. Troops of students with cases and arm-loads of books and papers passed by, changing classes. They sat a little stiffly over their coffees, as if unsure of what to say. Michael broke the ice.

'You teach Egyptian public health here, I believe?' he asked conversationally.

'What there is of it,' she said with a laugh and a shake of her head. For a moment, a curl of thick black hair escaped the *hijab*, but it was swiftly covered. Her voice, he noticed now, was low and musical. Her English was faultless.

The government, Leila said, was running down its programmes, reducing the provision of primary care and hospital services. They had never been very good – far too little for the needs of the population – and that was in the old slums; the new ones had nothing. And now public services in the old areas looked to be disappearing altogether, without private provision picking it up. Then there would be private hospitals for the rich and cemeteries for the poor.

Her eyes sparkled, contradicting the gloom of her words.

Meanwhile, the spread of primary education to most people living in cities had introduced them to the importance of medical care, and standards had risen – just as provision was declining. Mothers in the slum areas of Cairo took health care very seriously now. But often only charities provided any care.

She abruptly changed the subject. 'But how are you getting on in Cairo?' she asked. 'I hear something of you from Khaled – you and he seem to meet quite often?' Did he catch a note of resentment in her words?

'He's taken my education on modern Egypt in hand. I really ought to pay for the lessons, but as often as not, he won't even let me pay for his lunch.'

'I'm sure you're wrong. He's learning at least as much, and it is good that he gets out of the terrible treadmill of the lives we doctors lead.'

'I hear you are very active in the professional association of doctors,' Michael said.

Leila said the association had started a major scheme to recruit staff for their network of clinics in slum areas. Managing it took an enormous amount of time. Then there was raising the funds to finance it – patients paid a small fee when they could, but the rest had to be raised from charities or privately. But the work was very satisfying – meeting immediate needs; and people were very grateful.

Leila's face seemed to come alive, glowing with vivacity. She was like a young girl, chattering with enthusiasm. Not only was she

88

beautiful, he reflected, she was good, faithful to her craft as a doctor.

'When you said "we",' he asked, 'did you mean the doctors' professional association or a separate organisation?'

'It comes down to much the same thing,' she said, 'since we are active in the various organisations involved.'

It had to be the Muslim Brotherhood, Michael guessed, banned, yet caring for the casualties in that perpetual war of the slums.

There was a pause, and then she asked abruptly, 'And what do you do with yourself in this strange city?'

'I walk and walk and watch and watch, miles, through vast areas of the city. The more I see, the more I love it. The street life hums with excitement, always something happening, especially in the poorest areas, and you know better than me how unbelievably poor some districts are.' She nodded.

'But why are you actually here?' she asked, staring at him intently as if he might betray a secret purpose. 'What made you choose to come to Cairo?'

'I don't know. The AUC had a vacancy and I filled it. And Cairo is one of the more exciting cities of the world, and of course, it is a chance to get to know something about the Islamists.'

'Don't you have a family?' she asked.

'My wife died ten years ago,' he said. 'I have a son and daughter, grown up now, and a couple of grandchildren. And I am retired – so my time is my own.'

'So you are not a British spy as everyone says?' she asked with a mischievous grin.

'What? With so little Arabic? I would be hopeless,' he said with a smile.

She was gathering her things together, her curiosity exhausted. If he was hiding a secret motive, he was not going to reveal it to her. She checked her veil and finished her coffee.

'I am glad you like Cairo and you are enjoying yourself. But – as always – I must rush. Thank you for the coffee, and the talk – in English – more English than I've spoken for a long time. Goodbye.'

This time she shook his hand with a frank smile. With a great rustling of papers, she grabbed her briefcase under her arm, and with a billowing of black draperies, was gone.

Michael continued to sit at the table, watching her retreating back.

Her walk was full of confidence and the authority of a doctor. Hitherto, he had seen Leila as either actually or pretending to be a submissive Muslim wife, hiding behind her husband, but in reality, resentful to the point of rudeness. But this woman was quite different. There was no trace of either shyness or hostility. She was apparently at home with herself and completely in command. Nor, although it was too early to tell, did she fit easily into the mould of revolutionary heroine, everything subordinate to the political purpose. She was not a Nechaev even if she had once admired him. Did the Nechaevs sit and drink coffee, passing the time of day? It could not all be feverish meetings, churning out leaflets and plotting murder.

He gathered up his newspaper, preparing to return to his office. The student crowds had by now thinned out, classes were settling in. He saw Bob Ainsley, an Australian friend from the anthropology department, approaching with a grin. He slid into the chair next to him.

'Wow, you're taking your Islamism very seriously. If I'm not mistaken, that was the famous Red Leila who nearly burned down Cairo University in the seventy-seven riots – or at least that's what she is famous for. Now one of the leading sisters, if that's possible to imagine, of the Brotherhood. And stunningly beautiful – why does the other side deserve such wicked beauty?'

'She is good-looking,' Michael agreed shortly, hoping to divert the conversation. He was embarrassed to have been caught in such an encounter.

'Did you know I did research on the nineteen seventy-seven student movement last year? I had the luck to track down the ex-Professor of English Literature, who was in charge of Cairo University security then. A bit of an old twerp, but he was sure Leila was a Trilby.'

Michael looked blank. 'A hat?' he asked.

'Of course not. Don't you know your du Maurier? Edwardian best-seller, made into dozens of films. An evil genius, Svengali, takes control of the mind of a beautiful young girl, Trilby, and manipulates her, through hypnosis, into being a brilliant singer.'

'Who was Leila's Svengali?' Michael asked.

'Her husband, Khaled, instrument of the international communist conspiracy to destroy Egypt. According to the Prof. he plucked her out of the gutter, brain-washed her, and infiltrated her into the university as part of the Communist plot.'

'Sounds bizarre,' Michael said.

'The Prof. was a bit dotty, but completely convinced. I supposed his story was a literary embellishment on a story from Internal Security that made Khaled the evil genius behind the pretty face. Everybody thought she would end up in gaol or make minister, like most Marxists do. But one day, she just chucked it all in and joined the other side. She's no slouch. She'll eat you alive,' Bob proclaimed jubilantly. 'Or have your forehead pressed five times a day into the mosque floor.'

* * *

That was the innocent time of his stay in Cairo, Michael reflected, his Cairo youth, the overture when all seemed novel, exciting, promising. But the overture needed a closing movement; it needed a Colonel Mahmoud. If there was a heart of darkness, he must be close to it.

George, the affable and ageing head of the History department, held a cocktail party. He was English and somewhat foppish, medium height, entirely hairless and covered in fine wrinkles like old parchment, the reward of hours spent lying on Red Sea beaches. He called himself an unwrapped pharaoh. He had lived in Cairo, on and off, for 40 years, and was a thoroughly comfortable Cairene, incapable now, he said, of transplantation to any other location. 'My dear, one would just *shrivel up* in that *suicidal* English winter – and as for America: I doubt whether it is capable of *supporting* human life.'

The apartment was so crammed with antique furniture, books, paintings and bric-a-brac, it always seemed much smaller than it was. Michael arrived at the front door which opened almost immediately on to a large living-room, now crowded with people, spilling into the dining-room, the kitchen and the balcony. It was stuffy, with much talk, laughing and screaming with mirth or derision.

As soon as Michael crossed the threshold, he saw, towering over everyone and shaking with laughter, Colonel Mahmoud. Michael felt again that same strange mixture of feelings: pleasure, fear, guilt, hostility. And again, the lilt of 'Waltzing Matilda' came into his mind. It was bizarre.

'Michael! How perfectly delightful of you to come. The whole party now has a dimension of distinction. And congratulations on the publication of those Marx letters – but you're naughty to undermine the holy father.' George beamed. He was dressed in a

91

maroon velvet jacket, with a floppy cravat, the sort of thing artists used to wear.

'Come in, grab a drink.' He snatched one from a passing tray and passed it to him. 'And then you *must* meet Colonel Mahmoud before you do anything else. He is just leaving, but insists he must meet you urgently. Come and do your duty, and then you can have fun ...'

George led him, sliding himself through the congestion of people as if through a thick wood.

'Michael, this is Colonel Mohammed Mahmoud,' he said. 'Colonel, this is our visiting professor, Michael James, in whom you have a *special* interest. You should know, Michael, for your own safety, that he's a spy and knows *everything* about *everything* and *everyone* – probably including you.'

George laughed gaily, waving derisively at the Colonel. Michael had the irrelevant thought that perhaps they had once been lovers. George had some reputation in that area.

'George,' the Colonel protested. 'You know perfectly well I am *not* a spy, and even if I were, it would be most discourteous of you to say so.'

'But everybody *loves* spies, 007 and all that, and you were high up in military intelligence, and you still hobnob with the Ministry of the Interior, and that's *bulging* with spies.'

'Military intelligence was a long time ago, and I neither hob nor nob with the Ministry, which is bulging only with grey bureaucrats whose passion in life is parking fines, liquor licences, marriage certificates, all that great pageant, as you might say, of human pleasure and folly.'

The Colonel turned to welcome Michael with a great bear hug of a handshake. George sailed off hooting triumphantly.

'Dr James, how good to see you again. It is so long since we met – you have had time to become quite an old resident. How have you been? You haven't come on that felucca trip as you promised – nor riding at the pyramids.'

'Too much work, I am afraid, Colonel, and too many exciting things to do in this great city.'

'What a pity. But you still have lots of time ahead of you.'

The Colonel paused, and checked his watch.

'Please, forgive me,' he said. 'Sadly, I have an appointment coming up – just as you arrive – which I mustn't miss.' And then turning to look at him directly, he asked, 'And have you managed to get a handle on our own home-grown terrorists during your time here?'

'Oh no,' Michael responded, suddenly alert. 'I doubt that I could get near them, even if I wanted to – which I don't, given the density of your security services on the ground. In any case, someone who doesn't speak Arabic would be hopelessly lost in that world. But I understand from your newspapers that both Islamic Jihad and Gama'a Islamiya have given up on Egyptian targets, and, as a result, you've been releasing their militants.'

The Colonel's eyes narrowed as he looked at Michael. Was it suspiciously?

'I didn't see that report,' the Colonel said shortly. 'But in any case, there's lots more where they came from. New operations are being created all the time. Most of them die pretty quickly, but some don't. I've just been reading about one of the latest in a US embassy report. If you know your Islamists, I expect you have already seen it?'

'I don't think so,' Michael said, now doubly alert and keeping his gaze fixed obediently on the Colonel.

'The Americans speak of that Ismaili group from the early Middle Ages, eleventh to thirteenth centuries, in remote fortresses along the Syrian-Persian borderlands. The French called them the Assassins, a corruption of a word for hashish since those chosen to assassinate, the Fida'is or Fidawiya, were supposed to be high on hash. They were a secret brotherhood, blindly obedient to a spiritual head and dedicated to murder all opponents.

'Now it seems we have an outfit with the same name. Our young militants are perhaps not scholarly enough to know that the originals were named by foreign imperialists and that they were Shi-ite, unlike themselves who are, like all Egyptian Muslims, Sunni. Or else they want politically, as some say Al-Qaeda does, to abolish the enmity between Shi-ite and Sunni. But there again, perhaps they just want to preserve the old tradition of taking hashish before killing.'

The Colonel ended with a twinkle in his eye, but Michael was intrigued both at the length of this little scholarly lecture and the seriousness with which the Colonel continued to stare at him, as if expecting some reaction.

'How interesting,' Michael said somewhat lamely. 'I hope they don't have any success.'

'The hashish habit may save us,' the Colonel said. 'If they are all high and smell of it, we can sniff them out. I don't know where the Americans get all this information from – I suppose from spies in the Ministry of the Interior.' He giggled suddenly. And then, resuming his seriousness, 'So you can never assume it is all over. We thought that before, and then they tried to assassinate our President in Ethiopia, and blew up the US embassies in Kenya and Tanzania. There may be a lot of stuff to come. And then you can bring to bear your forensic skills to tell us all about it.'

Michael smiled and said he hoped the Colonel was mistaken. They moved off the subject and made small talk. There was more *badinage* about feluccas and horses, before the Colonel made his apologies, shook hands and moved away.

Michael found himself standing beside a woman in a flowered dress who looked vaguely familiar. Beside her there was a small slim man in jeans with a crew cut. Michael thought he might have been the man photographing on the balcony when the militia attacked the students. The woman, he remembered, had accused him of being mordant at the AUC welcome party.

'How's terrorism?' the small man said with a grin.

'Managing pretty well.' Michael returned the smile.

'They have to be exterminated like rats, no quarter offered,' the woman said scowling. 'This government knows exactly how to deal with them.'

Michael restrained himself, but was saved from making any reply by the arrival of someone who also seemed vaguely familiar. It was Emile Cyprian. Flowery dress and crew cut moved off.

'Michael, good to see you. And sorry not to have been in touch. We had a rush of new students, just as the semester was starting, far too many for our capacity in the Maths department, so I have been run off my feet.'

He seemed breathless with the effort to apologise.

'I had so much wanted to get a chance to talk to you, and apologise for that awful lunch with my brother,' he continued at a slower pace. 'I am a bachelor so I don't entertain at home. But maybe one evening, when you're free, we could go out for a meal?'

Michael realised he had rather forgotten Emile and looked afresh at this short, stocky man with the figure of a wrestler, so unlike his brother. His large fleshy nose gave him the look of an amiable frog.

'What about Wednesday of next week?' Emile asked.

'Certainly,' Michael said, surprised but without hesitation. In

Cairo – unlike the old days in London – his diary was almost always free in the evening. They agreed to meet at the entrance to the Greek campus.

Emile paused, as if preparing something. And then he began hesitantly, 'Did I see you chatting to my nephew's wife, Leila, in the Greek campus the other day?' He sounded uncomfortable.

'I didn't realise I was so closely observed,' Michael said with a smile.

'You could hardly miss her in the AUC, all in black among the multicoloured students.' Emile paused again, looking unhappy. Michael looked on encouragingly.

'I hate to do this, Michael,' he said at last. 'But I suppose I have some responsibility, and would never forgive myself if something went wrong. In fact, it was – to be frank – a little shocking that Leila, a committed Islamist, should sit like that in public, casually chatting to a man who was not related – and a foreigner at that. I mentioned it to my brother. He agreed with me that I should speak to you about it – come straight out with it.'

Again, he paused, groping for the right words, while Michael looked on puzzled.

'You see,' Emile began, 'she is so often … erratic, confused, even violent.'

'I didn't notice anything,' Michael said. 'She seemed confident and clear.'

'She changes her mood very quickly,' Emile continued, 'and not always to be trusted in what she says.' Again, he looked unhappy. 'I suppose what I am trying to say, and doing it rather badly, is that it would be wise to be careful with her.'

He stopped as if relieved that the ordeal was over.

'In what way is she untrustworthy?' Michael asked. 'I'm not a gullible youngster to be taken for a ride, nor in the age group to be swamped by a pretty face.'

'Well, no. I am sure you are capable of taking care of yourself,' he mumbled in embarrassment. 'But still it would be prudent to be extra careful, even if I can't explain very coherently why. Sameh agreed with me that I should warn you to be on your guard – and that is advice from some of those who know her most closely.'

Then suddenly he looked at his watch, and with obvious eagerness, said he was late for something and had to go. He shook hands once more, avoiding Michael's eyes, and fled in embarrassment.

Michael was mystified. He watched the square figure retreating between the tall slim people around. As he went, he was pulling his old black beret from his pocket, heading to thank George.

What had that been about? Was Leila psychologically unstable? There had been no signs of that, no tell-tale tremor of the lips or hint of hysteria in the eyes. On the contrary, she had seemed absolutely stable, completely in command of herself. If she was unstable, how did she hold down such a busy professional life?

And then there was Leila on whom he had hooked his images of the heroine, the incorruptible female Nechaev, storming the Bastille or the Winter Palace, facing the Prussians before Paris, courage to the point of suicide. He was more than ordinarily intrigued by this Leila. Or at least, he told himself, by the concept rather than the person. It was not because she was a woman or because she was beautiful, although that helped, but because of the idea of the supreme sacrifice in a cause, the secret conspiracy to overthrow tyranny at whatever cost.

16

Letter 9

Darling Jeannot,

I have been so longing for May for some warmth. The hedgerows of Cambrai must now be gay with flowers and merry with birds. The winter here seemed so long and wet and melancholy. But now the spring has at last come, you would hardly know it! We have so many long cold spells; only on Tuesday, there was some snow here in London!

There are so many foreigners exiled in London, mourning for their lost homes. It is a graveyard of crushed nations, all pining for a day of freedom. These melancholy thoughts were raised by Tussy, who, knowing our father's past, introduced me to a Polish émigré, a Mr Wladislaw Sobieski who was calling on Mr Marx. He is a maker of violins and well settled with his family here. It seems they live in the East End, which is very poor, and he has hundreds of children. He was driven to exile after the 1863 rising failed. He is pleasant and polite but my knowledge of Poland and Polish was too weak to encourage intimacy. He knew of Papa's work and regarded me, as a result, with much undeserved respect. However, meeting him reminded me so much of the great anguish of our Papa – do you recall? I was nine or ten, I think, and too young to understand what was happening. Poland was just a name then. But I do remember Papa's rage at the massacres, at the cruelty of the Tsar's Cossacks, and then his great hopes that Poland would be reborn in the rising. He longed to go, to volunteer for the partisans. But Mama's illness – and our existence – held him back. The rising was crushed even as she left us. No wonder the poor man was so downcast, so melancholy in our growing up. To have lost a darling wife, so young and beautiful, and to have lost all hope of your country's freedom! That evening, Tussy and I raised a glass of wine in tearful silence to the memory of poor, poor Poland – will she ever be free?

What other news do I have? Lenchen is ill. We take it in turns to prepare the food. I fear the standard of cuisine has much deteriorated! But we all rose to the occasion of May 5th, which was Mr Marx's birthday. Tussy and I prepared a grand feast, and all the old friends of the Marxes gathered to toast his health. It was very merry and, I think, touched his heart a little. I think I saw a glint of tears in his eyes when Mr Engels proposed his health. Mrs Marx was of course quite unable to control the waterfalls!

The first proofs of the French translation of *Das Kapital* have arrived. The translator was chosen very carefully but it seems it is not good, and much more work will be needed to get it right. I doubt whether I shall ever read it! We are all longing to see the picture of Mr Marx in the front of the final publication!

I am so glad your Russian madman has disappeared. I expect the Swiss police must be on his tail! But perhaps he has gone off with his friends from Bulgaria (I do not even know where that country is!), or to put bombs under the Tsar's train! I look forward to hearing how you find his *Catechism of a Revolutionary* if anyone will ever translate it for you.

The prospects for the International, I fear, grow no brighter. I expect you have heard that the General Council was blamed for the fire in the Milan Agricultural Academy? Mr Marx was much amused: 'along with the recent sun spots' he said! The governments may fear the hydra-headed International with its legions of fierce workers, but the quarrels within the organisation grow no weaker. Mr Engels held forth at dinner the other day on 'the score' of supporters in preparation for the next Congress of the International. He says your Mr Bakunin, and his 'Alliance', hold almost all of Italy. Spain is very divided. The Germans will be only weakly represented since membership of the International is illegal there. The Belgians are unreliable and the Americans hopelessly at loggerheads. Our countrymen here and in Geneva cannot agree, and the Swiss – the 'Jurassian Federation' – are with the Alliance. If all send representatives, with between 30 and 50 from Italy, we shall be lost and then all those terrorists will take over the International and provoke massive repression. The prospect is very gloomy.

But I shall end on a more cheerful note! What a grand secret! For now you have met your charming young lady from Perpignan, I hope there will be much more sweetness in your life. Has my intuition told me right? But how will you be able to afford to prosecute your suit? Is it impossible to find work there? I hope for your sake it is not.

Your most loving and devoted sister,

Natalie.

17

Letter 10

Dearest Jeannot,

Now – at last! – some measure of joy! London has suddenly stopped being the old awful black prison of the winter, but a new place of light and colour! The change is astonishing – even the terrible fogs seem to have decided to give us some peace. But people are not consoled – they say it cannot last and will soon return to rain and grey again!

But what excitement! Tussy has confessed to me that she is secretly engaged to be married to Mr Lissagaray! Another Frenchman! Three brave communards are invading this heavy Germanic family and taking it over! But it has to be a great secret. Do not breathe a word to anyone or it may get back to here and ruin poor Tussy. The family is entirely against it. Tussy loves her parents deeply and it will break her heart if they refuse her. Mr Marx dislikes L., saying he is too flamboyant and untrustworthy. I do not know why he says this, but it is sadly his view. And then L. is twice her age and she is still very young. I do not know what is to become of it, but for the moment Tussy is dizzy and glows with excitement (her mother cannot fail to notice).

More attacks on the General Council by the sections. They seem all agreed that Mr Marx is a great despot (in this they are at one with your Mr Bakunin and his friends). But Mr Marx protests that despots have armies, police and prisons to enforce their despotism, but he has nothing but the power of ideas and persuasion. Here in his home he is a complete model of reasonableness, even if sadly overworked with the endless business of the International and his writings. He labours mightily over the French proofs of *Das Kapital*

100

at the moment. At dinner last Thursday, he agreed with Mr Engels that he must leave the General Council and most urgently if he is to complete the second volume of *Das Kapital.* As you know, Mr Engels is financing this project and so cannot be pleased if in reality he is financing the General Council! But how can he leave the General Council when he and Mr Engels are the guiding hand and the light of the International?

Of course, there is the terrible possibility that they might be driven out! There are so many rebellions and quarrels. There is another frightful row on the General Council itself. An old close associate of M. and E. with the curious name of Eccarius has, it seems, turned against Mr Marx, quarrelled with him and resigned. It has created quite a storm. I cannot think what is going to happen to the International if Mr Marx leaves. I feel a despair that after its fine record, it may yet founder in its noble cause – and more from the internal quarrels of its friends than the machinations of its enemies. However, Mr Marx appears quite steadfast in his decision to leave the General Council at the next Congress.

Your letter had much to delight me, especially the vivid account of the walks with your friends around Geneva. I am so sorry your arm still gives you much trouble. Perhaps it is the weather (or the altitude), which leads to such aching? But I am very pleased that you have been able to resume drawing.

I was saddened by what you report of Mr Bakunin's comments on Marx – that he no longer has the 'instinct for revolution', that 'politics' has corrupted him since the days when he organised a secret International in the 1850s. I am sure Mr Marx does not want a strong State after the revolution just so he can concentrate power in his own hands. But I do see now how Mr Bakunin sees Mr Marx and M. Blanqui – and the Jacobins – as the same in this respect, in the belief in a strong State; 'the dictatorship of the proletariat' (there! Are you not mightily impressed that I know this phrase of M.Blanqui?). But Mr Marx is too afraid that the new State will be overthrown by its enemies unless it can defend itself properly, and that requires centralisation etc.

As to your *Catechism*, I think your Mr Nechaev is a madman (or a scoundrel), set only upon murdering as many people as possible. All this talk of his amazing 'single-mindedness,' his 'total self-sacrifice' to the cause does not impress me against the reality of his hatred. In this, I agree with Mr Bakunin – power corrupts, and if Mr N. came to command the State, he would turn Russia into a charnel house. I write this knowing how much you long for the spirit of total dedication which you think he displays, of suicidal courage. But he does not love humanity, only himself.

End of sermon! I am sorry to prattle to one who actually made a revolution while I slumbered in Cambrai! I hope you will forgive my impertinence – it comes only from love.

Your faithful and loving sister,

Natalie.

PS But you did *not* tell me about the young lady from Perpignan. Not a word. How can I bear my impatience. You *must* tell me or I shall never write to you again.

18

Leila III

Emile was at the Greek campus gate at seven in the gathering shadows of a mid-winter evening, hunched up in his beret and a short black leather jacket, the uniform, Michael thought, of the Latin American designer left in the 1970s.

'Ah, Michael, good to see you.' His English was good, with a slight French accent. He clasped both Michael's hands in his own. They agreed it was too cold to sit out so they would get a taxi to the Odeon enclosed roof garden.

The tiny lift took an age rising. They emerged into an airy wood-panelled restaurant with glass tables, shaded lights, potted plants and boxes of flowers. The pictures on the walls were David Roberts' old Cairo. Michael gazed out over the darkened roofs of the city, stretching to the skyline, with street signs flashing now. They took an unobtrusive table, in a corner behind a short palm tree.

The cuisine was Lebanese, and Emile favoured lots of different *mezes*, starters, with hot pittas as long as they liked, and then if they were still hungry, a main course. Getting serious alcohol was a problem now the government was making concessions to the religious. But, Emile had a deal with the owner, an old friend, and he would mix some Lebanese *raki*; he got a special supply from the Embassy. But it would make too much of a display to drink it Lebanese-style with lots of small glasses:

Michael waited a little impatiently while the ceremonials of ordering took place. He was longing to find out why Emile had issued such a peculiar warning about Leila.

When the ordering was done, they settled back awaiting the *raki*. Emile lit a thin cheroot.

Tentatively, Michael began, hoping he was not about to ruin the evening:

103

'Leila said her father was very ill.'

'Really?' Emile said quickly. 'I didn't know that. He's quite an old acquaintance of mine, although, as a pillar of the Church, we belong to quite different worlds. He's famous as a preacher among religious people in his Heliopolis church, even if he has gone down a bit of late. But I can easily check if he is ill.'

To Michael's surprise, Emile took out a mobile telephone and started to press the digits.

'No, as I thought, her father is not ill and has not been ill in the recent past. But he is very frail and old so he could easily be ill.'

Before they could continue, a tall angular man in a suit stopped at their table and with a nod at Michael, spoke in a low rapid tone to Emile. He left with another nod, and for a moment, Emile sat thinking as he smoked.

'Dear me,' he said to Michael slowly. 'He was passing me a message for Butrus that his friend Dr Ismael Khan has died in prison. Such a pity, a most talented psychiatrist. Butrus will be very upset. He says also that he thinks another crackdown is coming, and Butrus must be careful.'

At that moment, the drinks arrived and they were silent while the milky liquid was poured out.

Michael tried to return to the issue of Leila in Dokki. He reasoned – deviously – that Leila had sworn him to secrecy only with her husband, but not to anyone else.

'How odd if Leila's father is not ill,' Michael said. 'She told me she got news of her sick father whom, for some reason she no longer saw, from an official in the Coptic Church. In fact, quite by chance, I also caught sight of him.'

Emile smiled quietly, and said in a low voice, 'I wonder who that was? Was he a big bear of a man, bald with a cropped white beard, bushy eyebrows, dressed all in black with a big gold cross on his chest and lots of rings?'

Michael laughed at the accuracy of the description.

'That was Pierre-Georges, head of security in the office of the Coptic Patriarch.'

'Why would Leila, an Islamist, want to see him?'

'Well might you ask! Who knows? Perhaps he is an old friend from the days before she became a Muslim. Perhaps – as she said – she was getting news of her father, but without the illness.' He continued, with a slight laugh, settling back comfortably on his chair. 'You must know that Leila is a creature who collects rumours like a magnet collects iron filings.'

The stories were legion and contradicted each other on every point of the compass. She was said to spy on the Islamists for the Copts, on the Copts for the Islamists, on the Islamists for the Ministry of the Interior or one or other of the security services. Another rumour had it that she was once the mistress of a former head of Military Security, a Colonel Mohammed Mahmoud – and that was why she never spent long in prison (just enough time to earn her credentials on the Left). Others said she spied on the security services for the Islamists, which is how so many managed to escape capture. Or that she did all these things at the same time! Emile did not know where she got the time.

'Is that why you warned me the other day – at George's party – to be careful?' Michael asked.

'Oh Lord, Michael, I'm sorry about that. I made a fool of myself, not giving you any reasons. It was stupid. My only defence is that in a crowded place like George's party, you cannot speak openly. I thought tonight I owed you an explanation of more substance.

'But I have to put together the bits of my recollections of the story, and I have forgotten a lot. So be patient,' he said with a smile.

Leila had a difficult growing up, so difficult it would have been miraculous if she were not damaged. She was talented, but you did not always know which of her many worlds the talents were operating in. Her father had been perhaps the most talented Copt of his generation, from a family line of high Church dignitaries and clan chiefs of Upper Egypt. The great family house in Minya – almost a bishop's palace – was crammed with religious books, a lot of them written by ancestors of the family. It was of course preordained that he should go for the priesthood while his elder brother managed the great estate. His exceptional abilities marked him out early as a candidate for high Church office.

But, after all that youthful glory, everything had started to go badly wrong. Or rather, he had made one dreadful mistake. He had fallen in love with an extraordinarily beautiful girl – that's where Leila's good looks came from.

Emile paused. The *raki* was now singing in their veins. The food arrived, on a mass of small plates. The waiter, having surveyed the table, bowed and moved away. Emile resumed.

Fatimah was Leila's mother. The catastrophe was that she was Muslim. As a foreigner, Emile said, Michael would find it almost impossible to understand the sheer ferocity which these issues provoked, the obstinate violence of the bigotries.

Fatimah's family was important – clan chiefs, big landlords, ancestral lines of governors of the province, generals and judges. It might just have been possible if Leila's father had been willing to become a Muslim, but he could not. The clans mobilised for war – the Muslims believing one of their high-born daughters had been stolen by the Christians; the Copts believing one of their most promising sons had been seduced by a wicked Muslim harlot.

The couple did the only thing they could. They ran away. To Paris. There Fatimah was baptised into the Coptic Church and they married. This was such an outrage against Islam, it could have led to the couple being murdered even in Paris. They lived in exile for a number of years – Leila was born there. The young militants had not been able to get through to kill them.

Then the miracle happened. Both families had been shattered by the experience and were sworn to vengeance. Both were ruling families in the province. In fact, the fathers had gone to school together and been moderately close friends. They had both been ardent nationalists, and in those far off heady days, had sworn that religion would never divide them as Egyptians dedicated to freeing the country of the British. But they hadn't seen each other for twenty years, and both had inherited the chiefdoms of hostile clans. Fatimah had been the favourite child of her father, and Leila's father had been the rising star of his family.

But – and this had been the unbelievable part – the two old men met by accident, out riding along the Nile. It seemed impossible that they had not immediately turned with their followers and galloped off, or else pitched into an open fight. But they didn't. They sat in their saddles and talked, and grieved together. They say they were just weeping, and only the other really knew the grief of each, the loss of a treasured child.

The two old men had finally agreed to do everything they could to call the dogs off – not to kill the couple. Young hotheads on both sides wanted revenge. For them the agreement was almost treason. But the old men had given their word to each other, and committed the honour of the clans. They held it and faced down the opposition. And in those days, the deal, sanctioned by, as it were, the lords, could not be broken by the zealots. The couple could return to Egypt, but of course, not to Minya.

They came back and settled in Cairo. Leila's father, despite everything, was still held in some esteem by the elders of the Church, and so, ultimately, he was able to complete his ordination as a priest. He had of course ruined his career, but he or his family still had enough friends in high places. With a bit of string pulling, he was put in his present church in Heliopolis. The rich Copts there were a bit more laid back on these questions – and appreciated a first rate preacher. He had been there ever since, but was now getting very old. Most people had forgotten – or never found out – how he came to be there. Only the ancients like Emile remembered.

They were now well into the meal and slowing down. Michael was engrossed in the storytelling, in the food and floating on *raki*.

Leila grew up in Heliopolis, Emile continued, and when she was nearly in her teens, there was a second daughter, Esther. Emile did not know how much of the story of her parents Leila knew or how far it influenced her. But as she approached her teens, she had become pretty wild, well beyond the capacities of her poor mother. It had been worse since Fatimah had been diagnosed as psychiatrically frail with occasional schizophrenic episodes.

Leila was severely disciplined by her father who, although he adored her, knew nothing about bringing up children. She had begun rebelling by the time she was twelve. And she was both beautiful and looked older than her years. Her father could not control her, whatever he did. She was as intelligent as she was stubborn.

Emile remembered meeting the father at some function and he was discussing sending her to Paris to get her into a new environment. But in the end, he decided it would be worse having her run wild in Paris than Heliopolis.

Just after her fourteenth birthday, she ran away. She left a note saying she could no longer bear the family and was determined to lead her own life. It was unheard of – the sort of outrage that normally would be a major news story or bring in the police. But, fortunately for the family, the story did not get out, at least not beyond the Heliopolis Copts. Copt parents with daughters panicked, locked the door and threw away the key!

Her father was heartbroken. And the shock for the mother was probably what started her terminal decline. The father drove himself crazy, tramping the streets, looking for her, cornering his friends – and hers – to cross-examine them on where she might be, on whether she was still alive.

It seemed – Emile heard later – she had set off searching for some boy she thought cared for her. He lived on the other side of Cairo. She had managed to reach the river and that was some achievement, since she knew little of the city outside Heliopolis. Once she'd crossed Zamalek and the bridges, she got lost, and panicked as it grew dark. She was then, though she didn't know it, in Mohendeseen district, and desperate.

A kindly man had taken pity on her. He was a rich Bedouin, a businessman from Qatar, on holiday in Cairo and staying in his own apartment in Mohendeseen. The inevitable happened. He set her up in his apartment, guarded by three Qatari bodyguards and a cook-housekeeper. There they kept her, a pampered plaything for the occasional visits of the sheikh. Of course, he, being a scrupulous man, had gone to the trouble of going through a temporary marriage ceremony with her to make sure it was all legal.

She went into strict purdah – very rarely left the apartment, and then only with her minders.

She was there about a year, and Emile supposed it had given her time to realise what a catastrophe she had brought on herself. Emile did not know how she had got hold of narcotics – perhaps her bodyguards found it easier to control her sedated. But she became hooked on heroin, or something equally hard, and perhaps that deadened the pain. The only saving grace was that her patron did not ill treat her, no physical abuse.

Then, to crown it all, she had become pregnant. One disaster had followed another. It was a wonder she did not take her life.

She was visibly pregnant when the terrible incident took place. Leila's father had continued his search with increasing desperation. He completely neglected his flock, and they looked on with horror at the madness of his grief. No one dared reproach him . The bishop chose to look the other way. The old man looked amazing in his black gown, with a haggard insane face and wild loose black beard, tapping his staff as he went, like the spirit of death, the Grim Reaper.

Then someone had told him they thought they had seen Leila in Mohendeseen, in a black burka, and possibly pregnant. It drove the old man even more crazy. He redoubled his efforts, virtually living on the streets, tramping the pavements one by one, sleeping when exhaustion made it impossible to go on.

Leila was rarely allowed out, so it would seem impossible for him to find her. But as luck – or some crazy intuition – would have it, he found her. Emile said he had heard the story from Khaled years later. Her patron had taken her on one of those rare outside trips, perhaps as a reward for her giving him a baby, possibly a son. They were coming back, and as she stepped out of the Mercedes, her father at the end of the street saw her. He started running towards her, shouting hoarsely and waving his stick.

The minders closed in swiftly. They pushed Leila back into the car, and turned together to attack the old man. She must have seen it all from the car window without being able to do anything. Khaled said that the old man lashed about him in his mad rage with extraordinary strength. He did them a lot of damage, but that only redoubled their fury. He was lucky to escape with his life. They beat him without mercy, and left him, a broken bundle in the gutter, and drove off.

Someone finally found him and recognized a Coptic priest. The Coptic hospital took him in. He was six weeks recovering, with a broken leg, arm and fingers, multiple gashes and bruises to his head and shoulders, stamped on hands, but luckily his sight and his hearing were intact.

The police knew all about the Qatari, but of course were not going to do anything. The government would not risk irritating the Gulf Arabs. They were too important politically and financially, certainly compared to the Copts. In any case, as Leila's patron would have told the police, they were legally married, and she was not being held against her will – hah!

The old man had been heavily beaten in his body, but that was not as severe as the beating to his heart and mind. There was nothing he could do to save his daughter. Friends gathered round, even people who hardly knew him, to try to hold him up. The Church took it up and made representations, without effect.

The story had swept through the community and finally got out. The Copt account was that a foreigner, a Muslim, had kidnapped a Coptic girl and held her by force as a sex slave. There were letters of rage to the President and anyone else. The story in the press was something different – a Coptic terrorist had, without provocation, attacked a Qatari tourist in broad daylight on a Mohendeseen street. It was said to be the same as when Islamists attacked the German tourists in Luxor. The government expressed its anxiety that this was not the beginning of a wave of Coptic terrorism against Muslims, and commented that Muslims could not indefinitely be expected to tolerate unprovoked attacks without retaliating! The hotheads tried to rally a crowd, but fortunately not much happened. Little more got through the censored press, and the incident was soon forgotten, except among Coptic fathers with daughters.

The train of disasters that fell on Leila's family was not over. Her mother, driven to distraction by the shame of what had happened to Leila and her father, had become quite inconsolable. Calmly and quietly, she tidied the house, and then took her small daughter Esther to a high building near their house, and holding her hand, jumped off.

Emile said he did not know how Leila's father hung on to his sanity. For a

109

long time, he had not, and in his delusion, saw all the scourging as the just punishment for marrying a Muslim. The bishop sent him to a monastery in the western desert to recover.

After some months, to everyone's surprise, he did make some partial recovery. He was made of stuff as rugged as his daughter. He pulled through, even though he remained a picture of gaunt misery. His preaching was black despair at being alive. But his sermons were still full of anguished eloquence, and this made them in written form, paradoxically, popular among Copts of a certain age. As his fame in Egypt grew, his Heliopolis following for the spoken word, had shrunk. But he was so old and frail, the establishment would, sooner or later, persuade him to retire back to that monastery in the western desert.

Leila was so ashamed at what she had done to her father, she never dared face him again. That fight on the street in Mohendeseen was the last time she saw him. It was cruel, because he would have been proud of her as a doctor if he could have got over her being Muslim, which Emile doubted.

Emile stopped and looked seriously at Michael. 'We've eaten all the food and drunk all the wine. Would you like coffee and a smoke?'

'A hookah, a shisha?' Michael asked brightly.

Emile nodded and ordered two, with tassels and pipes clad in striped felt. The glowing coals arrived in tongs along with coffee, and soon the clouds of soothing smoke billowed out, the water gurgling like a mountain stream.

Leila was shattered by what she had seen happen to her father. She was hysterical, tied to her bed for days to prevent her doing herself damage. There was an idea that the shock would force a miscarriage, but it didn't.

When she came to herself, she knew she had to act. The Qatari was so excited by her pregnancy and the possibility of a son (he didn't care about a daughter), she knew she had to do everything to deprive him of that pleasure. This was to be her revenge. But to do that she had to escape, and with enough money to pay for an abortion. Emile did not know how he knew all this, nor how she thought she would, on her own in a strange part of the city, find an abortionist.

She set about the task with the zeal and intelligence that was her strength. Over the weeks, she gathered together a pile of money that lay around the apartment, and while the Qatari was in the Gulf, one afternoon pretended to take a good dose of heroin – or whatever – to give her bodyguards the slip. Then, while they were in a drunken stupor, she escaped.

110

She walked as far away as she could, and then booked into a cheap hotel. She had to be careful since a woman on her own, even if in a burka, *was a prostitute to a hotel keeper, to the police or anyone else. She told some story about being from Upper Egypt – complete with the accent – just arrived and searching for her father who had changed addresses without telling the family. Fortunately, they did not ask to check her papers, and her money was sound enough. Once located in the hotel, she spread out and ultimately tracked down a back street abortionist, though she was probably medically far too late to risk an abortion.*

They did her no kindness. It was a botched job. She could not have children after it. Worse still, they stripped her of everything she owned, including her money, and dumped her.

Emile did not know how she survived. She took to the streets, wandering as a vagrant, dodging the police and sleeping rough. She took whatever man she could, provided he could pay and she could earn enough for a shot of heroin. If there was anything left over, she would get something to eat. She must have become exceptionally streetwise to survive at all, and had perhaps learned a ruthlessness that served her well. But she could not have gone on for long. AIDS would have got her, or being beaten up by some sadist. Influenza or something else would have carried her off. Then she would have been food for the dogs.

Emile paused, as if imagining the horror of Leila's descent into hell, drawing the smoke deep into his lungs before letting it out in streams.

She was found by someone, curled up, trembling and moaning, under the steps up to one of the bridges across the river. She had been beaten up, and was nothing but a bleeding bundle of bones and sores. They took her to a local clinic for the poor run by a Coptic charity. It was at night, and, by chance, it was Khaled who was working there as a part-time volunteer doctor on the night shift.

Khaled had led a sheltered existence and the clinic was his first experience of real life. He was overwhelmed by the tragedy of this young girl. It became a challenge to him to save her, to bring her back from the edge of death. He wildly overran his time, treating her, bandaging her up. Then they filled her up with drugs, food and care, patched the problems of the botched abortion, and in time, slowly began to prise her loose from heroin. Khaled said he was amazed at how quickly she responded. She arrived as nothing but a filthy skeleton in rags, wounds, scabs and sores all mixed up. And it seemed only a

111

matter of weeks before she had filled out, found some renewed energy and even, he said, smiled. She would say nothing about her past and how she had come to be where she was – Khaled learned that years later. But everyone assumed she was Christian – she had some kind of Christian family symbol tattooed on the inner wrist of her left hand.

When she had become strong enough to leave the clinic, Khaled found her a home in the house of a Coptic widow in Ma'adi, a woman who had been a nurse.

He was now committed to restoring Leila fully. Without letting his parents know anything, he paid any costs involved, and ultimately settled an allowance on her. There she convalesced. In time, Khaled began to take charge of her education. He hired a local tutor, and then, as she developed, other teachers. She had become his only daughter and he lavished on her his great resources of affection and care. Leila was a responsive pupil. He says he was as astonished at her capacity to learn as he had been at her physical recovery. Her father and a good school in Heliopolis had perhaps given her a sound grounding. Even when she had been a captive of the Qatari, she had filled her time with reading.

Khaled began to think that, if she could get the entrance qualification, she might even make university. She did so well at this, he then began to think she might make medical school, which seemed to attract her. And that is how it turned out. She was admitted to Cairo University's medical school. Khaled was quite short of money at that time, particularly given how much unpaid voluntary work he did. He had turned to Emile for help to conceal the matter from his parents (in case they thought he had a mistress). Emile agreed to help until Leila started work.

What Khaled hadn't allowed for was that Leila would also pick up his politics, his Marxism. She developed her own brand of militant feminism. She had become a leading figure in the students' union and in campus politics. There were all sorts of agitations in those days and in a lot of them, she was one of the leaders, and came close to being expelled or arrested several times. Emile supposed her work as an agitator is what pleased Khaled most – she really had been recreated by his care.

Leila was too much of an individualist to be a proper Marxist. She was no good at being a routine party member. She was for the spectacular deed that would inspire the millions. She was fascinated by the story of the Latin American guerrillas in the 1960s. The style and verve of the act was more important than building the party bureaucracy.

When Khaled wanted to marry Leila, Sameh and Yasmine were horrified. Emile did not think they ever stooped so low as to think they might get a society *wedding in the cathedral, packed with distinguished guests, but for Khaled to marry a street vagrant was too much.*

Emile stopped, musing, gazing into the middle distance, exhaling slowly a thin cloud of smoke. The pipes were nearly finished. Then he said, reflectively:

'Each generation reversed the trick. Fatimah became a Christian and her daughter returned to Islam. I suppose since Leila can't have a daughter, the spell is broken.'

He paused again, and Michael realised the story was finished.

'What an astonishing account, Emile. I'm only sorry that my curiosity and your indulgence has wrecked your evening and your meal.'

'There is a final note' Emile said.

Leila had finally gone to gaol, but only for a year. It was crucial for turning her into a Muslim. Islamist women were not supposed to be active in the world, but there were some university feminists who became Islamists. In gaol, she met the rare women militants of Jihad and Gama'a . They were no walkover for dialectical materialism. On the contrary, they went on the attack on all that was wrong with Marxism. When she came out, she said nothing to Khaled and certainly did not put on the veil. She saved it up until she had him on his own, and that happened with the term in Cambridge. Other things happened that nearly parted them. Leila became very close to a Palestinian doctoral student and that swept her into the politics of the Occupied Territories. She did not volunteer for Hammas but it was very close.

Emile had now paid the bill. He sat, silently smoking.

'Of course, Michael, this is all in confidence. It is strictly between us.'

In the street, Emile took another taxi, and gave Michael a lift to the Nile so he could walk home. It was dark and quite cold, but a lot of people were still about, walking along the river bank, and the traffic seemed as thick and noisy as ever. The high-rise hotels – the Nile Hilton, the Semiramis, Shepheards – were a mass of lights. People were working late in the Foreign Office building. He stood for a while under the October 6th bridge, watching by the light of the street lamp the family of dogs who lived there, scavenging for food dropped by the passers-by. He had a new image of Leila now, crouched under the bridge, trembling, moaning.

113

19

Letter 11

London, 3 June 1872

My dear Jeannot,

What a to-do! It seems my letters to you are all about betrothals! Are they not the most exciting things in all the world? Yet the excitement does not make ordinary life easier. Mr Longuet is finding it most difficult to find work. He went to Oxford to see if he could set himself up as a teacher of French, but it came to nought. Perhaps the English do not want to learn the language of the *communards*! It is so hard for young people today to find a place, especially if they are of the respectable sort, and even more if they are foreign – and worse still, Parisian. People even look at me, if I have occasion to confess to being French as if I might carry a head under my arm or have blood on my dress!

Meanwhile, the point of weddings is to prepare. They – Jenny and M. Longuet – are to marry in mid-July, possibly the 18th or 19th. So we must all prepare. Think of the haberdashers and tailors, think of all the immense quantities of hats, scarves and waistcoats that have to be got ready and all the immense anguish and hopes that must be experienced in choosing this or that! I have written to dear Papa beseeching his agreement for a new and exceedingly grand dress, with simply miles and miles of linen and silk and brocade – I shall look like a princess. Tussy and I have already spent hours working out what this should be before we take it all to Mrs Buttonnose, as Tussy calls her, to be made into a dream. Perhaps all this talk of marrying *communards* will also suit me! Dear Papa will have much to say on that!

But the other news is much less delightful. The troubles for the International come thick and fast. The leaders of the Danish

114

Federal Council have been arrested. The Belgians held a congress in Brussels and decided the General Council had grown over-mighty and the rules should be changed at the next Congress so that it will be no more than an office to collect information and exchange correspondence (a view, I believe, shared by your Mr Bakunin).Then each national section would have *complete* authority to manage its own affairs as it thinks best. Tussy makes great fun of this, asking then *how* the poor Russians could ever get help from outside?

Herr Liebknecht, Mr Marx's great friend whom I mentioned before, has just had his sentence for treason confirmed in Dresden. Tussy is quite cast down and sends comfort continually to her old friend, Alice (Herr Liebknecht's daughter).

I met again Mr Vaillant. He came with friends to meet Mr Marx to discuss how they can guide the General Council back to good sense and save the International. I think Mr Vaillant has been entrusted with the task of revising the rules of the General Council, though to what end, I know not. He seems a most gallant gentleman.

All the family now speaks of nothing but the *infamy* of Mr Bakunin and his Alliance. It is most sad that it has come to this. Yesterday, Tussy said what a pity it was that Mr B had sunk so low when once – on the barricades in Dresden in 1848 (according to her father) – he was such an heroic figure. Yet now she feels B. is ruined, perhaps by the years in a Russian prison or in Siberia, reduced to being a conspirator, consumed with the desire to corrupt all the sections and destroy the International, so doing the work of its enemies. And now that this wretch, Nechaev, is involved – he who believes that the only deed to start revolution is murder and terror – what can be made of it all? Tussy is almost tempted to believe Mr Bakunin must be a paid agent for Count Bismarck or the Tsar! I know how much you admire him and tell you this only so you can see how terrible, and destructive, are these divisions among those who, at heart, all agree on the main questions!

But we should speak of more delightful matters. Why do you not mention the delightful mademoiselle from Perpignan? Is it now too close to your true heart, too sacred, to be reduced to the banality of letters to your sister, even though she longs to hear such news?

Your loving – and puzzled and muddled! – sister,

Natalie.

20

Letter 12

London, 17 June, 1872

Dearest Jeannot,

A short letter since we are to go shortly on an expedition to the dressmaker – in search of wedding glories! Jenny, Tussy and I (with possibly Mr Engels' dear friend Mrs Burns, and her niece, Pumps). We shall make such a merry party!

The important news is that the General Council has at last settled the date – early September – for the next Congress of the International, and the place – Holland. It has caused much excitement, and an immense increase in activity, with furious writing of letters (by Tussy, and I suppose, by her father and Mr Engels) to all and sundry. They fear that without the greatest efforts to rally their supporters, the Italians, the Swiss, the Belgians and the Spanish will swamp them all. Mr Marx said at dinner yesterday, with great solemnity, that the life and death of the International was at stake. It could disintegrate into warring factions – to the immense delight and amusement of Bismarck, M. Thiers and all the rest. I was quite astonished to hear that there are especial fears that many will come to the Congress with 'forged mandates', false credentials, and they will then be able to outvote those who have been genuinely elected by their national sections. Is it possible that such things can be done in a noble cause?

As if these tribulations are insufficient, the news from Madrid is not good. Mr Marx's only grandson, Schnappy (Tussy calls him 'Fouchtra'), may be failing fast. The Spanish climate has done nothing for him, and the worries of all this political activity cannot help his parents to care for him with single-minded devotion.

Mr Vaillant, it seems, is ill, although Tussy says he is now somewhat improved.

In haste – they are calling – your loving sister,

N.

21

Mona

He saw Leila only once again, and it was much later. There had been many trips to London, many bundles of letters to be posted, buried deep in his luggage in the hold and carried obediently through the airport and airline security controls. Each time, he swore firmly that he had not accepted to carry anything for anyone.

The weather was still cool in Cairo. But there was now a promise of spring in the air. He was able once more to resume sitting over a beer on his balcony in the evening, watching the moon mingling with the glow of the setting sun, the women taking in their washing from the clothes lines on their balconies, men in singlets sitting in the cool of evening, the lights of buildings around going on or off. The great mysterious house below with its enormous glassed-in balcony stood, as usual, dark and empty, a silent monument to a bygone age of great pashas and beys, giant landlords of the Delta. Once it had felt the cool breezes from Alexandria, across the delta, but now it was ringed by higher buildings. Beside it, he could see the grand white house behind high steel fences, with splendid gardens, green and full of trees and shrubs. People said it was the home of the American ambassador, but there were no signs of habitation. A terrorist, he thought, could lob a rocket from his balcony into it, without the six or seven policemen at the gate being able to do anything.

At sunset, lines of birds wheeled across the sky, black at one angle and then as they turned, becoming pale grey and almost invisible. Sometimes he played a cassette, Saint-Saëns' Fifth Piano Concerto, *The Egyptian*. It was briefly his passion. The flight of flamingos rising from the Nubian Nile in the first movement intoxicated him, though he could also hear the gruff disapproving voice of Helen's father, deploring such 'programme music' – music should be pure sound, not painting a picture of birds wheeling over a muddy river.

118

With the warmer weather came the morning mists or traffic smog. On his morning walk to the AUC, along the river, the high buildings in the city centre were often invisible in fog. It was cold at that hour, and he passed old men with shawls over their heads, blowing on their fingers and stamping their feet, or sipping steaming tea from saucers. The police, still in their thick black winter uniforms, were as always loafing on the street corners of the richer neighbourhoods.

That last meeting with Leila was the most bizarre. She was a different person each time he met her. This time, the new personality was off his mental map of her range. She had been by turns resentful, frosty, warm and welcoming, and then – what word was right? – good, a person of integrity. He wondered if she reinvented herself each time, for his benefit or her own amusement?

This time she accosted him. It was late morning as he was crossing the crowded Greek campus quadrangle, He heard her low voice call – 'Dr Michael'. He turned with a smile. This time she had someone with her, a woman, a massive figure with rolls of fat and immense spherical bosoms, ill-concealed under her coloured *gallabiya*. She was a study in conjoined globes, model for some Picasso lithograph of a bather. On her head, she had a kind of spongy coloured bathing hat. He assumed it was a token hijab. As she walked towards him, she swayed from side to side, like some great ship under full sail. Beside her, Leila looked tiny and fragile.

Michael recognised her almost instantly. She was the woman on the balcony behind the photographer taking pictures of the student demonstration outside the Greek campus.

Leila was smiling at him, a welcome so warm he thought she must have made a mistake. But she had not. As he reached the ill-assorted couple, she seemed more vivacious than he had ever seen her.

'How good to see you after all this time,' she said. 'Let me introduce my aunt, Mona – Mrs Sharif.' She turned to the large lady. 'This is Dr James of the AUC, a good friend of Khaled and his father.'

'Pleased to meet you,' Mona said in a low husky voice, staring at him with narrowed eyes of appraisal. 'You're the terrorism man, aren't you?'

Then, to Michael's greater surprise, Leila said, 'Do you have time for a cup of coffee with us?'

They made their way through the usual crowd to the tables and chairs outside the refectory. Michael noticed Bob sitting at one of the tables, reading the *New York Times*. He nodded, and Bob raised his eyebrows derisively as if to say: not again, flirting with danger?

For Aunt Mona to sit in one of the wicker chairs was a major enterprise, fraught with danger. Michael was impressed that she was even willing to try. She clasped the arms of the chair behind her and gently and slowly lowered herself. The chair crackled and seemed almost to groan. But she held it so it did not tilt and spill her to the ground. Michael guessed the width between the arms was not wide enough for her hips. She overflowed in unpredictable directions. He unconsciously positioned himself to try to break her fall if it came. But all was well. The chair did not collapse, and Mona finally arrived, fanning herself at the great effort involved. Michael wondered how she was going to get out.

When he returned with three plastic cups of coffee, the two women, heads close together, were giggling like schoolgirls. Michael smiled with them. He carefully put the cups on the table.

'Oh, Dr James,' Leila said in excitement, 'you will be shocked at our frivolity. My aunt takes twenty years off my life and reduces me to silly giggles. Aunt Mona was picking out the boys around that she fancies. She has this word – it may be English or American – "dishy".'

The two went off again into hoots of laughter. Mona's vast globes heaved as she cackled and dabbed her eyes. Leila tried to pull herself up sharply and put on a straight face.

Michael admitted to himself he was shocked. Frivolity – with sexual innuendo – did not fit his picture of Leila.

'You must stop, Aunt, here of all places. You'll ruin my reputation as a serious professor. And poor Dr James has his academic dignity to look to.'

'Leila, don't be a bore,' Mona said. 'Just because you are dressed in this awful black and read the holy book every twenty minutes does not mean there is no room for fun in the world – for "cakes and ale", isn't it, Dr James?' she asked archly. 'The fun of coming to the AUC is to inspect the boys – you do have a superior variety. You don't let yourself have as much fun as you ought, Leila. I am sure Dr James is old enough to take all this in his stride.'

'Aunt Mona lives outside Cairo now,' said Leila, 'so I hardly ever see her. Then she descends on her broomstick and turns us into giggling schoolgirls.'

Michael was astonished at her gaiety. Her cheeks were flushed with excitement. Her bottom lip seemed now particularly plump and red – surely there must be a trace of lipstick there? Her eyes were merry, sparkling with mischief. Could this be the austere Islamist?

'You're not shocked, are you, Dr James?' Mona asked archly. 'The English are supposed to be more relaxed about sex now – wasn't London one of the centres of free love in the sixties? I remember an English film from that time that really impressed me, what was it called? Oh, yes, *Tom Jones*. Did you see it?' she asked Michael innocently.

'It was all the rage. But it's not much of a guide to the sexual habits of the English.'

'What a pity,' Mona said. 'I was astonished by it as a teenager.'

Michael felt the conversation was getting close to dangerous topics, and glanced nervously at Leila. But she was smiling broadly. Could this Mona be an intimate of his ice-cold terrorist?

'I haven't seen it,' said Leila, 'and if I get the drift, it sounds as though I shouldn't. And, Mona, stop trying to shock my friends.'

'Dr James, if I'm not mistaken,' Mona said loftily, 'and I had the privilege of being alive in the sixties, the age of liberation. I lived in New York in those days, Dr James, and it was wonderful. And,' turning to Leila, 'since you didn't have that privilege, you shouldn't be so sniffy.'

Mona finished her coffee and looked at her watch. Michael noticed how tiny the watch looked on that vast wrist, buried in flesh.

'Oh lord, look at the time. I'll be late for Sharif and you know how irritable he gets. We fixed to meet in the Nile Hilton and here I am miles away. Look, Leila, no time for chatter. I'll see you this evening – in the lobby, and then we can have a heart to heart.'

Leila jumped up to help her aunt out of the chair. It was another major operation with much stress on Mona and the wicker chair. As she struggled, she caught Michael's eye and said with a girlish grin:

'Oh, how the years of excess catch up on me – years of beans and beer!'

To Michael's astonishment, she winked, and finally broke free and rose to her feet. Leila hugged her and gave her a kiss.

'Good to meet you, Dr James,' she said, waving her enormous hand, the fingers like sausages, except that they were cut by countless rings. They shook hands, and she murmured, 'Hope to see you again.'

She lumbered off, waddling slowly, like an immense hippopotamus, nosing its way through the willowy saplings of the students.

'And I must go too,' Leila said, suddenly quick and businesslike. 'She's not really my aunt, but she was good to me years ago, and she's fun. She asked specially to meet you – you're famous!'

'Goodbye, Dr James.'

'Could you not call me Michael,' he said suddenly.

She stared at him in surprise, those penetrating green eyes looking directly at him. She held his glance for a moment, and he felt his heart miss a beat.

'Of course, Michael – though the Egyptian form is more courteous, "Dr Michael". And I'm Dr Leila.'

'Dr Leila,' he said with a smile.

She gave a wave and was gone in a rustle of black skirts.

Michael continued to sit at the table in the now warm sun, reflecting on the bizarre encounter. Who was this aunt and how did Leila know her – or tolerate her frank sexuality and frivolity? How was it consistent with all that black puritanism? How could Leila even know a person like Mona, let alone meet her in a public place? This Leila was no austere revolutionary, no Nechaev. This Leila enjoyed the world too much to risk her life overturning it.

Bob slid into the seat next to him. 'You *are* mixing with dubious characters,' he said mockingly. 'Not only Red Leila but now the formidable Mrs Sharif, Mohammed Mahmoud's watching eye on the students, though not the most agile spy. She must be busy, now that Bush is getting himself ready to bomb Iraq.'

122

22

Letter 13

London, 30 June, 1872

Dearest, dearest Jean,

Well, now at last it is warm, beautiful and sunny. I cannot believe it is the same place – nor the same people, because we are all now so delighted and rejoicing at the blue skies. The house of the Marx family is on a slight hill, above the city, and so we have some views when the weather is clear although sadly, we cannot see the river. We take long walks on Hampstead Heath with all the family (and all the pets). It is quite a grand procession with all our hats and dresses and parasols. Last Sunday, we met a group of *communards* there, also taking the air, so we all promptly sat down on a grassy hill and began 'political talk'. The men had brought some beer and that increased their liveliness and argumentative excitement. I fear I lay in the grass and dozed delightfully, unaware of the great events being conducted all around me!

Can you imagine? My dress for Jenny's wedding is going to be the most beautiful in all the world that ever was! It is a delicate shade of mauve, with grey and white, with an enormous skirt and a short coat. And the hat! A hat with streamers to match. And gloves and a handbag. And the gloves are a gentle grey and of a leather so soft, you must think it is linen! I grieve that you and Papa will not see me in all my finery. You would not know what a grand lady your sister has become, not at all the little Cambrai dormouse.

That is the good news. The bad is that Mr Marx is so gloomy that he will never finish his great book. He is now consumed every minute of the day with managing the affairs of the General Council, and whole days can go by without seeing him at all. It drives him to distraction, saved only by his wonderful sense of humour although he is much ill-used and often angry. He seems beset on all sides with the fiercest enemies. There are endless meetings here and at the home of Mr Engels, and weekly at the headquarters of the General Council in Rathbone Place. To prepare for the Congress, they have created an executive committee, and this takes much of Mr Marx's time – they meet from the afternoon until past midnight. Poor Mrs Marx worries all the day long that his health will not stand so much strain, and Tussy labours even more to protect him from doing silly unimportant jobs.

However, Tussy is also quite pessimistic. She says the combination of Mr Bakunin's Alliance, the Proudhonists among the *communards*, and the English trade unionists (who do not want a revolution at all lest it soil the gown of their own dear Queen!) can destroy the International, especially if everyone knows her father is to leave. It would be a terrible outcome at a moment when, Tussy says, prospects for revolution are emerging everywhere, when the International is so vindicated on all sides. Yet what hope is there if the most clear-eyed and resolute leaders are so at odds over issues, which often seem quite childish! There! I have said it, and if you will, you may dismiss me as a silly girl who knows nothing! But I think grown men, brave leaders of their society, should exercise more self-restraint and calm.

As for me, I am a little homesick, and would much love some quiet and peace in Cambrai. Here, all is noise and movement, coming and going and fierce discussion, as if it were a military headquarters in the midst of a great battle. But if I were in Cambrai, could I ever grow to love the peace there again? I might now be spoilt by all these great events, and just wither away in dullness.

I long to see dear Papa. His letters hide his sadness in his solitude. But also I am torn, longing to see what will pass at the Congress – what am I to do?

And leaving to the end, the saddest news. What a pity about the young lady from Perpignan. I am sure you are wrong and it was not your arm which persuaded her parents to discourage her. But, then, if she were so persuaded by such a matter, it is far better for you to leave her. There are, fortunately, many more and many more worthy fish in the sea!

With much love,

N.

23

Letter 14

London, 15 July, 1872

Dearest Jean,

Ah me, what a great sadness! Little Schnapps – Tussy's darling Fouchtra – finally gave up the long struggle! The whole family is plunged in grief. Tussy wept for two whole days – I thought her heart would break. Mr Marx hid himself in his study, and Mrs Marx also disappeared. Poor Lenchen kept us all going, weeping as she did so. A creature so small deserved much more from this world. Now Mr and Mrs Marx will never see him, not even his tiny grave in a foreign land. His mother and father must be quite inconsolable, for it is the third child to pass away, and they must feel Providence has condemned them for ever.

As a result of poor little Schnapps passing away, Miss Jenny has of course postponed her wedding to Mr Longuet (it was to have been very shortly). Mr Marx, already exhausted from his work and the daily press of urgent affairs in the International, is so cast down, he has now gone with Mr Engels to Ramsgate to try to distract himself there. If we can, Tussy and I may go down there for a day or two to join them – I have heard so much of it, the beaches, sea and shops. But I fear it will not give Tussy much comfort for her loss.

So it was a sad sad Bastille Day on the 14th, the saddest I have known since poor Mama passed away. I hope that you at least and your friends were able to toast that great time and all that followed. I fear we dearly need such memories of past glory to console us for the present darkness when all seems lost, the enemy triumphs, and even friends can agree on nothing.

I am glad you were again able to attend the meeting where Mr Guillaume addressed the assembled Jura workers and they

125

responded so enthusiastically. It is sad to think that, if they become a little more prosperous – like the more prosperous watchmakers you mention – they forget all about the liberation of the people and become 'bourgeois'. This seems to be the picture here if Tussy is right. The skilled workers are well organized in 'trade unions' and have comfortable homes and wives who wear many petticoats and bonnets, but they show little favour towards the lot of the majority of the poor. Those who keep the fire alight are the unskilled, but so often their day-long toil and lack of means make it impossible for them to read enough to know what future society holds. I grieve for your mass of poor cottage watchmakers, threatened with imports of cheap watches from America. Here, the Irish building workers, those who labour in the great London docks, in the carriage works and some of the factories, are in the same position. I suppose they see the corruption of the better-off workers and those who claim to represent them to the great Mr Gladstone and the Liberals, and identify it as politics, so all politics is corruption. Mr Bakunin would then be right: all politics, all matters connected in whatever way to the State, are necessarily corrupt and corrupting. But I still think Mr Blanqui has some merit. Can the proletariat defend itself if it just tries to abolish the State? And if the victorious people create a militia to defend themselves, how will we protect the new society from the corruption of the militia? The optimism of Mr Bakunin – that all will live in harmony and love once the oppression of the State is removed – is splendid, but I cannot rise to the level of such hope. There are too many who preach the interest of the people but betray it as soon as they have an opportunity to gain.

You see, your sister's faith is a little lacking, but not at all in her brother!

Your most loving sister,

Natalie.

(Editor's Note: if Natalie wrote her normal fortnightly letter to her brother on 29 July, 1872, a copy was not included in the bundle recovered from the Cambrai bureau and no trace of it has been found elsewhere.)

24

Khaled in Flight

The spring arrived in Egypt and the heat became slowly more oppressive. He survived the period of dust storms, marvelling when he returned from London at the carpet of dust coating the apartment and furniture. The air-conditioning now became vital, and Michael noticed how instinctively he now avoided the sun, kept to the shade, or dashed between islands of air-conditioning. It was impossible to walk to work any longer without getting soaked with sweat. There were rumours of big trials of Islamist activists, of possibly a major police round-up of suspects; but as usual, the government allowed little information to leak out.

Before the heat became too extreme, he made a short trip to Yemen. In Sana'a, the Yemeni men had abolished women – or rather, turned them into black letter boxes, scuttling through the streets like daleks. Sometimes there were eyes peering out of the tent.

When Michael returned to Cairo, it was already time to start planning the end of the second semester and what he would do during the long vacation – perhaps a couple of months in England, catching up on his life, and then back to Cairo for a month to work in the libraries before his second year began.

He saw much less of Khaled now. He seemed very busy, but not so busy that he did not have time to bring the usual bundle of letters to his office for the monthly trip to London. Khaled was full of apologies and much gratitude. But what had started as a small service – in exchange for learning about the Islamists – had become a tiresome chore, and the exchange had broken down. Many of the letters were not addressed in Khaled's handwriting. Michael had become a general mail service – and to what end, he dared not think. Most of the letters were to addresses in England, but some went to other destinations – Hamburg, Milan, Vienna, Madrid. Almost all were directed to Muslim names. He had become part of a communications network, the purpose of which he did not know or share.

It was mid-May and unbelievably hot when Michael at last had a call from Khaled, suggesting they have lunch once again. They were to meet at the side entrance to the Greek campus. It was less conspicuous than the main entrance. Michael sheltered in the shadows of the entrance, feeling the waves of heat lift off the tarmac outside. The woman in a purple gown who sold chocolate bars on the pavement was sheltering from the sun on a broken sofa in the shade of a side street; some people said she lived there permanently.

Khaled was late. It was unusual. Thirty minutes passed. Michael felt the sweat running down his front, his shirt sticking to his back.

When Khaled finally arrived, he was out of breath and distraught, tight-lipped. He was dripping with sweat, carrying his jacket. He seemed nervous, and almost ran into the entrance as if seeking to hide from the street. He was carrying a small case.

'Something has happened,' he said in a low voice, eyeing the security guard on the door who was checking the students in and out.

'I can't go to lunch with you today, I'm afraid – sorry. Can we have a word in your office?'

Michael showed the guard his pass again, and Khaled was waved in. He followed him through the corridors to his room. Khaled slumped into a chair, and allowed himself to cool in the chilled air. Michael had never seen him in such a state. His normal suave polish had deserted him.

'What's happened?' Michael asked.

Khaled hesitated, as if weighing his words carefully, and then began, 'You've heard of the second set of trials now just completed?'

'The Jihad group?'

'And many others. Nine are to be executed, seventy-eight given long prison sentences. The prisons are so bad, it's better to get the death sentence. And what a mockery of a trial – trumped-up charges, forced confessions, bribed witnesses, and so-called evidence that, if it were not so tragic, would be laughable. Just think, the defence lawyers are not allowed to see the prisoners at any stage! Some of Egypt's finest are going down.'

Michael suddenly remembered Calcutta in 1972: 4,000 executed,

12,000 gaoled, 'some of the finest of a generation'. Another time, another place, but still the same terrible slaughter, the blood sacrifice of the young.

Khaled was abstracted, musing over one of his friends who was to be executed. 'He was a doctor, excellent physician and as fine a man as you'll ever meet. He went to his death, defiant to the end. They were all singing as they were led out of the Haekstep cage. What kind of a world is it where the best are slaughtered? The mothers and sisters and wives were weeping at the prison gates, banging their heads on the bars. The terrible waste of it all.'

Michael thought Khaled might weep, but he stayed dry-eyed and bitter.

'And what are they doing to the villages and small towns of Upper Egypt, where nobody can see – or to the slum areas here? – laying waste and arresting all the adult males. Many never return. Thousands of arrests and hut demolitions. The government denounces what the Israelis are doing in the West Bank and Gaza, but they do exactly the same here to their own people. It's a reign of terror.'

Khaled was silent for a moment. 'Anyway, there's a general crackdown, which, as always, catches more of the innocent than the guilty. I have to disappear until it is over. That's why I can't come to lunch. It's always the same – a brutal campaign to terrorise the population, and then, when the police have filled their quota of arrests, they call it off.'

'But why you?' Michael asked. 'And what about your patients?'

'They arrest anyone, with or without suspicion, so it is as well to keep out of their way. As to the patients – my colleagues are understanding and will cover for me.'

'Where will you go?'

'I don't know. We used to have a series of small hotels run by friends in the slum areas where, suitably disguised, we could hide up for a time. But the police have got wise to that. I'm waiting to find out where I might go. The main thing is to keep away from country areas where strangers are easy to spot.'

Then Michael heard himself say, on impulse: 'What about my place in Zamalek? That will not be on their list of suspect areas. The porter is often not around so you could slip in without being seen, and, provided you lie low there, who is to know?'

Even as he said it, he wondered what he was doing and why. The golden rule in his trade as political voyeur was never to get involved, never to move from observer to activist, never to be complicit. But finding refuge was complicity.

Khaled looked at him silently and in astonishment for a moment, turning the idea over. Then slowly and thoughtfully he said, 'It is a possibility. You might be right. It would not fit their thinking – Islamists don't live in Zamalek nor in the AUC. But it is an impossible thing to ask and very dangerous for you. If they catch you, they could throw you out of the country or into gaol. Will you take that risk?'

'Yes – it is only a few days, and I'm sure they won't be looking there. After all, I live across the road to the American ambassador!'

'But you must hurry. Look, take my door key – I have a spare – and let yourself in. There's a spare bedroom and bathroom, and food in the fridge. I'll draw you a map, and when you've got the idea, you can destroy it. Ma'arashli is the street, where the Coptic cathedral and the AUC student hostel are.'

'I know it,' Khaled said. 'This is an astonishing piece of generosity in something that is not at all your war.'

'But what about Leila,' Michael said suddenly.

'Oh, she's already gone to ground – she'll be all right,' Khaled said almost carelessly.

They shook hands, and Michael took him again through the corridors to the entrance to clear him past the security guard.

He returned to his office and sat for a time. Why had he done that? It was weird. He was an old timer in this game, yet here he was behaving like a novice. What was it to him? He was in principle opposed to Islamism, not even a sympathiser, yet here he was courting arrest, scandal, over something in which he had no part, no interest. Yet despite the almost absent-minded questions, he was already being overwhelmed by a sense of urgency, into action mode.

He started to plan – he must buy more food. A bachelor's fridge was usually inhospitable, so he'd better stock it for two. He wondered in sudden alarm whether there was any pork or bacon in the fridge. He thought not, but in any case, Khaled was no sheltered violet; in Cambridge he must have come across these things. What should they eat this evening?

He need not have worried. When he arrived home that evening, carrying the shopping from Al Saud's little supermarket, the apartment was empty. Khaled had not followed his advice. It was not wise: the more he went in and out, the more likely the porter would be to challenge him. There were shaving things in the second bathroom, and some pyjamas in the guestroom, but no sign of their owner.

Nor did he return while Michael was awake. He lay still in bed, trying to hear the front door open above the hum of the air-conditioning, but heard nothing. He woke with a start at two, panicking that the police were already pounding on his door. But the apartment was silent – a distant car roared, a dog bayed and a foolish cockerel prematurely heralded the still distant dawn.

So it continued in the days that followed. Khaled seemed to be there in the morning but sleeping. Michael left him a glass of fermented milk with a note suggesting they meet for supper. But when he returned in the evening, there would be a note from Khaled, apologising that he would be held up.

On Thursday morning, Michael reflected, he would be sure to see Khaled on Friday since he would be home and the AUC would be closed.

That Thursday at the AUC stood out in his memory afterwards. The class began at 4.00. He gave them an overview of the role of terrorism and anarchism in the socialist movement in preparation for their final examinations. When he finished, one of the brighter graduate students suddenly burst out:

'But what was it all about? Socialism, Communism – from Russia to Nicaragua. Why did so many people believe it so strongly and kill for it? It seems all so senseless. Why did Nasser make such a massive mess of everything here in Egypt, and why did people adore him while he was doing it?'

Michael was taken aback. He sat down, scribbling some notes. Why indeed? Why had we all believed so strongly and been so wrong, or at best, half-wrong? He stumbled into some kind of conventional answer. The State, *their* new State, had seemed to offer people hope, an escape from the new work disciplines of capitalism, from foreign domination, from poverty. And there were fresh audiences for this new religion of national liberation – peasants swarming into the cities; new masses of students pouring through higher education; new social classes rising through the State bureaucracy and the military.

But also the world was a dangerous place. Newly independent

131

governments had to defend themselves against a return of British imperialism and the threat of their neighbours. That promoted centralised power and militarisation, the disciplines of which often seemed the same as socialism. But before the project was even near completion, globalisation undermined it all. The State was no longer salvation, just one among many predatory agencies.

He knew his answer did not grip the minds of his listeners; it was abstract and remote. The old State agenda had not been intellectually refuted, only forgotten, so that today's young could no longer feel what had been at stake. For Michael's generation, the Russian revolution had been a part of their lives; now it had slipped away into history, along with the Ming dynasty or the Incas or the Reformation.

Had it all been a mistake? The passions, the hatreds, the martyrdoms. Was the struggle for universal freedom just an illusion? Or were there so many byways, so many covert matrices of power beneath the surface, that nothing could ever be the simple achievement of purposes. The Bolsheviks set out to free the world, and ended up with one of the most terrible tyrannies ever seen. Was therefore even the attempt wrong?

He was tired and deliberately put aside the questions. He walked to the Estoril for a drink with Bob and another friend, three solitary bachelors. Universal liberation must wait.

25

The Horror

Michael did not stay long with Bob and James in the Estoril. Then he made his way through the traffic to the edge of the river. As he walked home, the twilight was still heavy with the day's heat, though there was now a blessed breath of a breeze from the north, from Alexandria, ruffling the surface of the river and gently swaying the palms. The traffic horns blared from the road, but it did not disturb the courting couples lingering along the river bank, furtively cuddling. He crossed the October 6 bridge, passing the two homeless old women in black, curled up asleep on mats on the pavement, turned down the steps on the Zamalek side and crossed the road, passing the Grand Youth Art Gallery on the corner – 'Treasures of Romanian Young Painters'. On July 30th Street, he passed the pork and cheese shop, again wondering as he always did how the Coptic shopkeeper could be so public in flaunting his differences.

The lift refused to move. So he climbed the dark stairs slowly, skirting the great sacks of garbage left by the collectors and groping for the light switch on each landing. He passed the door to the Taiwanese company on to whose balcony his socks fell when the breeze blew them off the clothes line on his floor; by now they had developed some passing relationship when he reclaimed his socks.

He felt physically weary as he climbed, wondering, yet again, what he was doing in Cairo. Helen had been the anchor in the golden days. But even those had been vulnerable. So many times he had driven to Heathrow to meet her, rejoicing that once more she had escaped bullet and bomb in some far-off war.

On his floor, he again groped for the landing switch. In the sudden light, he found his key. And paused, listening. There were no sounds from the apartment, only the distant street noises. He unlocked the door. The double lock was not secured so perhaps Khaled was at home. He always hated entering an empty apartment and was pleased in anticipation that Khaled might be there.

As the door swung open, he saw that one of the table lamps was on and was pleased. Then he noticed, with a start, what seemed a tiny figure, crouched on one of the carpets. It was a woman, hugging her knees with both arms, her head bowed. She was, he thought – although it was difficult to tell in the low light – in a dark green gown and head scarf. She was smoking, one of his ashtrays beside her knees. Was the hand that held the cigarette trembling? it was not possible to be sure.

He must be in the wrong apartment. But the key had worked. The woman was so abstracted, she had not heard him turn the key and open the door. He closed the door firmly to make a noise, and then the woman turned her head.

'Leila,' he said softly. She stubbed out the cigarette and rose gracefully to her feet. It was the first time he had seen her in anything except black, or the plain grey she had worn in the Cyprian apartment. Her hair was gathered up inside the scarf, tied below her chin in a way that had once been fashionable. She was completely silent, motionless.

She turned to face him, staring dully, her eyes unfocused. She looked awful, her skin dull, puffy and grey. Part of her gown seemed to have been torn, and when he looked more closely, there were dark patches on the hem. His eyes grew used to the semi-dark, and he noticed that several chairs were knocked over, a small table overturned, and perhaps more dark patches on some of the rugs, and black smears on the white marble floor. One of the carpets was scuffed up in a tangled heap.

'Leila,' he repeated, more insistently. 'What has happened? Where is Khaled?' His voice rose as he tried to penetrate her abstraction. She continued staring at him blankly as if she had not heard his question. Then she lowered her eyes wearily.

'Leila, what has happened?' He almost shouted at her. He was tempted to stride over to her and seize her to shake some sense into this lumpish mute.

Then, at last, she spoke. 'He's gone,' she said stonily, tonelessly. He did not recognise her voice. 'He had to go.'

Then – long afterwards, the memory kept the power to chill him –

he witnessed the first transition: a sudden surge of rage swept through her and seemed to spark her back into life.

'He had to go – Nazarene scum! He was a police spy. He worked for the Americans …'

She trailed away, as if the rage had exhausted her small stock of energy. She returned to apathy. Her eyes sank down and her shoulders drooped.

'How can that be, Leila? How do you know?'

'We have our people – in the security services, in the Ministry, in the US Embassy, everywhere,' she said dreamily.

And then, with more force: 'The police are everywhere. The organisation is too vulnerable – it could so easily be destroyed. And then the last hope for Islam and Egypt would be gone.'

She was talking to herself in a low tone, or talking herself out of her mood of apathy. Michael felt he was eavesdropping.

'There must be no breach of security,' she continued. 'We cannot afford the risks of keeping a spy in our ranks just in order to fool the enemy. It was necessary that he be removed.'

The last words tumbled out, the tone a mixture of rising rage and bureaucrat-speak – the 'necessities' of authority. How the rebels mimicked the official communiqué, donning the garments of officialdom to pretend to an authority they lacked.

Michael felt the menace in her voice, the tone of controlled rage. Her body exuded a tangible hostility, an acidity. He was frightened, sensing her powers of violence, of aggression. He must treat her with the utmost care. She was either already deranged or coming close to it, and her reactions were not predictable.

The menace and the official tone faded. She returned to musing to herself:

'He was never a real Muslim. Where was his beard? I know how he slipped away on Sundays, and secretly ate pork sandwiches.'

Michael was tempted to giggle at the banality of pork sandwiches in the face of the great issues of mankind. The temptation showed him how tense he was and he made an effort to relax.

'But you were both good Muslims,' he said soothingly.

She stared at him and a flash of fury seemed to strike her, 'I am not a Muslim,' she shouted, 'and never will be.' She stopped abruptly, tears choking her voice. 'But of course I am,' she said more gently. 'I will go to my grave in the faith of the Arabs, and with great joy in it.'

The fury returned. 'But you know all this, don't you, Dr James?'

she suddenly sneered. So she had recognised him; that was a small step back from the brink, from madness.

'Of course, you know it perfectly well,' she continued. 'You knew more about Khaled than any of us, didn't you, Dr James? You were his contact with British military intelligence? All those cosy lunches, little chats, and then the monthly mission to London for debriefing and opening the mail you carried. We are not fools, you know ...' And then, more menacingly, 'And we believe in vengeance. We are not Christians who turn the other cheek. The payment for betrayal is death.'

The rage brought more colour into her face, pink patches on each of her cheeks in a white death mask. She was panting for breath. Her body was angular, as if composed of sharp hostile edges.

Michael curbed his alarm. All this must be part of the syndrome, he thought, periods of apathy broken by vengeful paranoia. But how to humour her out of it, calm her?

'Go, Dr James, go while you are still alive and can decide to do so. If you don't, you also will descend into the nightmare.' She paused again, abstracted, and then suddenly shouted, 'And why are you here? You do not belong here, you have no place.'

Her face had started to become firm and resolute. Her eyes were now exercising authority over him. And then, another transition, as if waking from a dream, she was swept by panic. She crumbled, suddenly tiny and vulnerable, a frightened child, twisting her fingers in the corner of her dress.

She pleaded plaintively, 'You won't betray me, Michael? Oh, please say you won't betray me.' She approached him and put her hand gently on his arm, staring intently into his eyes. 'Please, at least do that for me.'

'There's nothing to betray,' he said soothingly, patting her hand to comfort her, much relieved that the rage had cooled.

She turned and moved away from him until she was a couple of metres away. Then she turned and faced him. Those enormous glistening green eyes now held him, fixed in their stare as if mesmerised – or mesmerising. The cobra had him in her gaze. Then, with one swift gesture, she whipped the scarf from her head, all the time watching him. An immense swathe of black hair fell about her shoulders, glistening in the lamplight. He caught his breath for the hair transformed her face. Her beauty was like a blow to the head.

That was only the first impression. It seemed to him that she was, as if by a conscious act of will, growing more beautiful. This was the strangest transition of all, and it disarmed him. She stood, perfectly still, half-smiling while she willed herself back into beauty. The colour returned to her face – the dead fish pallor of her skin became suffused with gold; the pale thin lips seemed to grow full and scarlet; the blank eyes widened and glistened, seeming to glow as they held his gaze. The sharp edges of her body rounded, the angularity of rage or resentment softened.

He could not believe it. It must be some trick of the light, the filmmaker twisted the lens and dreary black and white was transformed into glorious colour. She was still half-smiling as if proud of her trick, her lips slightly parted, gazing at him – he noted with some alarm – as if she were in love. He tried to remember the transitions – from apathy to fury to pathos, and now the simulation of a courtesan. The courtesan was submerging him, turning him from voyeur to participant, exactly as Khaled had done.

At last she spoke. She seemed completely normal.

'Michael,' she said in a low voice. 'I am so tired, so very tired. I will tell you the whole story, but first I must rest, I must have a little warmth and comfort to restore my courage ...'

She was calm and majestic, completely in control of herself – and of him. With slow deliberation, she was undoing the line of buttons down the front of her gown.

Michael began to feel alarm. 'What are you doing?' he asked, but she made no answer. Despite his sense of panic, he also felt his excitement mounting. It was absurd, a corny striptease. The thoughts raced through his mind. She was a psychiatric case, needing help, not sexual abuse. She was not responsible for her actions; it was his duty not to exploit her vulnerability. She was another man's wife, a man who was his friend and to whom he owed the duty of protecting his wife. And what if Khaled should suddenly arrive back? The penalty for adultery was stoning. And adultery with a foreigner not of the faith probably earned an even more drastic punishment. Above all, he was a foolish old man with a woman young enough to be his daughter. Who would ever forgive him?

The gown slipped from her shoulders. Beneath, she was wearing a short muslin jacket with pale blue trousers. He noticed she was not wearing a bra and wondered in confused fashion whether this was a relic of her feminist days. As she slipped the jacket off, she braced her shoulders back so that her breasts stood out more prominently. Michael watched himself observing her breasts, marvelling at their size. But perhaps that was already the distorted sense of the voyeur. Her hips were larger than he had thought.

Still her smile held his eye, fixing his attention. She seemed to rejoice at the panic in his eyes, at the power she had over him, mocking the vulnerability of men, their foolishness. Her derision seemed so palpable, he was for a moment also amused by his own absurdity.

His loins were long unfamiliar with the feelings now swamping him. But they were swinging into the centre of his consciousness. He remembered some saying that an aroused man loses half his brain. He had not protested. He was already complicit, compromised.

She was now naked. The striptease was over, and she was moving towards him, supremely confident in her command of him. It was virtually rape, Michael thought. But why? Why was she going through this ritual? Or was it part of the psychiatric condition? He was an old man with wrinkles and a paunch, and knew that, even if once he had been attractive, that was long ago. Indeed, ruefully, he reflected that after all the years of celibacy, he might not even be able to raise an erection. He was tempted again to smile derisively at the thought – after the great seduction scene, the male member refused to perform.

She took his hand to her lips and kissed the tips of his fingers gently, still gazing at him. He stared as if without a will of his own. She put her hand on his shoulder and leaned her head against him. He was engulfed in the warmth and scent of her body. His qualms were being melted away. He remembered her plaintive, 'Do not betray me.' Was that it? Was this a bribe to keep him silent about something he was yet to discover? Was she binding him, like a husband, to the implicit vow made when a man sleeps with a woman? His detached thoughts were being subverted by his loins. She must know how weak he was. Not only would he allow himself to be seduced, he would accept the bribe for his silence, his complicity. His price was pathetically low.

His arm encircled her waist. He knew that now he had made the decision. She began to take his clothes off, until he too was naked. He tightened his embrace, and then with sudden surprise, felt her fondling his genitals, her proud eyes smiling frankly into his as she did so. He was intrigued at her care, her measured and methodical exploitation of their mutual sensuality.

She pulled him across the room, away from the scuffed rug and bare marble floor. She folded herself to the carpet, pulling him down as she went. And pulled him into her.

Afterwards, as sleep invaded his mind, he remembered briefly half opening his eyes. She was lying on her side, curled up beside him, her head against his shoulder. Her hand rested loosely on his pelvis. He noticed, now close up, the tattoo on her wrist. Was it a flower? Or a stylised cross, or a cross shaped to resemble a stylised flower? He noticed also that there was grime in her fingernails, on the nails themselves, slight traces on her skin. It was the hand that had so carefully coaxed him. He decided he could not now face whatever those traces meant, and allowed sleep to engulf him.

He cannot have slept long. When he woke, the flat was in darkness, outside lights glinting through the windows and the sounds of cars passing. He was covered by a blanket, though his back was cold from the marble floor below the carpet.

He reached out in the darkness to touch her but she had gone. He got up, clutching the blanket around him like a child. By the dim light from the street lamps through the glass doors to the balcony, he stumbled to a table lamp and switched it on.

His clothes were scattered about, but of Leila, there was no trace. Except a hairpin on the white marble floor and a few long black hairs, He called softly, but there was no sound in the apartment. His body reeked of her, as if she had anointed him, made him, even if only temporarily, part of her domain.

He stumbled across the room in his bare feet, putting on more lights. Absent-mindedly he straightened the scuffed rug and bent to examine the patches on the carpet and the smears on the marble. It seemed, as he had half-surmised, that it might be dried blood.

He stumbled along the corridor. The door to Khaled's room was wide open and he put the light on. The room was in chaos, the bed clothes churned and half off the bed, the chairs turned over and more blood, if blood it was, a lot of it, streaking the sheets, great black patches on the carpet, on the wall. He noticed one pool on the marble, which was not yet dry, and felt sick.

He turned back to the corridor and made his way to his own room. The door was open. He hesitated. He switched on the light, and caught his breath. It was impossible to believe. Some immense struggle must have taken place. The blood was now everywhere, and he heard himself cry out, his legs weak with shock. The smears on the walls were like a child's hand-painting, and there were more pools on the marble, wet stains on the carpet.

And then he glimpsed through the door into his bathroom something else. He could not stop now. He put on the bathroom light gingerly, and saw at a glance. Khaled, naked, bluish-white, like a slab of meat, half floated in a bath that seemed full of blood. He noticed the terrible eye cavity, exposed to all the world, a hole into his head.

He thought he must be screaming, but he wasn't. He stopped, panting and retched convulsively.

Khaled's throat had been cut, but there must have been a great struggle since what could be seen of his body above the scarlet waters was marked with multiple stab wounds, long lacerations and dark bruises. As he looked, he thought he saw amid the gore of the cut throat, a wire. Was it possible, he thought stupidly, both to cut a throat and garrotte someone? The single eye, wide open and in terror, stared at him, as if defying all the evidence around, as if mocking him that he should be so impressed by this elaborate staging.

He stumbled out, breathless, still carefully stepping to avoid the contamination of blood. His mind was racing. He remembered for no particular reason, Macbeth – who would have thought the old man had so much blood in him?

He tottered, as if drunk, leaning heavily on the wall, and made his way unsteadily to the kitchen. It seemed endless.

There, with a trembling hand, he poured himself a tumbler of raw Scotch. He drank it, coughing, and poured another. Then he made his way slowly back to the sitting-room. He sat, crouched, shivering in his blanket. He felt so cold, so tired, so old, and thought he heard himself softly moaning.

Then the pity of it came upon him. Poor Khaled. He had grown fond of him. He was a fine man. And now cut down. Could she have done it? It was not possible – even if she were strong enough, her gown would have been more torn and blood stained. Unless she had changed her dress. But he had seen no torn and blood-stained black *gallabiya*. Perhaps her madness had given her the strength? She was, he assumed, capable of murder, but not of a struggle suggested here. How could she have been so calm and calculated in seducing him if all this had preceded it? Perhaps seduction was a routine that

140

calmed. If she could have done this, then perhaps she was, after all, his female Nechaev, pitiless sword of retribution cleansing a world of filth?

Slowly, the drink burned his stomach, and he emerged from his confusion. His trembling ceased, he returned to some measure of calm. What was to be done now? He would have to go to the police and face all that, face being beaten up, perhaps tortured, perhaps gaoled for a long time or even forever. Should he get a lawyer, or was that just a bad joke with the Egyptian military tribunals? According to Khaled, defending lawyers were not even allowed to see their clients before their trial. Other prisoners just disappeared.

Then he remembered the hairpin and the long black hairs. He dropped the blanket and, naked, crawled over the ground, inch by inch, searching for incriminating evidence. There was nothing. He collected the hairpin and the hair. How strange that there should be so little material evidence to show what had happened. He dressed to get warm, although the evening air seemed normally warm.

He felt he could not face the bedrooms again, but forced himself to do so. Averting his eyes from as much horror as he could, he searched but again found nothing. Leila had left no trace. No doubt the forensic bloodhounds of the police might sniff out something extra, but there was nothing obvious.

In his own bedroom, he retrieved the picture of Helen from the floor. The glass had smashed and there was a streak of blood across it. His eyes filled with tears as he tried to wipe it clean. But then he noticed something else. On the mirror, there was an Arabic sentence with an unfamiliar symbol beneath. It was dark red and at first he thought it was blood, but when he looked more closely, it seemed to be paint – or lipstick.

He flushed the pathetic pieces of evidence down the lavatory in the guestroom and carefully wiped the handle. He returned to the sitting-room and again sat, thinking. He should ring the embassy, at least to record that he had once existed before disappearing into the Gulag.

'You are in a bit of a pickle, old man,' the jaunty night duty officer at the embassy said. 'What a thing to come home to – body in the bath! You need Agatha Christie. You know she was once in Cairo?'

The man gave a cough of laughter at his whimsy. Was it possible he could be so gross?

141

'The Egyptian police are a bit rough on this kind of thing and we can't often do much to help, but we'll try. I'll get a lawyer in the morning – Galal is good and we'll try to track you through the labyrinth. Any next of kin you want informed? I'll have to tell the ambassador tonight and he may want to have someone speak to the Ministry of the Interior. He'll want to keep it out of the newspapers if he can – these things really do muck up normal diplomacy. The key thing from your point of view is not to give up hope – you know we'll be beavering away outside to get you out.'

Afterwards, Michael again sat in silence, sipping his third drink. He felt warmer. Did he now go and report to the police? Did he ring them up? But probably no one would speak English. Should he call the porter and get him to call the police, but the porter spoke almost no English. Could he call the police in front of the ambassador's house?

He thought suddenly of the children. Will was abroad, but Jane might be contactable. He rang and, to his surprise, got through with one attempt. He could almost feel her trembling as he told her what had happened, those tiny veins in the side of her forehead throbbing as panic swept her.

'In your bath,' she said incredulously. 'But how?' He tried to explain.

'But, Dad, what a fool to let him stay with you,' she said angrily. 'How could you? He's sure to be a terrorist.' And then – 'But can't you just hide up? Can't you take sanctuary in the embassy until it's sorted out?'

'No, I wouldn't get in. Only diplomats get that sort of privilege. I have to grin and bear it. As soon as I get through, I'll call you. Don't worry, it will sort itself out.' He didn't believe it, but there was no point in alarming her.

'No!' she said firmly. 'As soon as I've fixed the children and I can get a flight, I'm coming.'

'But you can't do anything,' he protested. 'Who knows how long it will take – you can't leave the children. There's nothing to be done until the police have had their chance.' He felt weak and tired, overwhelmed by events.

'I'm coming,' she said, 'so don't argue.'

'Please don't,' he said weakly. 'But I have to go – it will look suspicious if I am too slow in reporting to the police. Fortunately,

I'm well covered in terms of an alibi. I was drinking with Bob and James until seven, before I came back, so if the autopsy can pinpoint the time of death, it will be clear I was not here.'

'What?' Jane exploded. 'The Egyptian police and accurate autopsies. You must be mad. They'll kill you, Dad: be serious.' Then she stopped, and went on, 'Maybe the embassy can fix an autopsy?'

'Maybe,' he said, without much hope. 'But I must go – love to you all, and to Will. Let him know when you can.'

He rang off, feeling he was cutting the umbilical cord to life. He sat for a time, thinking, exhausted. It was already nine o'clock and it had taken so little time to collapse his life. Was there any point in packing a bag, or would the police just steal it? He got some paracetamol and plasters. And sat again, as if disabled.

He reflected that what he had seen in the bathroom was terrorism. He had devoted his professional life to the subject but never actually seen the blood. Now he was drowning in it. And this was just one body – imagine the torrents of blood, of limbs, of torsos, of mass graves in war, a battlefield. There was nothing heroic here, no noble young men and women putting their lives on the line for what they believed. It was – like every war – just butchery, what mad dogs did. To glorify it was to enter into the madness of nations, the fantasy that there was anything fine in war; that it was splendid to throw away young lives so carelessly.

As he was getting ready to leave the apartment, he remembered Sameh. Poor Sameh and Yasmine. He had a responsibility to break the news, not leave it to the police or the newspapers. He turned back. He rang, wondering as he always did whether the security services monitored his calls. It didn't matter now.

'Sameh – Michael James. I am afraid I have some terrible news for you.'

'What?' Sameh said hoarsely. 'Is it Butrus? Is he dead or hurt?' How swiftly we leap to our worst fears, Michael thought.

'I'm afraid you must prepare yourself for the worst,' Michael said in a low voice, as gently as he could. 'He has been murdered.'

'Oh, my God!' He could hear the old man beginning to cry, his words strangled before they could come out whole.

'The silly fool. All that idiotic politics. How could he run such risks? What happened?'

Michael tried to explain, as briefly as he could, leaving out the details of the flat and the struggle. Sameh seemed hardly to be listening. He suddenly interrupted Michael violently.

'It was that witch that did it, wasn't it?' He broke in, and Michael knew who he meant.

'Who?' he asked.

'Leila, of course. She always hated him and tried to destroy him. She corrupted him with all this Islamic nonsense, used him and then, when she'd sucked him dry, got rid of him.'

'Don't say that,' Michael protested, with as much firmness as he could muster. 'There is no evidence of her involvement at all,' he said, lying calmly. 'And it is most dangerous now to say so – the police will only need your word to let their bully boys loose on her. Let's not prejudge the issue. The poor girl will be distraught when she learns – will you tell her?'

'Poor girl!' Sameh sneered. 'She hasn't slept with him for years, so stupendous is her love for him. Being a Muslim, he could have divorced her instantly, but he was too good for that.'

'Sameh,' Michael interrupted. 'I have to go to the police now and report.'

'You can't do that,' Sameh said, suddenly emerging alarmed from his grief. 'Give me time to get some advice and ring round what contacts we have in the police – or hide in your embassy. Let me ring Hosni and see what he says. Otherwise, the police will kill you – or at least, torture you.'

'No, I can't delay any longer. The longer I delay, the more they'll think I have something to hide. I'm very sorry to have had to bring you such terrible news, Sameh. It is such a blow for you and Yasmine. Please tell her how much my heart goes out to you both.'

'Wait, Michael, wait,' Sameh pleaded desperately. And then, on an impulse, 'What about ringing that chap who teaches at the AUC – Colonel Mahmoud. He was something high up in the government and I think you know him. He must know what to do. I have his home telephone somewhere – hang on.'

Michael was aware of a strange sense of relief at the mention of Mahmoud's name, of comfort, followed swiftly by the old feeling of guilt and of an anguish so strong he felt tears come into his eyes.

There was a sound of rustling, a drawer being violently opened. Then Sameh's heavy breathing returned.

'But he's security and military,' Michael said, 'not homicide and civil.'

'Oh, Michael, those things don't make any sense here. He'll know who to contact. Please, Michael, for my sake. I'd never forgive myself if I let you be taken by those thugs.'

Michael wondered why Sameh had Mahmoud's home telephone number, but he copied it down. He waited a moment, reflecting on his strange emotions – who could it be that Mahmoud reminded him of?

He rang. Again, surprisingly, he got through.

'What a happy surprise, Michael!' He heard Mahmoud growl in his deep smoker's voice and Michael found it soothing. 'I was just thinking that I had cleared my timetable enough to think about our felucca trip on the Nile – perhaps with a little gathering afterwards for dinner in the Officers' Club in Zamalek. They have quite a good cellar there, though they don't like it mentioned anywhere.' He gave a laugh.

Michael explained as briefly as he could why he was ringing. The Colonel was suddenly silent throughout the exposition. Michael was not sure he was still there.

'How very curious, Dr James,' he said finally, breaking the silence. 'In my line of business, I notice I never quite lose the capacity to be surprised.' And then after a pause, 'It must have been a terrible shock for you. I suppose the man in your bath was Khaled Cyprian, the Copt doctor turned Muslim? And husband of the charming Leila?'

'But how did you know?' Michael asked, alarmed at Mahmoud's knowledge.

'Oh, just a lucky guess,' Mahmoud said, clearly thinking hard as he spoke. 'Some of the pieces of the jigsaw may be falling into place.'

'You know the Cyprians?' Michael asked.

'Yes, we know them.' He paused. 'You were very wise to come to me, Dr James. Otherwise, you might have fallen into entirely the wrong hands, and then you really would have been in trouble. Now you live on Ma'arashli? Overlooking the American ambassador's house, if I'm not mistaken.'

'Indeed, I do. How did you know that?'

'Oh, you probably told me sometime. Now, stay where you are, and I'll come and pick you up as soon as I can get across the city. Do not leave the apartment, whatever you do. Just sit tight, and I will come to you.'

145

Michael poured himself another drink. Alcohol was now barricading him from reality. He felt somehow comforted, secure in the knowledge that he was in Mahmoud's hands. He went out to the balcony, and sat, for a time, thinking about what would happen to his appointment at the AUC. Would this mean the end of his time at the university? The authorities there couldn't stomach any hint of scandal and this was a scandal and a half.

The night air was cool with a slight breeze blowing from the north, but he felt hot, his clothes sticky with perspiration. It was unusually quiet. The cars that normally streamed down Ma'arashli had disappeared. He looked down at the cross roads. The dogs that slept on the steps loped across to see each other.

Then, he saw by the street light that the police, who normally loafed about outside the ambassador's house, had formed up in line, with, unusually, an officer in charge. Three of them charged their guns and marched in step towards the entrance of his apartment building. Three more disappeared to the side of the building, leaving three in front. Meanwhile, the officer positioned himself immediately opposite the apartment building, training a pair of binoculars on Michael's balcony. Michael waved, and the man put the glasses down for a moment before resuming his observation.

It took twenty minutes for Mahmoud to arrive. When he did, Michael noticed that the police who remained at the crossroads were standing to attention. The car was large and had smoked-glass windows. It had a military driver, who jumped out and ran to open the rear door. The officer with binoculars ran over, saluted and said something to the man in military uniform climbing out of the car. Mahmoud emerged, unmistakable in his bulk, with another officer in uniform behind him. Mahmoud waved his arm at the police and then, with the other two, crossed the street to the entrance to Michael's block. The lift was working now and Michael heard it creaking as it rose to his floor.

As Michael opened his door, Mahmoud saluted him with a smile. The two other officers, much younger, were distant. Mahmoud introduced them as his 'boys'.

'Can the boys look around a bit?' Mahmoud asked with a kindly gesture. Then he took a seat and motioned to Michael to sit opposite.

'And no one was here when you got back from the drink with your friends?' Mahmoud asked.

'No.'

'And tell me again why Khaled Cyprian was staying here?' Mahmoud stared at Michael intently.

'He was having some row with his wife and needed to get away somewhere for a few days to think matters over. He said he was going home tomorrow.'

'You know his wife?'

'I met her at her father-in-law's house and have seen her a couple of times at the AUC – she does some teaching there.'

'Have you been in touch with her since this,' Mahmoud beckoned to the bedroom, 'happened?'

'No. I don't know where they live. I spoke to the Cyprian father and asked him to break the news to her.'

One of the younger officers came back to the sitting-room and spoke to Mahmoud in a low voice. He rose:

'Excuse me for a moment, Dr James.'

When he returned, he looked again at Michael inquisitorially.

'Did you notice what was on the mirror, Dr James?' he asked.

'I noticed something had been written, but my Arabic is not good enough to read it, or perhaps, I was in such a state I could not concentrate.'

'Ah,' Mahmoud murmured. 'For your information, it says something like: "Executed as a traitor by order of the high command. God is Great." And the symbol beneath is of the organisation I mentioned to you when we last met – the Assassins.'

Michael said nothing. He stared at Mahmoud.

'What's more, it is written in lipstick.'

26

Into the Gulag

Michael double-locked the front door to the apartment, but then Mahmoud took the key with a smile.

'We'll need to come back for the body,' he said, 'and make a more thorough search. We'll pack your stuff up so you have no need to worry on that score.'

The four squeezed into the lift, each staring away wordlessly. The porter was at the bottom, looking rather frightened, bowing convulsively. Outside in the dark, there was a small army of policemen, all bristling to attention. Passers-by stopped to stare. Michael noticed the thin man from the shop for dry-cleaning whose ambition it was to buy a farm in the Delta. Mahmoud waved his hand at the policemen while one of his aides briefed the officer in charge.

The car inside was surprisingly large with an extra line of seats in the middle where the two aides sat, cut off from the back seat by a glass panel.

'We're going to the headquarters of the Military Security Agency,' Mahmoud said. 'I'm afraid you'll get a fair old grilling there, so you should prepare yourself.'

'Is this a security case then?' Michael asked.

'Of course.'

'Because of the Assassin sign?'

'That among other things as you'll no doubt find out in due course – that is, if you don't already know. This case is only a fragment of a whole.'

Mahmoud took out a mobile telephone. 'Please excuse me for a moment,' he said as he tapped in a number. He spoke into the phone in Arabic and then changed to English: 'Sorry to ring you so late, George, but this is just to confirm the details I gave you earlier.

It is now accomplished.' He paused, listening. 'No, of course not. You know all about it. And thank you so much for all your help. The speed was impressive – and invaluable.' Another pause. 'Yes, you may be right, but we have to check everything. If there is any news, I'll let you know. Oh, and I owe you and your charming wife dinner – I'll be in touch when this has blown over.'

He rang off. Michael presumed it must be British intelligence or the Americans.

'I've let the British know,' Mahmoud said, 'so we don't get into any diplomatic tangles. They have been very understanding, first-rate bunch. So,' he turned to Michael, 'you need not feel neglected – your ambassador knows all about the case.'

'So you are not just a retired army officer?' Michael said. 'How are you involved in this business?'

'I suppose there's no point now in beating about the bush,' Mahmoud said. 'I have some residual duties in the security apparatus, one of which was keeping an eye on you.' He smiled disarmingly. 'No one wanted the great international authority on terrorism to end up a victim.' He gave a gruff laugh. 'It was one of my more pleasing assignments, although I am sorry we didn't get to know each other better.'

They drove through the night at speed with headlights blazing, crossing red traffic-lights as they went. They used one of the city's overhead highways, and Michael could see below, the streets still full of lights, market stalls teeming with people. They were heading eastwards but he had not seen how they had left Zamalek to guess the destination more precisely. He felt, as he was increasingly to feel, cut off from the world, trapped like a fish in a bowl. They knew all about him; he knew nothing about them and their agenda.

Finally, they drove into a tunnel-like entrance in a high nondescript building, passing guards who saluted. They swung into a large illuminated courtyard with office doorways and more guards. The car slewed to a halt before one of the doors where a man was waiting. He was in military uniform. The driver jumped out of the car to open the passenger door. Mahmoud heaved his great bulk out of the seat, and stood for a moment, stretching his arms. Michael scrambled after him.

'This is one of my boys, Abdul – he'll take good care of you, and I'm sure you'll get to be great friends.'

Mahmoud smiled. Abdul did not, but he made a polite salute towards Mahmoud.

'Captain Abdul Rahman – this is Dr Michael James. Look after him and he may reward us with a little bit of his vast knowledge or,' and here he twinkled, 'we might get a mention in one of his footnotes.'

The Colonel shook Michael's hand and passed him over to Abdul Rahman, gave a perfunctory salute, turned and got back in the car. Abdul made a slight bow and shepherded Michael into the building. Michael felt deserted.

Abdul and the guard who accompanied him said nothing as they led the way through apparently endless corridors, each pitilessly exposed to glaring strip lights. They saw no one. If this is Lubianka, Michael thought, where is the blood, the screams from within? They came finally to a large office, full of people coming and going, and telephones ringing. Michael was required to complete forms, translated by Abdul, to pass over his belongings and collect a tunic. There was a changing cubicle where he put on the coarse prison shirt and trousers. His clothes were folded in a plastic bag and hung in a metal cupboard.

Then again the corridors, now somehow moving downwards into the depths of the building. At least it was cool. But as they proceeded, he began to feel increasing apprehension. He remembered thinking that it was good for his soul to experience the growing despair of prisoners, those stripped of all power, identity or significance, an insect under the tank tracks of the State. He remembered also wondering about his capacity to withstand examination. How astonishing it was that some prisoners, completely reduced by intimidation, became increasingly stubborn. It was as if all they had left to embody their identity was their refusal to submit. The means to force information out of them became perversely the opposite, a powerful incitement to withhold it. Except for people like him, he thought, who probably squealed without even being threatened, volunteering information under the illusion that they could win the affection of the inquisitor.

The cell was, by the standards he had expected, not at all bad. It was tiny but he had it to himself, with a short narrow bed, a small table and a rickety stool. Some writing paper had been thoughtfully supplied so he could write his confession. There was even a tiny WC attached, not just a stinking bucket. There was no window. By the

150

look of the vents in the ceiling, it must be air-conditioned, which was an astonishing privilege. But this was only a temporary lodge, a way station on the road to hell. And he was here, courtesy of the British Embassy, as a privileged foreigner. How ironic that he, who had always wanted to be a free citizen of the world, without nationality, was now so pathetically dependent on being British.

Abdul showed him the facilities, saying, 'Of course, they are vastly superior to what the majority of prisoners get.' And then, with perhaps a touch of resentment, 'But you have friends in high places who cannot be offended. I'll leave you to have a rest – I presume you've eaten – and later on, we'll have another word.'

He turned and left. Michael heard the guard locking the door and footsteps retreating down the corridor. He reflected that Abdul's English was too good, almost free of accent and with casual Anglicisms, which suggested he had lived in Britain.

He was alone. Silence flooded in, trapping him at its centre. It was unlike what he had imagined. He had had an idea of bare stone walls, cold and sweating, perhaps with running water down the side; chipped and covered in graffiti; a urinal stinking in the corner; an eye permanently at the hole in the door; and bunk beds with three or six prisoners in them. He'd seen too many films. This was none of those things, but more like a Spartan student hostel room, a hospital room or the sergeant's cubicle in a better class of barrack. He was very privileged – for the moment.

He stretched full-length on the bed, his feet sticking out at the foot. There was a deep weariness at the back of his head, soaking into his bones. Now he had a little temporary space of his own. The illusion of security allowed his fears to subside. Sleep was invading him although he felt he ought to remain awake to meet Abdul again. He could not stay awake, even though the centre light seemed to shine into his head.

His sleep was troubled. Doors slammed continually, the sound of running boots clattered down corridors, voices shouting questions he could not understand.

'You're mordant, mordant, mordant!' someone shouted, and it seemed he cried out, 'I am not, I am not – I'm just a teacher ...'

He was woken roughly by a guard who was indeed shouting at him and in Arabic. The guard cuffed him, dragged him off the bed and pushed him into the corridor. By some oversight, they had left him his watch and he noticed it was just after 2.30 in the morning. He was

151

shoved to make him speed up as he slowly recovered from sleep. Again, endless doors. Were these all specially privileged prisoners, he wondered. It seemed a long way and he lost any sense of direction.

Finally, they arrived and he was pushed into a dark room, illuminated only by one shaded light, hanging from the ceiling and shining on one chair. Ah, he thought groggily, this is more like the films, all ready for the sinister KGB interrogator.

He was pushed into the chair beneath the light, and sat and waited, his heart beating uncomfortably. Slowly his eyes became more accustomed to the dark, and he thought he could detect other furniture, including a desk and two chairs facing him.

How should he behave? he wondered yet again. He could not do other than behave normally. He was part of no conspiracy to commit acts of terrorism and in that sense had nothing to hide. But it would be foolish to think his basic innocence would protect him. Indeed, it could unknowingly implicate him since he did not know in what games he was being employed as a pawn. Perhaps Abdul needed a killing in the competition between different bureaux of the Military Security Agency. Perhaps different sections of the security apparatus were competing in pursuit of the Assassins. Perhaps the military aimed to steal a march on the Ministry of the Interior. Then nobody had an interest in his guilt or innocence, only in how he could be used – and if need be, framed – to win a point in the contest. In that case, he could even be – regrettably – shot 'while trying to escape'. His Excellency, the Ambassador for the United Arab Republic of Egypt would call on Her Majesty's Principal Secretary of State for Foreign Affairs to express his government's profound regret at this unfortunate accident – and the deepest sympathies of his government to the family of this distinguished scholar. He was day-dreaming again.

Abdul arrived in a hurry, carrying a bundle of papers. Dimly, Michael was aware of a second man following him, and he sat quietly further out in the darkness. Michael thought he could make out in the gloom a crew cut and jeans, dark glasses. Was he not the small American, taking photographs on the balcony above the student demonstration? And at George's party with the English Literature professor – the 'mordant' woman? The man made no sound, crossing his knees and observing. But how could he see anything in dark glasses?

'I know you've done some of this before,' Abdul said curtly, 'but we need to run over it again just to make sure we've got it right.'

Michael took it that this was by way of an apology.

'Michael Thomas James, aged sixty-eight, retired Professor of Government at the London School of Economics, widowed with two adult children – Jane Forsyth, architect (married to Alexander Forsyth, architect, two children) and William, unmarried, computer engineer. Normally domiciled at thirty-five, Laurel Lane, Alresford in Hampshire, UK, currently Visiting Professor in the Department of Political Science at the American University in Cairo.'

His voice was toneless. At the end, Michael agreed.

Abdul looked up from the form and stared at Michael coldly.

'And now will you tell me exactly why you are in Egypt, Mr James?'

'You have already said – I am Visiting Professor at the AUC.'

'Mr James,' Abdul scowled, 'I am conducting this examination and you will kindly answer the questions directly whether you think you have answered them, or not. Why are you here?'

'I am Visiting Professor at the AUC.'

'But why did you accept such an appointment – to leave England and your home in Hampshire? Alresford, isn't it?' Michael nodded. 'You left your family and friends and for so long – why?'

'I have increasingly specialised in the politics of the Middle East, so it seemed an opportunity to get to know the largest Arab power – and learn Arabic.'

'But you are retired. What is the point in learning a new specialism?'

'I try to keep my hand in, to continue my interests.'

'And you want to learn Arabic? A difficult language at any age and you are well past the time when people normally do it. It is a strange story.' He paused, and then continued, 'How did you know Khaled Cyprian?'

'I met him through his father who also teaches at the AUC. We became good friends, and for a time, used to meet occasionally for lunch.'

'Why was he in your apartment?'

'A few days ago, he came to me and said he had some trouble with his wife and wanted to live apart from her for a short time. I had a spare room so I offered to put him up. He was to leave tomorrow.'

'How did knowing Khaled Cyprian and being in Egypt relate to your lifelong interest in terrorism?'

'It didn't – Khaled was just a friend and my interest in Egypt was general, not specific to terrorism.'

'I find that difficult to believe, given your lifetime preoccupation. Let us just check some of that. You did your doctoral work on the Russian nihilists and terrorism in the nineteenth century – with a special study, I believe, of Sergei Nechaev, and,' his voice hardened, 'the assassination of Tsar Alexander II?'

'Yes, but that was over forty years ago, long before I became interested in the Middle East.'

'Then you moved to the University of Washington to make a study of the roots of American anarchism, the terrorist tradition and the assassination of President McKinley.'

'Yes'

'Then you were in Lebanon during the civil war, interviewing Palestinian leaders before moving on to Jerusalem to look at suicide-bombers, before the Israelis moved you out.'

'In Lebanon, I spent a semester at the American University – much as I'm now spending four semesters at the AUC. I was preparing a short study, which was later published.'

'And it seems that you were involved with the Provisional IRA in Northern Ireland?'

'I did some work on the issues there and wrote some articles.'

'The British authorities have a feeling that you did more than that – weren't you once expelled from Belfast?'

'That was a mistake.'

'Ah, a mistake. As when you clashed with the French police in Corsica, looking into the terrorist movement there? Or with the Japanese police in Tokyo when, by accident, you happened to be looking into the Japan Red Army? Or when you tried to cross the Turkish military lines into the Kurdish areas of northern Iraq? Or when the Peruvian military police arrested you in Arequipa, trying to contact Chairman Gonzalo and the Senderistas? The record speaks rather loudly, Mr James, doesn't it?'

'Civil disorder and political terrorism have been my lifelong professional interest. It is the topic of the course I run at the AUC.'

He felt his protest sounded weak in the face of this immense body of lifelong mischief-making. How could he have done so much in so many different places? The record must be from British military intelligence, tipping off the Egyptians. Abdul's English was indeed excellent – he must have been a beneficiary of a British Council scholarship to Sussex for an MA in methods of scientific interrogation. He summoned up a half smile to himself.

'And then you were in Pakistan, sniffing round the old Afghan refugee camps until you were picked up by the Pakistani police – or so they tell us – looking especially at the *madrasahs*, the religious schools where the Taliban were recruited. And did you visit Afghanistan, by any chance, perhaps to interview Osama Bin Laden?'

'No, I didn't – and I know nothing of Bin Laden. I went to Pakistan to do an article, and did no more than any other journalist would do. As a specialist in the field, I used often to get asked to do such jobs.'

'I think the evidence suggests you were in Cairo on the same mission, whether, as you put it, "to write an article",' he sneered, 'or something less innocent.'

'I have no contacts here and had no intention of doing anything on this question.'

'You have no contacts, Mr James?' The tone was exaggerated astonishment. 'You do surprise me,' he continued. 'And I had hoped you were going to help us.' He paused, staring directly at Michael as he said, 'Who do you think was in your bath?'

Michael was flustered. He must be careful. Abdul was perhaps just trying it on, fishing for anything he could get because he had so little to go on. But there was a danger that Michael might, by accident, implicate himself in something.

'The doctor, Khaled Cyprian.'

'And who was he?'

'A doctor at Cairo University and at hospitals and clinics elsewhere – I don't know where exactly.'

'You don't know where,' Abdul mimicked. 'And what did it say on your bedroom mirror?'

'Colonel Mahmoud said that there was a message and a symbol of something called the Assassins.'

'Executed as a traitor by order of the Military High Command.'

'What does it mean?' Michael said, panicking.

'That's what I want you to tell me. Even a person without your intelligence might be tempted to put two and two together, might they not? That Khaled Cyprian was mixed up in something to do with terrorism – and got caught by it?'

'I don't know – I know too little about the terrorists in Egypt.'

'Such a pity for you – the mirror is the key clue, isn't it? You

155

wouldn't get far on the Falls Road if you missed such clues, Mr James.'

Michael's confusion increased. Was Leila acting for the Assassins or as an accomplice? Was she working for the police? If the Israelis could murder and call it 'selective assassination,' so could the Egyptian police.

Again, he marvelled at Abdul's sophistication. This was no PC Plod. British military intelligence had flooded him with information. And now the British must be laughing up their sleeves. This had done, once and for all, for that little shit, James, and without us being in any way involved.

'Mr James,' Abdul began again, this time with an air of finality. 'I have tried to be fair with you. I've given you far more information about the direction of our enquiries than is customary in the hope that this might persuade you to co-operate. As an admirer of your work, I am eager to learn from your experience. But you tell us nothing. I am most disappointed .'

'I'm sorry,' Michael began. 'I don't know what it is you think I know. I knew nothing about the Assassins until Colonel Mahmoud told me about them, and I know no one with any connection to them. I don't know who murdered Khaled Cyprian, nor whether the sign on my mirror is authentic.'

'Mr James,' the Captain said wearily. And then suddenly, swinging his chair towards him, he glared at him, his fists clenched. Michael thought he was going to hit him and flinched. Abdul shouted, 'How do you know Khaled Cyprian?'

'I told you – we met through his father and we became friends.'

Michael was trembling, his palms and his back suddenly cold with sweat. Abdul's glare was violent.

'And that's why you lunch with him every week? That's why you offer him sanctuary, hiding him from us in Zamalek. Instead of doing what ought to be your duty – telling us where he is.'

He was shouting again, his eyes bulging. His forehead was shining with sweat. 'Do you know what these people are like? Shall I get the photographs from the Luxor massacre and show you? Do you know what a massacre looks like?'

'And,' Abdul's voice sank almost to a whisper. Michael leaned forward to hear him, 'with people like this, you instruct them on a weekly basis in terrorist tactics, obtaining arms and methods to defeat us?'

'No, no, no,' Michael protested. 'It was not like that at all. He was a friend and we met purely socially. He was introducing me to Egyptian life. We didn't meet every week and I didn't at all act as an instructor.' He knew it sounded weak, lame.

'Egyptian life,' Abdul said scornfully. 'More like Egyptian death,' with almost a smile of derision. 'Cyprian, as you undoubtedly know, which is why you chose him as a friend, has a long record of association with those in violent opposition to the Egyptian government. He married a notorious terrorist who set fire to Cairo University in the nineteen seventy-seven troubles. I am sure he was an excellent introduction to Egyptian life.'

Michael felt the ground crumbling beneath his feet, a hollow feeling in the pit of his stomach. His protests seemed so weak. The trembling had returned and a cold sweat was soaking through his clothes.

'I didn't know all this,' he said weakly, recognising his lie.

'You didn't know!' Abdul burst out with indignation. 'And in all those charming tête-à-têtes in Felfela, *foules-mesdames* and stuffed pigeon, you never had a sneaking suspicion, nor wondered why he had made a friend of you?'

'No, none.'

'You must think us great fools, Mr James.'

Abdul stopped abruptly, looked searchingly at his fingernails, and then began to scoop up his papers. The guard at the door braced himself in a position of attention; the American – if such he was – stirred in the semi-dark. Abdul stood and looked at Michael.

'You are a foreign national and, more specifically, British. We have good relations with your government, good co-operation, and we have no wish to jeopardise this. So in our hands you have a remarkably privileged status – you would not get such treatment as an Egyptian. But there is a limit to our patience and to your privilege – you must co-operate. We have to know all that you know or,' and here his voice took on a menacing tone, 'we shall have to start treating you like an Egyptian. I think you would find that most disagreeable. And don't think that, being British, you cannot just disappear. Your press would shout, there would be questions in parliament and your ambassador would fuss for a few minutes for British public opinion. But you would be quickly forgotten, particularly if there were inspired reports from "normally reliable sources" in the *Daily Telegraph* and the *Daily Mail* that you had been working as a liaison officer between Al-Qaeda in Afghanistan and the Assassins here, through a London control centre.' He paused, and then continued.

'Think about it carefully, Mr James, and we'll meet again. But this session has not been very satisfactory – I had hoped one session would have been enough and we could release you. But it seems not. You may have to stay quite a long time with us.'

Abdul turned to leave. The American stood. He was shorter than Michael remembered. He followed Abdul, and then at the door, the Captain stood aside politely and allowed him through first.

They did not meet again for what became an age. Days moved into weeks, and, it seemed, perhaps months. Without daylight it became impossible to follow the passage of time. The batteries in his watch took the opportunity to run out, so time ceased. He became more familiar with the walls around him than his own skin, with the endless tedium of his own thoughts. The only breaks were food – gruel and bread – and an exercise session where he saw no one. None of the guards spoke English.

It was then, in one night of turbulent sleep, that he had a strange dream. He thought he was riding on the shoulders of Colonel Mahmoud who was dancing up and down, singing what seemed to be 'Waltzing Matilda'. It was impossibly funny and he was laughing hysterically; he felt he was going to be sick all over Uncle Jack. His mother stood watching them, her face radiant with delight. And as he was jogged, Michael felt another presence, a misty image at the other end of the room, an image that seemed to him intensely sad, so sad that Michael himself felt tears come into his eyes.

He woke, his heart beating so hard, it seemed he could hear it. Who was this Colonel Mahmoud? And then, suddenly, it came to him. It was Uncle Jack, that great bear of a man with a moustache identical to Mahmoud's. Slowly he began to reconstruct his memories. He had been in the Air Force, an Australian, full of fun and presents. Michael must have been five or so. And where was his father? It was then he half remembered his mother swearing him to secrecy, not to tell his father about the visits of Uncle Jack. For a moment he could not believe it; it was a rotten trick to play on a child. But he remembered now. And as he did so, the understanding of the adult slowly put together the fragments of a different truth. Was that why his father had been so sad? What had

158

his father died of? They said an illness. And what of Michael, the child, sworn to complicity in his mother's adultery and unfaithful to his father? To his astonishment, he began to weep, his chest heaving with the sadness for which there was now no remedy. He did not know how long he wept; in time he fell into a calm sleep.

Lesser interrogators took over, with less sophisticated methods, but still, it seemed, armed with an immense body of information about him. Life became a nightmare of episodes, broken by thugs, who when the mood took them, beat him. Most of the time he lay bruised and groaning on his bed. And the same questions revolved in his head endlessly. He knew that they had not yet written him off; he was not yet an Egyptian since there was no torture: no cigarette burns to his flesh, no legs broken, no electricity to his genitals, and the rest. He had still preserved his expatriate privilege so that he could be released without the embarrassment of clearly having been tortured. Yet the cross-examination rolled on as if there had never been a case of violence in the world in which he had not been involved.

'You visited Zambia to interview the ANC leadership, and then South Africa under apartheid? You were expelled and made a prohibited immigrant when the authorities discovered your links with,' the questioner hesitated and checked his notes, stumbling on the unfamiliar names, 'Umkhonto we Sizwe, the ANC's armed wing? And you went to Phnom Penh when the Khmer Rouge regime fell? You were a friend of Malcolm Caldwell who was murdered there. And you were in Nicaragua as the Sandinistas came to power? You interviewed the FARC in Colombia and were obliged to leave the country?'

Oh, what a long weary life, such a long war, so many deaths and so few victories, so much palpable injustice. And even when there were small triumphs, they went rotten so quickly – Cuba, Vietnam, Nicaragua.

'And you were in Sri Lanka to interview Prabhakaran just before the Indian Prime Minister Rajiv Gandhi was murdered by the Tamil Tigers?'

The interrogator – Michael called him Eustace for no particular reason – held up a copy of *The Red Mole*; Michael was unsurprised.

'You talked to the Sikh Student Federation in the Punjab in India just before Mrs Gandhi was assassinated?'

He nodded weakly. What did it all add up to – a wasted life? His mind was inexorably slipping into sleep until the guard slapped him across the face, and his ancient wounds were reactivated, his old comrades, his bruises, his cuts, his lacerations.

'And then there is Italy – your relationship to the Red Brigades and the habits of knee capping and the murder of Signor Moro. Was it an accident that you were in Bologna on August 2nd, 1980?'

Ah, Michael thought, they had not turned up the fact that in those far-off golden days he had been in Bologna, not on work, but in pursuit of the beautiful Luisa.

'I was interested,' he said with difficulty through puffy lips, 'in the activities of the P2 Masonic Lodge and the efforts of the Italian secret service to damage the Communist Party in their Bologna stronghold.'

'And just by chance, a bomb killed eighty-six people on the train leaving Bologna?'

'It was terrible – but I was just a journalist.'

'You attended the trial of …' Eustace checked his file, 'Angela Strappafelci, did you not?'

'Yes, but my Italian was not good enough to follow the proceedings properly.'

And so it went on, piling up circumstantial evidence on evidence, until he wanted to scream at the unremitting tedium and his longing to sleep. It went on through what Michael assumed was the long hot summer outside. Who knows what was happening? The second intifada, Venezuela in turmoil, the Congo collapsing: nothing, only the interminable silence.

At last Abdul returned, but without the companion Michael called the American. Michael almost smiled as if Abdul were a familiar friend. The tone of the interrogation improved and there were no physical threats.

'You haven't advanced us much, Mr James, in all these weeks, and I fear we are getting a little tired of this. You are exhausting our patience.'

Michael was tempted to smile through his bruises. Abdul's tiredness was as nothing compared to his own. Was he now going to be made an Egyptian and disappeared?

'I warned you – people do disappear. Even we lose track of them – who they are, where they are, what they are supposed to have done. And when they die, as some do, they are dumped far out in a desert

160

pit and forgotten.' He smiled, 'I suppose they may be discovered in a couple of thousand years' time, like the mummies, perfectly preserved in our dry climate. We will have created the next lot of antiquities.'

Another joke, Michael thought wearily.

'But to return to the question in hand. I notice from your file that you have never worked for British intelligence, which, given your background, might have seemed appropriate. Was it because you were always on the side of the terrorists? And in this business, Mr James, there are no neutrals.'

With difficulty, he mumbled through bruised lips. 'I admit that when I was young,' he paused to catch his breath, suddenly aware of his physical deterioration. He was very thin and his prison tunic hung loose about him. 'I admit I had a sympathy with some movements. But that did not prevent academic detachment. I did not compromise my independence by working either for a government or a terrorist organisation.'

He stopped again, coughing slightly.

'What were – or are – the terrorist movements with which you sympathise now?'

'Perhaps "sympathise" is too strong a word – understand is better. I can see, for example, that the Palestinians have no way out. The Israelis overwhelmingly dominate in military terms, continually stealing their lands while talking peace. The Palestinians have no way of fighting off the theft – what can they do?'

He knew he had chosen the right example. Abdul could not fail to agree and would not therefore persist in that line of questioning. Fortunately, the American was not there.

'Yours is a singular record, Mr James. What I can't understand is that you then try to persist in suggesting your relationship with Khaled Cyprian was innocent. How is it possible, with your record, that it was quite by chance that you came so close to yet another terrorist network?'

'I know nothing,' Michael said weakly. 'If I knew anything, I would tell you – I have no sympathy with Islamism.'

'But what Muslims do you know in London? It's an important centre for Al-Qaeda and other exiles.'

Michael felt that Abdul was giving up – the line of questioning was giving too much away. It suggested that, even though he might not escape, the hunt was coming to an end.

'I am,' he said wearily, 'an exhausted old academic, now retired – I don't think I know a single Muslim in London, let alone members of Al-Qaeda.'

There was a pause, a long pause. Michael raised his head, wondering if Abdul had slipped out. He had not. He was searching his papers. It was difficult for Michael to see in the darkened room. Abdul stopped, and raised his head, staring at Michael. And then, as if making a decision, asked suddenly, 'Were you and Khaled Cyprian lovers?'

Michael was stunned, and mumbled, 'No, we were not.'

'Why was he staying in your room?'

'He wasn't. He was in the guest bedroom.'

All the time, Abdul was staring at him. As he did so, the implications of his question slowly dawned on Michael.

'You murdered him and tried to stage it with all this stuff about the Assassins.'

Relief flooded through Michael. They knew nothing. He had won. This was Abdul's last throw, and it completely undermined all that the interrogation had been trying to establish. Abdul had failed.

'As you know, I cannot read or write Arabic sufficiently to do that,' he said with difficulty, suppressing his uncertain smile of triumph.

'I know no such thing,' Abdul snapped.

'Ask my Arabic teacher – I'm hopeless.'

Abdul was staring down at his papers as if to avoid Michael's eyes, to avoid admitting defeat. Of course, Michael reflected, defeat was only possible because he was a foreigner and the British Embassy were no doubt grumbling. It was not worth a diplomatic spat when they had so little on him. Had he been Egyptian, no one would have cared or had the power even to trace him. That was the privilege of being a native.

Abdul stood up, his head now in the darkness above the lamp. Michael could not determine his expression, only the flash of his eyes.

'Goodbye, Dr James,' he said. 'I may not see you again.'

He scuffled up his papers hurriedly and turned to leave. The guard, taken unawares by the speed of the conclusion to the interrogation, straightened up and opened the door. Then he turned to help the prisoner lever himself painfully out of his chair. Michael groaned, but he was also smiling.

They cleaned him up. He was taken to the prison clinic, and the doctor there patched his face and those parts of his body that had suffered. He was able to have a shower and brush his hair. Someone clipped his beard. His clothes reappeared, but they now hung like rags on his gaunt frame.

And one morning, he was led out into the world again. Back along the miles of corridors, shuffling painfully slowly to the gate office where he signed incomprehensible forms in Arabic. He was led out, across the courtyard, now bathed in the unfamiliar dazzling morning light. He was blinded. He caught his breath. It had seemed impossible that he might ever escape and yet now it seemed so easy.

The courtyard looked quite different from when he had arrived in the darkness so long ago. It was hot and, when he left the shadows cast by the building, the sun glared, burning through his shirt. He was cleared through the guards and led to the opening to the tunnel entrance. He felt he had been a lifetime in this prison, and yet now no one said goodbye or shook his hand.

He started to walk through the tunnel, the dark contrasting very sharply with the light at the end. He caught a glimpse of someone silhouetted at the other end, a woman, wearing, it seemed, a European skirt. Suddenly, by the angle of her body, he recognised Jane. He tried to run, stumbling unsteadily. She in turn saw him and began to run towards him.

She caught him in her arms, her face streaming with tears.

'Oh, Dad, what have they done to you?' She spluttered, holding him at arm's length to see his pathetic shape. 'You look terrible – you're as thin as a wire coat-hanger, and all those cuts and bruises.'

'I'm OK,' he mumbled, but also a little tearfully, still hardly believing he had escaped, expecting at any moment a cry from the guards to take him back.

'How long have I been in there?' he said unsteadily, continuing to stumble towards the light.

'About three months,' she said. 'It's the beginning of September. You went in in June.'

He could feel the heat now as they emerged into the light. A long dark car was parked at the side with a driver. A man was walking towards them. He was in a dark suit with a hat. He took off his hat and saluted Michael, trying to be gentle as he shook hands.

'Peter Hodges, British Embassy, sir,' he said in a clipped accent. 'They'd very much appreciate it – if you can manage it – if you could make your first call with them for a quick debriefing. You're going to be swamped by the press and we're anxious they don't get the wrong end of the stick. It could enormously damage our work here.'

Their work, Michael reflected, loomed larger than his experience in prison.

Then Michael saw, at a distance and behind some kind of barrier, a small group of people. The police were holding them back but camera lights were popping and he could hear questions being shouted in English:

'How's it feel to be out?' 'Were you tortured?' 'Will you be making a complaint?'

'You needn't talk to them,' the man from the Embassy said. But Michael stood and faced them, making a special effort to raise his voice.

'I was not ill-treated,' he called, 'and I'm delighted to be out.'

There was a chorus of new questions and more flashes of light, but he turned away towards Hodges and the car. The driver opened the back door and Jane helped him in. He moved with great care.

'We've been driven half crazy with worry,' she said, 'but I suppose that wasn't the half of it for you.' She squeezed his arm, but gently. 'I can't believe you're really out. Will was desperate to come, but he'd only just arrived back from Los Angeles so I made him stay put. He'll meet us tomorrow at Heathrow.'

'Heathrow?' Michael said in a puzzled tone. 'But what about the AUC? If I've been in gaol for three months, the new academic year is just beginning. What about my course? And the apartment?'

He was still mumbling almost inaudibly, and Jane leaned over him to hear what he was saying. The apartment. He suddenly remembered it; would all that still be there? He could never face it.

'The apartment,' Jane said, staring straight in front, 'is still in the hands of Military Security – and the AUC is complaining that they need it. They packed all your things up and the AUC shipped them to England.'

'To England?' Michael said in a puzzled tone.

'And here's what the AUC has to say,' she said, taking an opened envelope from her handbag and handing it to him.

His vision was a little blurred, and he could not now remember where his reading spectacles might be. But he made out the gist. It was from the AUC President:

> ... realise what an ordeal you have been through. All your colleagues and friends here feel the deepest sympathy for you in this terrible experience, and are now delighted that it is at last over and you have been released without any stain whatsoever on your record.
>
> However, you will also, I am sure, realise the position of the AUC as a prominent Egyptian institution and one responsible for the education – both pedagogical and moral – of the children of some of the most distinguished leaders of Egyptian society. Regardless of the rights and wrongs of your case – and none of us here has any doubts whatsoever as to your complete innocence – any hint of scandal is disastrous for the AUC and its long-term future in Egypt. Already reports have appeared in the American press as also here. Questions have been raised in Congress, and our Trustees in New York have expressed their anxieties to me that the University might be embarrassed. If our friends are worried, I need not spell out to you the slant put on these matters by the ill-intentioned both here and there.
>
> It is in this light that we feel that it is prudent both for us and for you if you do not resume your position here for a second year. I am sorry this has become necessary but I hope you will understand and might even welcome the opportunity to secure your full recovery from this ordeal at home. We have reorganised your courses so none of your students will suffer as a result of you being unable to resume your teaching.
>
> This is a matter of great sadness to me, to your colleagues and to your students who have gained immensely from your rich intellectual and professional contribution. Perhaps later, when all this has blown over, we will be able to welcome you back to the AUC – if you yourself feel able to face Egypt a second time. But for the moment, all of us pray that you will now have a little calm and comfort with your family in England after this terrible ordeal.

Michael scrumpled the letter in his pocket: not guilty but punished nonetheless. Jane was looking at him, trying to gauge his reactions but he betrayed none. The Egyptian experience had been terminated in one swoop.

He stared out of the window, amazed that the streets were still the same, the passers-by, the traffic. They swept over the river and he looked with neutrality at a view that had once given him much pleasure. The nurseries along the river banks were green and soothing, enough to almost feel the cool waters that sustained them. Temperatures must be high outside the air-conditioned car.

'We're staying at the Nile Hilton tonight,' Jane said. 'They've promised to keep the journalists at bay. We'll catch the early morning flight to London tomorrow. I'm sorry to rush you, but we thought it best for you to get out as quickly as you could. Then the nightmare will be behind you.'

The whole Cairo experience was to be ended abruptly, not with a bang but a whimper? He had lived so completely immersed in it for so long, it seemed impossible to end. He was an embarrassment to be bundled out of the country as fast as possible.

'Why did you tell the journalists that you had not been ill-treated,' Jane asked curiously.

'I thought I was staying. I didn't want to complicate matters by making a fuss. I'll say something in London.'

'Three people have been calling the Hilton for you. A man called Bob from the AUC saying that the reaction of the University is outrageous and the staff are getting up a protest, and can he see you in London on his next trip? And then a man called Sameh who wants to talk, and another called Emile.'

Jane was still talking but he found it difficult to listen. He felt anaesthetised, at a remove from life, in a silent film. He would not be able to talk to the Embassy for long without going into a doze.

* * *

Michael remembered the hotel from before. It looked hideous on the outside. But the shower was glorious, and the food so rich it was a shock to the system. In the evening, they sat on the terrace of their suite. He could barely sit still, continually changing position to ease the aches. But it was a joy: the warm evening air and a rising moon, the twin necklaces of city lights strung along each bank of the river, the traffic thick and noisy as always.

Jane brought him a Scotch with ice clinking in the glass, and sat opposite him.

'I think your adventures better come to a close now, Dad. Will and I hated it when you decided to push off to Cairo on your own – and for two years. It was weird. We couldn't understand it. Now I want you back home where we can keep an eye on you – and fatten you up. You look like a scarecrow!'

He grunted and continued to stare at the city. He had lost the habit of small talk, of talk at all and needed time to absorb the complexities of normal life. He had also lost the habit of drinking Scotch – it went straight to his head now.

'I've brought any mail that looked interesting,' Jane said. 'And I listened to your answer phone and made a note of the messages. There was one from a dramatist – I couldn't catch his name – launching a trilogy at the National. He wanted you to check his portrayal of Bakunin.'

'I think I know who that is,' Michael said, 'and thank you, Jane, for life saving your foolish old father.' He squeezed her hand.

The door buzzer rang. It was Emile, black beret in hand, his square face with the great nose, smiling. Jane was suspicious he might be a journalist, but Michael reassured her, so she introduced herself on the doorstep and brought him in. Michael levered himself up, and Emile, with great gentleness, put his arms round him.

'My dear, dear friend,' he said. 'What a terrible experience! And what a dreadful outcome of your stay in a city you had come to love. I'm sorry to call when you're barely released, but you're off to London, so this is the only time I could catch you.'

Michael remembered the French 'r's. Jane brought Emile a drink.

'And all because of the Cyprian family,' Emile continued.

'Well, really, because of the Egyptian government,' Michael muttered.

It was hard work for Emile when Michael spoke so little. In the silences, Jane and he chatted – of the AUC and of Michael's colleagues.

At last Michael summoned up the strength to ask: 'And what of Sameh and Yasmine?'

'Ah, a sad story,' Emile said regretfully. 'They were shattered, as you can imagine. Sameh had quite a severe illness – a lung infection and that developed complications. He was in hospital for about six weeks. But he'd given up hope, I think. He resigned from the AUC,

167

and when he left hospital, he left Cairo. I inherited the family apartment. We had always had a little place in Asyut, our little crumb of feudalism, he called it. He and Yasmine have moved there and have taken up growing cacti. Bulus is staying with me now in Garden City while he finishes at the AUC. I told Sameh you were here and he may ring this evening.'

'And Leila?' Michael asked at last.

'Not a thing. She disappeared that evening without trace. We don't even know for sure that she knows Khaled is dead. Of course, it's always possible the police picked her up and kept her in one of the women's prisons – God help her if they did. Another theory is that she was so shattered by Khaled's death, she just fled abroad to hide. Some people even think she volunteered for work in Afghanistan. There's always work for doctors, but the Taliban don't let women work. Maybe she's gone to be the Al-Qaeda medic.' He gave a grim laugh. 'But nobody, so far as I know, has heard anything of her.'

When they parted, Emile again held him gently in his arms, hugging him with care, and kissed him on both cheeks.

'Take very good care of yourself, Michael, after this terrible time. Try not to think too badly of us Egyptians. Some of us loved you and will sadly miss you. Maybe after some of the wounds have healed, you'll come back. Bring your daughter,' he nodded at Jane. 'Remember, if you decide to come, there's always a bed for you in Garden City in my apartment. I have your card, so if I come your way – which is unlikely – I will certainly let you know.'

He shook hands with Jane and left. Michael was moved. He had indeed loved Cairo and Emile was part of that golden time, the first flush of his romance with the city.

Later Sameh rang. The line was not good, crackling intermittently, with a periodic mysterious overlay of other people's voices.

'Oh, how good to hear your voice, Michael,' Sameh said, 'and know that you escaped. We were so worried, fearing the worst. Prisons in Egypt are a serious risk to the health! I hope you have suffered no lasting damage. And I'm only sorry we are not there to greet you. But I've funked life since Butrus went. Yasmine does everything, holding me up. She is a saint. We ran away here to a place outside Asyut. I can't bear the thought of Cairo now. And I fear

168

I've got very old rather suddenly. The zest for life has rather gone out. My greatest pleasure now is growing cacti.'

They chatted of this and that – of Yasmine's poor health and Bulus' prospects – but it was hard work with a poor line and Michael's befuddled silences. Then suddenly Sameh asked:

'Did Emile tell you about the Islamist press?'

'No, what of it?'

'I don't like to tell you, Michael. I don't want to alarm you, especially when you've only just got free. But the Egyptian press generally was full of the line that this was a homosexual quarrel that got out of hand. They got that from the security services. We were outraged but what can you do? The government controls the media and there is no way of challenging it.

'However, what there is of an Islamist press had a different spin – or rather hinted at one, since they couldn't openly flout the government. In essence, they denounced the story about homosexuality as a lie put out by who knows? They said – and this is the nasty bit – that Butrus was one of the most promising rising young leaders of the movement. The Americans and the British were alarmed at how important he was becoming. British Military Intelligence was given the job by the Americans of taking out Butrus as a warning to the Egyptian Islamists . I don't need to tell you who is supposed to have been given this job. Then, they say, the police here covered the affair up by arresting you and pretending it wasn't a political assassination.

'That's not all. The Islamist press has promised revenge – to pay you back. I understand from Emile that a death threat was found pinned to your office door in the AUC. Various other people seem to have been warned that you would not stay alive for long after you left prison.

'Of course, all this will be known to the security services and I'm sure, despite their normal incompetence, they will have you watched to make sure nothing happens. Nor do I think that this is more than wild talk. Lots of people speak loosely of revenge. Fortunately, in most cases, the bark is louder than the bite. But anyone who wants to, can find out where you are, so it is wise to be a bit extra careful.

'I'm sorry it all ended this way, Michael. My life is over now though we still have Bulus to watch over. I shan't leave here, so unless you come this way, sadly we won't meet again. Yasmine and I send you our heartfelt love – and an immense hug. And we'll always be sorry that your interaction with the Cyprian family ended so disastrously. God speed – and take care of yourself.'

Michael burrowed down into himself. He did not tell Jane what Sameh had said. There was no point. The old life had disappeared, it seemed, and no one was asking those questions any more – Had Khaled been a traitor? What was his relationship to the Assassins? Who wrote that message on the mirror? Did Leila murder Khaled? Did the security services murder Khaled? Had they murdered Leila? If they hadn't, where was she? How could she have known his astonishing weakness – one quick lay and he was sworn to silence, to protect her. The Egyptian State had closed the file. No one cared any longer.

*   *   *

At Heathrow, they feared the ambush of journalists, but the steward assured them they would be filtered through the VIP lounge to evade them. They need not have bothered. The terminal was almost empty. It was eerily quiet. Michael leaned heavily on the trolley carrying Jane's case, using it like a walking frame. As they came out of customs, they saw how deserted the terminal was. Small groups of people stood around, hushed, almost whispering.

'It's weird,' Jane said, glancing from side to side. Then she noticed the departure monitors. There were no flights scheduled. At that moment, they heard Will calling them as he raced towards them, breathless. He embraced Michael with relief.

'Dad, how wonderful to see you and for you to be safe. But, my God, you look to have had a beating.'

'Will,' Jane interrupted him, 'What is going on – why is it so quiet, and no flight departures listed?'

'Don't tell me you haven't heard? The reason I'm a bit late is that we're all glued to the television. There's been a terrible accident in New York – a plane crashed into one of the two towers of the International Trade Centre. It's all on television.'

Then Jane noticed that there were more people than she had at first thought, but all clustered round the television monitors in the lounge area. They crossed the terminal. For Michael, it seemed vast. But when they reached the area, people moved aside, sensing he was ill. And it was then that they saw the full horror of Manhattan.

170

27

Letter 15

Dear darling Jeannot,

What an *excitement*! And for Mr Marx, at last some relief from the great worry about the next Congress. Have you already heard the news? It seems that Mr Bakunin's followers in Italy have held a Congress at Rimini a week ago and decided not to attend the Hague! It seems they wish to create a new organization, outside the International, and hold their own Congress in Switzerland at just the moment when the International meets in Holland! Of course, it is sad that so many good people in Italy will not now be in the International, but for all of us here, I fear, the prospect that the General Council might be *defeated* at the Hague Congress outweighed any regret at the loss of the Italians.

It does seem to me however that the *natural* revolutionaries like these Italians are instinctively inclined to Mr Bakunin. To follow Mr Marx requires much deep study, which distracts from the need to *act* now. It is too much to ask of the fiery wild young men (and women!) who respond to the call to turn all the world upside down to go back to the library for the best years of their life!

Mr Engels has now done a new list of those who will and those who will not support the General Council. Without the Italians, the prospects appear much more promising. It is possible the International will be safe after all, provided there can be some strictness about forged mandates, the number of false delegates. Mr Vaillant is busy working on the revised rules of the International and it is here perhaps that the *forgers* will be snared!

There is also another quarrel on the General Council. This time it is between a Mr Hales and Mr Engels.

13 Aug. *continued.* I fear at that point I had to break off since Tussy rushed into the conservatory where I was composing my letter to you. She was *beside herself* with excitement. So I was obliged to put my letter on one side and have only been able to resume it today. But what caused so much excitement? It seems that Mr Marx has heard from St Petersburg a curious and shocking story about your Mr Nechaev, the great follower of Mr Bakunin and leader of the revolutionaries in Russia (or so he seems to tell everyone). The story is that Mr Bakunin ages ago signed a contract with – and accepted a considerable financial advance from – a Russian publisher to translate Mr Marx's *Das Kapital,* but had been unable to complete the work by the time Mr N. came to him in Geneva. Mr Bakunin was evidently much *troubled* by this betrayal of trust, and, it seems, was unwilling to undertake any other tasks until he had completed this one. He therefore refused to divert his attention to drafting the manifestos and brochures that Mr Nechaev required of him to employ in Russia to build the revolutionary organisation among different sections of the people. Well, Mr Nechaev was most vexed at this, but persuaded Mr Bakunin that he and his organisation in Russia would ensure that the matter was settled amicably with the publisher and the contract dissolved. It is now said that Mr Nechaev did not repay the outstanding advance but instead wrote to the publisher in St Petersburg, threatening him with death if he tried to secure the execution of his contract (and the return of the advance).

Mr Marx and Mr Engels believe that this is so *wicked* a way to behave – and it is, if true, most *shocking* although it seems all of a part with what you have told me of that *dreadful* young man – that if they can secure and publish the letter, it will completely destroy the reputation and following of Mr Bakunin! As you can imagine, my mind was not at all settled on this question, for I do not know that Mr Bakunin had any idea of what Mr Nechaev was doing. Furthermore, this seems a question of the *morally reprehensible* behaviour of Mr N., not a refutation of the political positions of Mr Bakunin and his followers. But as you can imagine, the family are much overjoyed that their enemies – or at least some of them – may be quite cast down and overcome by this means.

Now, dear Jean, you must tell *no one* of this story – and certainly not the most important person there with you – lest my betrayal *come out* and be used to destroy the family that I have grown to love, especially Tussy. I am not convinced that even if the letter is found it will influence the sage counsels in the Hague!

After all this time, living so close to the debate – unable to *escape* it! – about the future of the International, I have such a *longing* to go to the Hague for the Congress! All the Marx family will go, and Tussy is very enthusiastic that I should accompany them. I have therefore written to dear Papa to ask if he *might* allow me this additional excursus and expense. It is a little hard on him but I am hopeful since the Congress is so close to *his* concerns, and it is a great historic occasion with which I can, for years, one day regale my grandchildren! I await his reply with *great* impatience.

Dearest Jean, my time in London is drawing to a close, but I fear I shall never again experience the *intense excitement* of this time and in meeting so many fine and *dedicated* heroes. I only wish your time in Geneva were also coming to an end so you could plan your return to Cambrai. I pray with all my heart that this will come about very soon!

Your most affectionate sister,

Natalie.

28

Letter 16

London, 26 Aug, 1872

My dearest Jeannot,

Hurrah! Darling Papa has said I may go with Tussy and the Marx family to the Hague on my way home. I shall therefore proceed from the Hague after the Congress direct to Cambrai. You cannot imagine how my feelings are torn at losing my dear friends here, being in the Hague for this great occasion, and yet the *immense* excitement at going home after all this long time.

Papa says I must be very careful in the Hague since the place will be full of police spies and policemen, anxious to arrest anyone they can. But I can hardly be *clandestine* when I am travelling and staying with the family of the great Mr Marx, himself one of the leading persons of the occasion! Perhaps I should wear a *moustache* and dress in boots and trousers! Tussy says we will not be allowed into much of the Congress since we are not delegates, but at least I shall hear something of the *gossip* from around the meetings. You cannot imagine how excited I am, delirious! I feel as if I personally had *prepared* it all and shall now see the final outcome for the International!

The poor Lafargues are also coming, from Spain. I fear it will much sadden the occasion; I do so *grieve* for them. I do not know *how* I should bear such a thing if I were Laura (you see, living in the family, I feel I am already intimate with her although I have never seen her!). She has lived through a *terrible* nightmare.

It seems that the Rimini conference – I mentioned it in my last letter, but your reply does not say whether you knew of it already – definitely decided not to attend the Hague. Now I hear – and you may know much better than me – that some of the Swiss delegates plan to walk out of the Congress of the International when the deliberations reach resolutions attacking the Alliance and Mr Bakunin and his followers. If this continues, the General Council may triumph over its foes, but in an empty Congress hall!

The news from you about your Mr Nechaev (and I forget what his real name is although I know you have told me) is most fitting – that he was *betrayed* in Zurich by a Serbian student, working for the Swiss secret police and arrested as a common murderer. You say Mr Bakunin had completely broken with him last year and knew nothing of his evil letter to his publisher in St Petersburg. But why then did he protest so much at Mr N's arrest as a common murderer rather than a political prisoner. I know that the Swiss will not allow the extradition of a political prisoner, but it seems Mr N was indeed a *murderer*. I cannot think that I would have done as you did and go to a demonstration of protest at Mr N's arrest – let alone, as your Serbian and Polish friends did, try to spring him from prison. I know this will grieve you since you think Mr Marx and his friends have tried to destroy the reputation of Mr N., a great hero and real son of the people, just to attack a great and noble revolutionary like Mr Bakunin. But he can never be a hero if he planned and carried out the murder of one of his comrades, just to bind all his followers together. Surely this is *entirely intolerable* and the evil man concerned deserves *no* sympathy whatsoever?

What will the police do now? Hand him over to the Russians?

So, I am to go to the Hague Congress! I am only sad that you will not be there. What a joy it would have been for us to be reunited, even if for a short time. It is so long! I must be patient. Mr Thiers cannot last forever!

Your most loving sister,

N.

29

Letter 17

The Hague, 9 Sept, 1872

Dearest Jeannot,

I am here! Can you imagine? It is a quaint little place and full of ...
Dutch! With baggy trousers, puffing pipes and wearing clogs, just
like they are supposed to do!

This will be, I fear, the last letter sent without the eye of the French
police perusing it. And it is written *in haste* since I am just about to
start my journey south to Cambrai. I am so beside myself with
excitement, I can barely put pen to paper!

The time here has been even *more intense*, and *exhausting*, than in
London. On the journey here, Tussy and I *jabbered* every inch of the
way, including on the Channel steamer (the sea was on the side of
revolution and behaved splendidly for all the International
delegates, calm and smooth), hushing only when strangers passed
by!

Then, imagine, in the Hague, Tussy and I stood in the street and
watched the delegates as they walked in a troop from the railway
station to the hall of the Congress – for all the world like a school
outing! They looked very mild and uncomfortable before the great
watching crowds (half of Holland seemed to have turned out for the
occasion) and the line of very *fierce* and scowling policemen. There
were perhaps a hundred of them and they did not seem at all likely
to overturn civilization and spread chaos throughout the land! The
Hague's Mr Mayor in all his finery was there to greet them. It was all
very *respectable,* and I am sure, if Mr Bismarck or the Tsar or Mr
Thiers could have seen them, they would have slept more quietly in
their beds!

Now it is all ended, and the fate of the International is settled.

How will I now live peacefully in Cambrai after all this excitement? I feel I am leaving the eye of a great storm, living with 'history' in the Marx household and then in the Congress. I console myself that the Congress is the *crescendo* of the great torrent of music of the year, and it will not happen again.

True to their word, Mr Marx and Mr Engels both resigned from the General Council. But *then,* to *universal* consternation and shock, they proposed that the General Council should be moved to … *New York*! So loyal were a majority of the remaining delegates, that they all dutifully voted for this. Mr Vaillant and the followers of Mr Blanqui – about 30 in all – were *terribly* angry. They say Mr Marx used them to defeat the Alliance and Mr Bakunin, and to *increase* the powers of the General Council – but then *ran away* from the needs of the European revolution. They say the transfer across the Atlantic will be the *death* of the International! In protest, they walked out of the Congress. Think – it was the first Congress that the followers of Mr Blanqui had attended (as it was for Mr Marx), and now it is probably the last! It seems as if this was only the last blow, and the International is disintegrating. It can hardly survive this last shock, although everyone in the Marx family behaves as if it were all perfectly *normal,* and even, that the International ought to have its headquarters in the newest section of world 'capitalism', safe from the police spies who crawl about everywhere in Europe. I cannot see this at all. Everyone knows the Americans have had a great falling out, and how will the General Council be able to keep in touch with what is happening in Europe? They will be weeks late *after* the strike or the riot or the war! Can this be the 'leadership' of the world's working classes? It seems Mr Marx saved the International from its internal enemies, but only at the cost of its *suicide*!

I fear that, in my excitement and haste, all my jumbled thoughts just tumble *out* in a great stream! Please forgive your silly *goose* of a sister! Most of the main proposals from the General Council were *passed*, although some by quite narrow majorities.

But let me start at the beginning. The Congress began with a 'closed' session for three days to check the credentials of the delegates. Tussy and I explored the old city, which is very pretty although we were so *concerned* at what was happening in the Congress, we could hardly pay attention. Mr Engels said it was a 'nasty business' with much wrangling and the occasional fisticuffs! Then the Congress could get down to business. The Council usually collected a majority by allying the followers of Mr Marx with those of Mr Blanqui – for a strong centre. Mr Vaillant's changes to the rules carried this out. This also happened in the vote to expel Mr Bakunin and Mr Guillaume from the International, although the delegates refused to expel any more than these two (many more were proposed by the General Council for expulsion).

The case was not strong, I fear (and I am of course an absolute dunce in these matters, though Tussy was at my elbow!). They said Mr Bakunin had, against the rules of the International, tried to create a secret organization or faction within the International, had accepted bribes in Russia, had collaborated with the Tsarist officials during his exile in Siberia, and that he had instigated Mr Nechaev's letter threatening to *murder* his publisher (Mr Marx, it seems, has the letter but it was not shown). I say that the case was weak, but if the charges had been true, it would have been stronger, but there was no one to *prove* the charges. I am sure your poor Mr Bakunin, if given the opportunity to reply, could have defended himself against what seemed to be a tissue of *slander.* No one had much to say about the *political* divisions and what would be best for the International.

Finally, all the oppositionists – except the followers of Mr Blanqui – voted to send the General Council to New York!

There was much *confusion* and anger and noise, as you can imagine. It did seem that Mr Marx and his followers were playing a far from *democratic* role. The majorities were put together from those who disagreed and were disunited on all other issues. The followers of Mr Proudhon were *outraged* and some walked out early. Now different groups are setting themselves up as organizations to *fight* the International – where now is that wonderful international solidarity? The spies of Prince Bismarck and the rest must carry messages of great *delight* to their masters.

As you know, I dearly *love* Tussy and her family, so you can imagine how confused my feelings were. I was in a *great* turbulence of emotions and there was no one with whom I could discuss these matters without concealment. Mr Marx looked quite grim and old as the Congress proceeded. None of his victories caused him elation! It seemed as if he must *escape* at any cost! I felt very sorry for him – and Mr Engels – for they have poured their hearts and minds into the General Council for so long, and yet now, they seemed to have few trustworthy *friends* and an immense army of *enemies.* Yet I suppose, at the end, they had succeeded in what they had set out to do – to protect the International being taken over by the wilder people, to protect its name and to release them from its duties. Yet at what cost?

After the Congress completed its business, I went with Tussy to hear her father report the decisions to a meeting of Dutch members of the International. The speech was quiet and grave, very thoughtful. It made it sound as if all the tumult had hardly occurred. But he also said – and this struck Tussy and me most *forcefully* – that the institutions of *reform* and of *voting* in Britain and the United States, and possibly in Holland, had made it possible for workers to secure their salvation *without* a revolution! Perhaps this is what lay behind the decision to end the useful life of the International – sending it to New York where there is *no need* for a revolution!

Dearest, dearest Jean, I shall *miss* your letters most painfully, now I go back into the sad and gloomy silence of the Third Republic. I know you will write, but you can say nothing of what is in your heart, your real thoughts and actions. For that we wait for the darkness to lift. Now the time for my departure comes swiftly nearer, so I must finish this before I leave. Tussy has promised to post it for me.

When next I write, it will be from Cambrai! I would dearly love it if you were there.

All my love, my darling Jean – your sister,

N.

30

Epilogue

As they drove into London to Jane's house, they sat in silence. Michael realised he had only escaped Cairo because what was to become known as '9/11' had happened just after he had left the city. Otherwise, he would, almost certainly, have been re-arrested, kept and grilled – and grilled and grilled, possibly to his end. They would finally have extracted from him that he had been a half-conscious courier, and that Leila had been central to Khaled's murder. They would be only tiny pieces in the great global jigsaw and would not have been major finds, but they would have demonstrated unequivocally his complicity. People were hung, drawn and quartered for less.

They drove to Jane's house. Michael was supposed to stay there until he had recovered. But love his grandchildren as he did, he was eager to recover his own life. Despite Jane's doubts, he insisted on returning to Alresford, to an empty house with only the portrait of Helen to talk to.

At last, a healing silence flowed back into his life. The plant had its own resources of self-regeneration, independent of his will and mind; the sap began to flow once more, albeit more sluggishly. He recovered, although he felt ill from time to time, grieving for he knew not what. And there were many pauses, when he slipped helplessly into a reverie, a remembered sequence of events from which he could not escape.

He emerged, a little greyer and slower. One or other of the children came down almost every weekend, as if they had organised a rota to make sure he hung on to life. It was a trouble for them, he knew. It would be better if he were disabled and in a home so that then everyone could relax. But he was grateful to them for their care, even if he knew he could not tell them what had happened. He had already become ashamed of his moral confusion, of his complicity.

At the heart of his grieving was that idea of his complicity. As the mighty machinery of the Washington bureaucracy lumbered slowly into action, the names and the photographs of those who had flown the planes – now it seemed into the two World Trade Centre towers, the Pentagon, and a fourth ploughing into a field near Pittsburgh – were published, the networks outlined. And as Michael feared, they included some of the addresses to which he had posted letters.

But then surely he had always been complicit. His lifetime passion had always included that. He had not studied the Russian nihilists in order to hate them, nor the Red Brigades nor the Tamil Tigers. His professional devotion had always accepted that the struggle for justice was right and that the major users of terrorism were always oppressive governments. How could it be otherwise when governments, the Goliaths, were armed with aircraft, missiles, tanks, artillery, and the rebels, at best, with ancient rifles or even no more than David's sling and stone. Using civil aircraft as weapons against the Trade Towers was an act of insane genius, but it did not change the case – downtown Manhattan had became a ghostly echo of downtown bombed Baghdad. The State mobilised immense resources of cruelty, of brutality; it controlled the supply of information and the manufacture of lies; it 'disappeared' people, maimed them, murdered them, and created the legal rules to make it impossible that it should be held to account for its crimes. The prisons were the real monuments to terrorism. The rebel was, by comparison, impotent.

Yet not all violence was vindicated in this way. The fact that the Palestinians were powerless to prevent the steady theft of their land, did not justify any acts of violence against the State. The armed rebellion of the Tamil Tigers had produced, some said, the killing of 60,000 people, the laying waste of much of north-east Sri Lanka: could that ever be justified? To deliberately provoke the inexhaustible capacity of the State for mindless brutality against its own citizens or anyone else could not be justified on the grounds that, as in Palestine, there was no other way. On the contrary, unofficial terrorism here strengthened, enhanced, exaggerated official violence.

His experience in Zamalek had been trivial in the sum of things, trivial in comparison to what happened on a daily basis to countless unknown Egyptians. But it did not justify his complicity. He had assisted the Islamists and been a factor in facilitating the murder of Khaled. Of that he was now sure.

* * *

He wrote a paper for a seminar in Beirut, trying to distil something from the history of rebellion of the twentieth century for the Lebanese civil war. The press and the television news rolled on, the war in Afghanistan reached its crescendo, Osama Bin Laden disappeared.

The Beirut seminar was organised by old friends at the American University, the AUB. It was a delight to return to the city, now blessedly at peace. The handsome buildings, still bearing the scars, lined the ridge of the hill, looking far out over an azure sea. He came early with a weekend to spare to go with his old friend, Rafi, to the family home in the hills in a beautiful old town on the edge of Druze country.

Michael sat once more on the terrace in the morning sunlight, smelling the lemons and the oregano, hearing the goat bells and the crickets in the long hot grass, exulting in the physical joy of it. He remembered earlier visits when the shell holes in the terrace wall, now repaired, were visible, the bullet slashes along the side of the villa, mute witnesses to a time, now swiftly becoming unbelievable, when enough Lebanese strove with whatever means came to hand to kill each other. The events could be described, he reflected, but not credibly explained – why people who lived together in moderate amity for generations, went to school together, made love together, then turned to treating each other with unspeakable cruelty, with unrelenting and pitiless brutality. No babe too small or pathetic to have its tiny brains splattered against a wall; no ancient crone too bowed by years, to escape rape. The twentieth century's battle honours of brutality swamped any claims to civilisation. What would it take to turn the rage of suburban England or rural Vermont to the same unspeakable acts?

Rafi had survived, in the niches between the bands of killers. He was cheerful, and not at all permanently disabled by the years of horror. He could still joke and make love. Hana, his Shi-ite wife from the south, an immense smile on her pretty face as she brought him morning coffee, had survived – and more, for two toddlers clung about her skirts, thumbs in mouths. Bikini Atoll once more grew flowers too.

In Beirut, he stayed in the Mayflower Hotel, another old friend, and the receptionist greeted him as a familiar. He wandered in the little streets of Hamra, not unlike Zamalek, rejoicing in the bookshops, the antique sellers, the little galleries. Later he swam from the American University beach and looked back at the city, ringing the bay. Some of the downtown towers were still half-ruined, spattered like pewter with thousands of gunshots and shell holes. This is also what could happen with unlimited unofficial terrorism, a collective auto-destruction.

The seminar went well. There was a sympathetic hearing for his paper. On the last evening, the core group of friends decided to mark his departure the following morning by going out for a final drink and perhaps a meal.

'What about the Little Pomegranate on Bekhaz – near your hotel?' Rafi suggested.

'Not there,' Nadim said scornfully. 'It's so sleazy, and I hate all those ancient tarts.'

'They've cleaned it up,' Rafi said. 'It's all redesigned, and charming and close.'

The Pomegranate it was. The half-dozen of them walked from the university through the narrow streets, stumbling off the narrow pavements as they chatted.

The little restaurant had a long entrance of flagstones, lined with narrow ponds on either side, water lilies and a waterfall, pillars, and masses of potted plants and creepers; the arched windows had modern stained-glass designs.

'You see,' Rafi said triumphantly. 'They've transformed it.'

They passed the cloakroom woman and someone tried to guide them to a table, but they preferred to stand at the long bar. There were more pools, an opening to the sky, trees, potted plants, and a cobbled floor. The bar was virtually empty since it was too early for local patrons.

They were busy deciding what to drink. At the other end of the bar, a woman sat smoking. Of course, he did not recognize her at once because her clothes were so strange. But increasingly, he began to think it was her. In the noise and chatter around him, he became a moment of silence, stealing glances at the woman. It was impossible that it could be her, yet whoever it was had a striking resemblance to Leila.

183

'You look as if you've seen a ghost,' Rafi said in alarm, remembering the stories of Michael's ordeal in Cairo. 'Are you all right?'

'Yes, I'm OK,' Michael murmured. 'But I may have seen a ghost.' Rafi followed his gaze to the other end of the bar.

'That woman looks so like someone I used to know in Cairo, it is uncanny.'

'She looks rather beautiful,' Rafi said, 'a cut above the normal crowd here.'

The talk moved to other topics. Michael could not resist stealing glances. He realised he had never seen Leila in ordinary clothes – or rather, the clothes of a bar hostess. Even at this distance, the make-up seemed heavy. The skirt was impossibly tight across her quite large hips; her long slender legs were crossed. The neckline was low and she was wearing a lot of heavy jewellery. The hair was the same, although he had seen it only once, a shining black waterfall, now tied back to show off a slender neck. She was smoking, he thought, and watching them, perhaps hoping for a patron for the evening.

As the barman passed, Michael stopped him to ask who she was. He spoke some English but was a bit offhand.

'She's employed by the Pomegranate to entertain the guests,' he said. 'She sings when there's a crowd and the pianist is here.'

'How long has she been here?' Michael asked.

'I don't know – maybe six months.'

'And where's she from?'

The barman was getting impatient at being held. 'I don't know – she keeps herself to herself. But she speaks Egyptian Arabic so I suppose she must be from Egypt. Why don't you go and ask her? She's here to entertain the guests.'

Michael thanked the barman and turned away. The woman was still watching them, half-smiling, in welcome, aware that he was observing her. There was no trace of fear or embarrassment as she stared at him.

He excused himself from the group, and slid along the bar towards her. Her face broadened into a smile and she brightened. As he approached her, there was no flicker of recognition. But for him, it was increasingly clear that this was Leila.

When he reached her, he felt he was trembling slightly. He was engulfed in her scent – was it the same scent? Her lips were a violent red, and her eyes heavily ringed with mascara.

184

'Leila?' he asked.

'They call me Maha,' she said in English. The voice was Leila's, gruff and throaty. 'But you can call me Leila if you would like to buy me a drink.'

Close to her now, it seemed impossible to Michael that she was not Leila, even though her clothes and make-up were so out of character with the woman he had known. The lips were the same, plump and well shaped, even if now shockingly red. And her eyes were green.

I thought you were someone I used to know,' he said awkwardly, and summoned the barman.

'I'll have a Campari and soda,' she said. 'And who is Leila?'

'A doctor in Cairo,' he replied.

'Well, sorry, I'm not a doctor though I am from Cairo.'

'Whereabouts?' he asked.

'Nowhere you'd know,' she laughed.

'And what brought you to Beirut?'

'Work. In my job, you go where the work is. The owner of the Pomegranate saw me in Cairo and offered me this. It's OK as long as they don't start shooting again.'

Michael was suddenly overcome with confusion. What was he doing here, talking to a bar girl.

'Well, enjoy your drink,' he said lamely, 'and have a good evening. I have to join my friends.'

She stared at him with astonishment. He walked back to the group at the other end of the bar.

He could not absorb it. It must be Leila, but why was there no hint of recognition, no hesitation. It was not much more than a year since she had seen him.

He was tired so the group decided to end early without taking supper. She was no longer at the end of the bar as he left. He walked back to the Mayflower with Rafi and they said their goodbyes.

He went to the bar for a brandy, and sat for a while, turning over in his mind the mystery. And then he remembered – the tattoo on her left wrist. He had not checked whether it was there. He tried to remember how she had sat, her left arm resting on the bar, wrist downward and a cigarette in her right hand. But she had been wearing heavy bracelets that were big enough to hide the tattoo.

His heart was racing as he finished his drink quickly and stood to return to The Little Pomegranate. He must know. Why was she here? Perhaps she needed help. And then he remembered her blank stare. She could surely not have been pretending. She must genuinely have not recognized him. Perhaps she no longer remembered her life in Cairo.

He stopped. What was the point? This was not a love story. Neither of them wanted the other. Whether it was Leila or not was equally unimportant. He would have liked to know what had happened on that evening in Zamalek but she probably could not now tell him. Perhaps she had become another person.

She had paid him for his silence and that was now enough – there were no more debts or obligations. Nechaev, at last, was dead.

On the plane home, for reasons he could not fathom, he felt at peace.

Appendix

Michael James, 'An observer of the conflict between Marx and Bakunin in 1872', *Documentary Review of Political History*, Vol. 15, No. 3 (Autumn, 2001), Ann Arbor, Michigan, pp. 254–309.

Introduction

In 1998, M. Jean-Pierre Naireaux, an antique dealer in northern France and father of one of my doctoral students, Andre Naireaux, sent me a bundle of letters he had recovered from a bureau he purchased in Cambrai. These proved to be 17 letters, written between January and September of 1872, by Natalie Kolakowski, daughter of a Cambrai medical practitioner, to her brother, Jean, at that time in exile in Geneva. I am most grateful to M. Naireaux for his extraordinary generosity in allowing me to present these letters to a wider public.

Dr Stepan Kolakowski (1823–1888), born in Lodz, Poland; studied medicine in Cracow; was active in the 1848 Polish nationalist uprisings against Russian Tsarism; and was obliged to flee, finally settling and taking up a general practice in Cambrai in France. He married the daughter of a Cambrai merchant, Françoise Bernet (1834–1864) in 1852, and there were two surviving children, Jean (1853-1886) and Natalie (1854–1928). Jean was apprenticed to a firm of architects and engineers (1868–1871), led by Etienne Besançon (1832–1890), a friend of Stepan Kolakowski. A Proudhonist, Besançon was active in the Paris Commune. Jean was also active in the Commune, wounded and exiled to Geneva.

The letters have been translated into English and checked for accuracy by Professor Leon Nantes of Nancy University. The English is, of course, modern usage rather than the style of the times when they were written (but I have attempted to eschew any aggressive modernisms). They are now presented for the first time, the originals being deposited in the French departmental archives in Nancy.

We have no idea why the letters have survived. Presumably, the recipient, Jean Kolakowski, brought them back from Geneva when his exile was finally ended and he returned to Cambrai. Sadly, we do not have his letters to his sister, the hook on which Natalie often hangs her correspondence. However, much in the text of the letters is comprehensible without these.

The letters are of much interest even though they contain nothing of substance, which is new; that is, most of the details are available in existing sources. However, they offer the standpoint of a personal witness to what were for the Marx family the momentous events of 1872. Furthermore, although Natalie Kolakowski sees herself as politically naïve and inexperienced, she seems to have been highly committed, perhaps through the intellectual and political inheritance of her father and her brother, himself originally a follower of Proudhon and active as a supporter of Blanqui in the Commune. Thus, despite her youth and provincial upbringing, Natalie's observations are frequently more sophisticated, confident and perceptive than might be expected. Furthermore, her time in the Marx household constituted an intense education. In the end, she refuses to choose politically between the family in which she had lived and to which she was greatly attached, and the Bakuninism (one assumes) of her brother in Geneva.

Why was the writer part of the Marx household in that year? By reconstruction from the letters (and there are apparently no other sources), it appears that Natalie's father, Dr Kolakowski was an admirer of the work of Marx. Although he worked in exile as a provincial physician, he had inherited sufficient funds from his Polish relatives not only to make his family comfortably off but also to allow him to finance his favoured projects (particularly in Polish émigré politics). In the late 1860s, Dr Kolakowski came to learn that the Marx family were living in most difficult circumstances, so much so that Marx's capacity to continue his theoretical work was seriously constrained. At about the same time, Natalie's brother Jean was placed as a trainee in the architectural practice of Etienne Besançon and partners in Paris. It was through the good offices of Besançon

188

that the proposal was put to Marx that Natalie should come to his household as a paying guest in order to learn English and teach French conversation to the youngest Marx daughter, Eleanor, a subterfuge to allow Kolakowski the opportunity to relieve the poverty of the Marx family without any loss of face.

As it happened, historical events – the outbreak of the Franco-Prussian War, the collapse of the Third Empire, the creation of the Paris Commune and its subsequent defeat by the forces that were to create the Third French Republic – much delayed the completion of this project until early 1872.

*   *   *

The year 1872 constituted a climacteric in the lives of Marx and Engels. The Paris Commune had raised immense hopes, and when it was crushed – and vilely so in terms of the deaths and exile of a generation – those hopes were dashed. The ruling powers of Europe tried, yet again as they had in the days of the Concert of Europe, to make efforts to collaborate to prevent any recurrence of the French events.

However, although the hopes of European radicals were defeated, the reputation of the International (the International Working Men's Association) that Marx and Engels had created and intellectually sustained had never attained such a pinnacle of fame. It was allegedly the secret conspiracy – supposedly directed by Marx – which orchestrated every strike, riot, and demonstration, from Chicago to Moscow. It was held, notoriously, to have organised, financed and directed the Paris Commune.

The reality was somewhat different. Marx had his followers but they were few in number in Paris at that time. The leadership of the Paris Commune was overwhelmingly drawn from the followers of Proudhon and Blanqui (the sole Marxist was a Hungarian exile). This lack of significant Marxist influence in the Commune was repeated in even more extreme forms in social conflicts elsewhere.

Despite its notoriety among the ruling powers of Europe, the International could not prevent the demoralisation of the Left following the crushing of the Commune. 1872 thus represented the end of the 'innocence' of the International, its capacity to hold together in a single purpose so many divergent political and national groups. The divisions became insupportable. The immediate enemy might appear to those in London to be the anarchists followers of Michael Bakunin, but there were many other groups who demanded the removal of the leadership of Marx and the General Council of the International, not least the moderates and reformists of the English trade unions. The issue of the use of terrorism was a crucial element in the political disintegration of the International, with the anarchists seeing it as a vital instrument in the pursuit of revolution, the moderates as a powerful obstacle in the pursuit of peaceful reform.

At the Congress of the International in the Hague (September, 1872), Marx won the crucial votes, but almost by accident or sleight of hand. The divergent forces could no longer be kept in step. Each national section, once it reached a certain level of political importance, came to demand increased autonomy to relate to the peculiarities of each national context. Hence a majority emerged calling for the reduction of the General Council to no more than a 'corresponding and statistical bureau' (a favourite opposition formulation). However, at the Hague Congress, Marx won the vote for a *more* centralized General Council. It was a hollow victory because he was also about to end, effectively, the International. Marx had already indicated that he wished to leave the General Council to devote himself to his theoretical work, although whether this decision was the result of the rebellion in the ranks of the International is not clear. One can surmise that had a European revolution and a unified International been on the agenda, Marx would not have chosen that moment to give up his leading position in the General Council. In the event, to preserve the International from its divisions, he – almost single-handedly – exiled the General Council to New York and thus, as he must have known, sentenced it to death.

In practice, the opposition won. Over the following six months, seven of the eight national federations of the International reversed both the decision to transfer its headquarters to New York and the expulsions that had occurred at the Hague. Other favoured political positions of the Proudhonists and anarchists – as opposed to the Marxists – were reaffirmed.

However, these events reflected a deeper transition. Marx might identify the Paris Commune as the first herald of the arrival of a modern industrial proletariat and thus industrial society, but in reality it was rather the last of the uprisings of the revolutionary Jacobin tradition, based upon the sort of small group conspiracies and acts of terrorism that were both much closer to Bakunin's conception of revolution and to what Marx and Engels had devoted themselves to in 1848. That conspiratorial and terrorist tradition continued in the economically more backward parts of Europe: in Russia, Italy, Spain and eastern Europe. The new world that Marx so accurately identified in England, a world of a concentrated urban working class, of mass trade unions, great factories and cities of unprecedented size, made possible the 'self-emancipation of the working class' without the mediation of small groups of the educated, the revolutionary elite of conspirators. The old revolutionary sects of intellectuals became irrelevant if not positively obstructive (or risible). Marx was full of scorn for what had once been his own point of entrance to revolutionary politics.

Bakunin embodied that old agenda of secret conspiracies, of terrorism (as acts of retribution, of demonstration of the vulnerability of the ruling order, and as incitement to revolt) to lever the masses into action. Correctly, he saw the most promising terrain for this perspective in the less developed parts of Europe. Whereas Marx saw industrialisation as the route to creating a mass industrial class that could liberate itself, Bakunin saw that the new working class, with prosperity, would align itself with the ruling order. The more powerful politically the working class became, the more easily it could meet its ends without revolution, through compromise with the status quo. Workers would opt for reform, not revolution. Had Bakunin had occasion to study in depth the English case, he would have found abundant evidence for such a view. Indeed, Marx himself observed, after the Hague congress, that the demands of the workers' movement might be capable of being realised in Britain, the United States and possibly Holland without revolution. He is, it seems, almost accepting Bakunin's view that revolution is only possible in more backward parts of Europe. Economic development, by implication, creates mass society, but also neutralises the drive to rebel.

Did Marx sense the paradox at the heart of his system – the more economically advanced the working class, the less its appetite for revolution? Did he perhaps realise that henceforth serious revolutionary politics in developed countries would always be confined to small sects of intellectuals, and that that was not a world he – after the heroic experiences of the International – could any longer choose to inhabit? Where those revolutionary sects could on occasions be effective was in a relatively backward country with the mass of the poor. The trend that led to the ultimate collapse of the second International in 1914, also meant that the triumphs achieved in Marx's name in the twentieth century would all be in economically backward countries – from Russia to China, Vietnam and Cuba. Perhaps some such mood of pessimism underlay his failure to deal centrally with Bakunin's *political* positions, but rather to direct his attack on his alleged moral turpitude, or rather that of his claimed follower, S.N. Nechaev.

The dispute is not as arcane as it might seem. After all, Bakunin's perspective proved rather more accurate than Marx's. The intellectual force of Marxism, reinforced by the material power of the old Soviet Union, China and Cuba, trapped revolutionaries in Marxist concepts even when Bakuninism would seem to fit reality much more closely. The disputes among the leaders of the Chinese Communist Party – to reconcile what they had achieved in China with the orthodoxies of Stalinism – show the difficulties of, to employ another term from Marx, Marxism as false consciousness, theory as a means of concealing rather than illuminating reality.

The transition in Marx's views of revolution that we have suggested occurred in 1872 is relevant to the modern world in another sense. It is still the case that the politics of Bakuninism fit more closely many of the conditions in many developing countries than those of Marx, in particular, the revolutionary potential of that dangerous conjuncture of an alienated (and possibly unemployed) stratum of the intelligentsia, a mass of impoverished urban workers and small peasants, the social turbulence of rapid urbanisation, and a savagely repressive government.

Bakunin's instrument of revolution was a secret society of dedicated cadres (not so far from at least one of Lenin's conceptions of the party) undertaking acts of terrorism against the high offices of State, business and politics to precipitate the masses into action. Marx was loyal enough to that tradition to seek to align the International in support of the terrorism of the Irish Fenians and other such movements in Europe, even though the respectable English trade unionists were outraged at being associated with all forms of violence. They were no longer willing to embrace publicly the view that the terrorism of the ruling orders was always much worse than that of the rebels.

192

After Bakunin, the assassins came thick and fast in both developed and developing countries. Nechaev, who became the horrific model for pure dedicated destruction and who features in Natalie's letters, marked only one of the extreme cases for anarchists. (Lenin whose politics were always closer to the anarchist tradition than was healthy, thought most highly of Nechaev.) In the nineteenth century and shortly after, a tsar of Russia (1881), sundry high members of his ruling order, a king of Italy, a king of Spain, two American presidents, an empress of Austria fell to the assassin (with failed attempts on Queen Victoria of Britain and the Kaiser of Germany). In the following century, the Sarajevo murder of the heir to the throne of Austro-Hungary precipitated the outbreak of World War I. In *The Rebel* in 1892, Camus tells us, there were over 1,000 dynamite outrages in Europe and nearly 500 in America.

Today's concern with 'global terrorism' is, thus, not at all new. But the revolutionaries today are not, as they were in the main then, militant atheists, but Muslims. As in the nineteenth century, they are drawn from the educated middle class (in the case of the Islamists, overwhelmingly from the technical professions – doctors, engineers, architects), what Bakunin would have identified as *déclassé* intellectuals. They act in order to incite general rebellion, this time not among 'the People' but what in Muslim countries is the same thing, the faithful.

The Islamists are no less internationalist, and their politics are in essence Bakuninist within an Islamic framework. Is it pushing the logic too far to see the Islamist vision of the peaceful *ummah*, the harmonious community of the faithful, as much the same as the anarchist future of small self-governing communities, living in harmony and peace, once the predatory State has been removed?

For both the nineteenth-century assassins and the modern Islamists, martyrdom is the necessary condition of the moral purity of their acts, and lends quiet confidence to their deaths. In Camus' words, 'He who kills is only guilty if he consents to go on living or if, to remain alive, he betrays his comrades.' Indeed, far from there being a 'clash of civilisations', the Islamists appear to be solidly within the European political tradition.

However, apart from the religious inspiration, the significance of which some would rate more highly, there is another striking difference. Today, the assassin does not restrict him or herself to 'precision bombing', the killing of a person alleged to be guilty of a particular act, but specializes in punishing whole peoples, in slaughter of the innocent. The old assassins were morally fastidious, killing exclusively those who were seen as responsible for the acts of State terrorism. Camus cites cases where murder was not undertaken because it involved risk to the life of someone else – a wife, a soldier, a bystander. The modern terrorist, secular or Islamic, seeks to maximise – to use the US military phrase – 'collateral damage,' to punish whole nations or classes without discrimination.

If terrorism is the employment of physical coercion – or its threat – to achieve political ends, then acts of unofficial terrorism are pale imitations of official terrorism. It is the official wars of the twentieth century that removed the scrupulousness of official terrorism and so of unofficial terrorism. The German *Luftwaffe* bombed London, not the headquarters of the political leadership of the government. The RAF laid waste Dresden and Hamburg with the explicit aim of maximising the casualties of 'the innocent'. The US Air Force firebombed Tokyo with a horrendous death toll before dropping atomic bombs on Hiroshima and Nagasaki. The link between the criminal and the crime was hideously weakened.

The pitiless destruction of New York's twin trade towers in 2001 with over 3,000 casualties, assumes these moral precedents, as even an unofficial nuclear attack assumes the precedent of Hiroshima. Indeed, while states continue to rely so heavily on the use of terror to enforce their will, whether at home or abroad, the unofficial terrorist will continue to mimic them, albeit in a far weaker form.

The letters of Natalie Kolakowski offer us a small insight into the political and intellectual turbulence, and the injustices that prompt men and women to sacrifice their lives for great causes. Those who are required to sacrifice their lives in war are garbed in the heroic garments granted by the State, are martyrs to sacred causes, have tombs to unknown warriors. Those who decide to sacrifice themselves without a government are subject to universal repugnance, must dress in no more than their own home-spun virtue, striking examples of the moral tradition of western individualism, even when undertaken in the name of Islam.

The Characters, Events and References

Allende, Salvador (1908–1973). Chilean doctor and political leader – Minister of Health in the Popular Front government of the late 1930s; 1957 presidential candidate of united Left; President of the Senate, 1966; president of the Republic, 1970; murdered in US-backed military coup, 9/11, 1973.

Alliance for Social Democracy. The secret network of Bakunin supporters that Marx and the General Council alleged had not been dissolved as Bakunin claimed, but continued to orchestrate the opposition within the International.

Anderson, Elizabeth Garrett (1836–1917). Physician to the Marx family; first woman to qualify as a physician in Britain; founder of the Elizabeth Garrett Anderson Hospital in London (1866), and physician there (1866–1892); one of the first women mayors in Britain, in Aldeburgh, Suffolk.

Archbishop (of Paris). Georges Darboy, killed during the destruction of the Paris Commune and the taking of the city.

Baader-Meinhof gang (1968–c. 1977). German terrorist group. See Ulrike Meinhof, Gudrun Ensslin, Astrid Proll.

Bakunin, Mikhail Alexandrovich (1814–1876). Russian revolutionary, journalist, one of the founders of anarchism. Participated in the 1848 revolution in Germany; imprisoned in Russia, sentenced to exile, escaped to cross the United States back to Europe; active in Italy in spreading the International; in Lyons for the Franco-Prussian War; then in Geneva and Locarno; sought to turn the International to anarchism.

195

Bebel, Auguste (1840–1913). Leading German socialist; President, Union of German Workers' Associations from 1867; member of the International; deputy in the North German and Imperial Reichstags from 1867; one of the founders and leaders of the German Social Democratic Party; voted in the Reichstag against war credits for the war against France; tried for treason in Leipzig and sentenced to two years imprisonment.

Besançon, Etienne (1832–1890). Director of an architectural and engineering firm in Paris where Natalie's brother Jean Kolakowski was apprenticed (1868–1871). An active Proudhonist, supporter of the Commune but never arrested or charged. A friend of Stepan Kolakowski and likely link in arranging Natalie's placement in the Marx household.

Bismarck-Schönhausen, Prince Otto von (1815–1898). Prime Minister of Prussia (1862–1871 and 1873–1890); Chancellor of the North German Confederation (1867–1871); Chancellor of the German Empire (1871–1890).

Blanc, Gaspard Antoine (1845–1890). French Bakuninist; member of the Lyons section of the International; active in the Lyons uprising (1870); after suppression of the Paris Commune, became a Bonapartist.

Blanqui, Louis Auguste (1805–1881). French revolutionary and Communist; active participant in the revolutions of 1830 and 1848; key intellectual force in the Paris Commune, although he was already in prison.

Bradlaugh, Charles (1833–1891). English journalist, politician and radical; editor of *The National Reformer*.

Bonaparte (Charles Louis Napoleon) (1808–1873). Napoleon III. Emperor of the French (1852–1870); his regime, the Third Empire, collapsed in the Franco-Prussian War and he fled to England and settled in Chislehurst, a south west London suburb (1871).

Burns, Lydia (Lizzie), (1827–1878). Irish working woman, active in the Irish liberation movement; Engels' second partner.

Camus, Albert (1913–1960). Author of *The Rebel*, translated by Anthony Bower with an introduction by Olivier Todd, from: Camus, Albert, *l'Homme Revolté* (1951), Penguin, London, 1962.

Catechism of a Revolutionary. A publication attributed to Nechaev, written in Russian, possibly in 1869, in Geneva, but probably with the collaboration of N. M. Bakunin.

Centre des Études Sociales: the club of the *communards* in London. It held discussions and maintained some library facilities.

Cochrane-Baillie, Alexander Dundas Ross Wishart, 1st Baron Lamington (1816-1890), English politician and Conservative MP. His speech to the Commons on the International (12 April, 1872) was reported in *The Times*, 13 April, 1872.

Commune (Paris). Paris rejected the proposed peace treaty with Prussia to conclude the Franco-Prussian War, Feb. 1870, and in 1871 after the surrender of Emperor Louis Napoleon, popular forces of the Left seized the city and set up a commune to defend the city. Outside the city, Republicans proclaimed the Third Republic. The Prussians surrounded the city and it capitulated after four months' siege. The Republican army then advanced on Paris, bombing and killing possibly 20,000 or more.

Crémieux, Isaac Möise (called Adolphe) (1796–1880). French lawyer and politician; member of the Provisional Government (Feb–May, 1848); Deputy (1848–1851); Bonapartist.

Eccarius, Johan Georg (1818–1889). Leading figure in the German workers' movement; tailor and journalist; leader of the German Workers' Educational Society in London; General Council of the International (1864–1872), General Secretary (1867–1871); Corresponding Secretary for America; delegate to all International Congresses except the last (Geneva, 1873); close supporter of Marx up to 1872.

FARC (Revolutionary Armed Forces of Colombia) (1964–present). Started as the military wing of the Colombian Communist Party. Leader Manuel Marulanda.

Favre, Jules (1809–1880). French Foreign Minister (1871–1872); with Thiers, main leader in the suppression of the Commune, 1871.

Fenians. The Irish Republican rising of 1867 was suppressed by the British forces and numerous arrests made. Prison conditions were notoriously bad. By 1872, some 42 Irish political prisoners remained in custody. There was a major public campaign to secure their release.

Frankel, Leo (1844–1896). Hungarian jeweller; member of the Paris Commune (Deputy for the XIIIth arrondissement; Head of the Labour and Trade Committee; member of the Finance Committee); member of the General Council of the International (1871-1872); attended the Hague Congress; founder of the General Workers' Party of Hungary.

Free Officers. A group of young officers who reacted to the corruption of the Egyptian monarchy and its failure to end British rule in the late 1940s. Under the titular leadership of General Mohammed Naguib, they seized power and overthrew the king, July 26 1951.

Garibaldi, Guiseppe (1807–1882). Leader of the movement for the unification of Italy (1860); landed in Sicily with 1,070 men and defeated official forces before overthrowing the Kingdom of Naples and unifying Italy under the Savoy monarchy. Great European nationalist hero.

General Council. The London-based governing body of the International (IWMA).

Gladstone, William Ewart (1809–1898). British Tory politician, later leader of the Liberal Party; Chancellor of the Exchequer (1852–1855, 1859–1866); Prime Minister (1868–1874; 1880–1885; 1886; 1892–1894).

Guzmán, Abimael ('Chairman Gonzalo') (1934–present). Founder and leader of Sendero Luminoso (Shining Path) in Peru.

Grazdanov, Stephen. One of the pseudonyms of Sergei Nechaev (1847–1882).

Guillaume, James (1844–1916). Swiss teacher and leading Bakuninist; member of the International; delegate to congresses in Geneva (1866), Lausanne (1867), Basle (1869) and the Hague (1872); leading member of the Alliance for Social Democracy, and editor of the papers *Le Progrés* and *La Solidarité.*

Guevarists. Followers of Ernesto 'Che' Guevara (1928–1967); Argentinian doctor, second in command to Fidel Castro in the Cuban revolution in 1959. Cuban Minister of Industry (1961–1965); left in 1966 to spread revolution in Latin America; wounded in 1967 clash with Bolivian forces and died.

Hales, John (b.1839). British trade union leader; member of the General Council of the International (1866–1872); Secretary (1871–1872); delegate to the congresses in London (1871) and The Hague (1872); leader of the reformist wing of the British Federal Council (of the International) from early 1872.

International Working Man's Association (IWMA), founded in 1864.

Jacobin (Society of Friends of the Constitution). Set up as discussion group to prepare French Assembly debates during the revolution; by February 1790 there were 1,000 members; by June 1791 there were 2,400. Execution of the King split the group, and by 1792, the Jacobins represented the more radical wing of the revolutionary movement (see Terror).

Japan Red Army. Breakaway from Japanese Communist League Red Army Faction; series of high profile actions, led by Fusako Shigenobu: massacre at Lod airport (Israel) 26 killed, in support of Palestinians; hi-jacked Japanese civil airliner; tried to seize US Embassy, Kuala Lumpur.

Khedive. Originally title of the Ottoman Viceroy of Egypt, subsequently used to refer to the kings of Egypt under British rule.

Khmer Rouge (1975–1979). In the wake of the US overthrow of the Cambodian government (as part of the US war in Vietnam and the attempt to stop supplies to the Vietcong), the armed wing of the Communist Party of Kampuchea under Pol Pot launched a guerrilla war and seized power. They set out to purge Cambodia (now the Khmer Republic) and end cities, with a resultant famine; possibly up to 2 million died.

Kolakowski, Stepan (1823–1888). Born Lodz, Poland; studied medicine at Cracow. Active in the Polish nationalist risings and in 1848 obliged to flee and ultimately settled in France, as a general practitioner in the small town of Cambrai. Married Françoise Bernet (1834–1864) in 1852, daughter of a Cambrai merchant and had two surviving children, Jean (1853–1886) and Natalie (1854–1928).

Kropotkin, Count Peter (1842–1921). Leading anarchist thinker; intended for high position in the Tsarist order, he was arrested for critical views and gaoled in 1876; escaped to Switzerland, to France (1881); member of the IWMA (1883); arrested and gaoled in France; to Britain (1886); to Chicago (1899), and then back to London. Returned ill to Russia after the 1917 revolution at Lenin's invitation to tumultuous welcome. Voluminous writer.

Lafargue, Paul (1842–1911). Trained in medicine, active in the Paris Commune and the International (member of the General Council); in Spain (1866–1869), in France, Spain and Portugal (1869–1872); delegate to the Hague Congress of the International (1872); founder of the French Workers' Party; married Marx's middle daughter, Laura.

Lafargue, Laura (née Marx) (1845–1911). The second daughter of the Marx family, married to Paul Lafargue.

Lassalleans. Followers of Ferdinand Lassalle (1825–1864), German journalist and lawyer; active in the 1848–1849 revolutions; founded the General Association of German Workers (1863); supported the unification of Germany under Prussia.

Khaled, Leila (1944–present). Palestinian leader (Popular Front for the Liberation of Palestine); led a series of aircraft hi-jackings in the late 1960s, early 1970s. Held by the British and exchanged, with 6 others, for 56 hostages taken in the seizure of 5 airliners. Member of the Palestinian Parliament, lives in Amman with second husband and two sons.

Lenchen, Helen Demuth (1820–1890). Given to Marx's wife, Jenny, by her mother when she was 25(1845). As housekeeper, cared for the Marx family for the rest of her life.

Liebknecht, Wilhelm (1826–1900). Leading German socialist, active in the 1848–1849 revolution; member of the International; deputy to the North German and Imperial Reichstags from 1867; one of the founders and leaders of the German Social Democratic Party; voted against war credits in the Reichstag for the war on France; tried in Leipzig for treason – sentenced to two years' imprisonment.

Lissagaray, Hippolyte Prosper Olivier (1838–1901). French journalist and historian; participant in the Paris Commune; author of *Histoire de la Commune de 1871*; in exile until 1880; for a time secretly engaged to Eleanor Marx.

Longuet, Charles (1839–1903). Journalist and Proudhonist; member of the General Council of the International (1866–1867, 1871–1872); fought in the defence of Paris (1870–1871); member of the Paris Commune; exiled in London; married the eldest Marx daughter, Jenny.

Lubyanka. Headquarters of the secret police of the Soviet Union, from the Cheka to the KGB, and now in Russia, the FSB. The most notorious centre of prisoner torture.

McKinley, William (1843–1901). Elected US Congress in 1877; Governor of Ohio, 1891; President (1896–1900) during the US imperial expansion; assassinated in Buffalo by anarchists.

Mazzini, Giuseppe (1805–1872). Italian national revolutionary democrat; leader of the movement for Italian unity; head of the Provisional Government of the Roman Republic (1849).

Meinhof, Ulrike (1934–1976); married Klaus Rainer Röhl; mother of twin girls; left husband in 1970 and joined Baader-Meinhof gang seeking to free Andreas Baader from gaol; captured June 1972; suicide by hanging in custody, May 1976.

Moro (Aldo) (1916–1978). Former Christian Democrat Prime Minister of Italy, murdered in 1978 as he was about to launch a government to be supported for the first time by the Italian Communist party. He was kidnapped by the Red Brigade, held for two months and left dead in a car boot in central Rome.

Mubarak, Mohammed Hosni (1928–present). Former pilot and Commander-in-Chief of the Egyptian Air Force; Vice President of Egypt under Sadat; President from 1981.

Muslim Brotherhood. Founded by Hassan Al-Banna (murdered 1949) in Egypt, 1928, four years after the end of the Ottoman Chaliphate, for an Islamic revival and the creation of Islamic states and societies. Spread rapidly in, it claims, 70 countries, and became in some countries politically influential. Savagely repressed in Egypt after a failed attempt on Nasser's life. Restored under Sadat, but again semi-suppressed under Mubarak. From mid-60s, groups broke away to undertake terrorist attacks on the regime.

Nasser, Gamal Abdel (1918–1970). Attended Military College (1936); on active service helped form the Free Officers, which overthrew the monarchy and expelled the British to the Canal Zone in 1952. Deposed Naguib in 1954 and became President; set in train social revolution under the rubric Arab socialism. Nationalised Suez Canal to drive out the British and withstood British-French-Israeli invasion; radical land reform and widespread nationalisation. Resigned after Egyptian defeat in 1967 war with Israel, but drawn back into office. Died in office 1970. (See Free Officers.)

Narodniks, Narodnaya Volya (Freedom of the People). The result of an 1879 split in Land and Freedom, for a more activist policy. Series of spectacular assassinations culminating in the murder of Tsar Alexander II, March 1881.

Nechaev, Sergei Gennadiyevich (1847–1882). Son of a waiter and sign painter of Ivanovo-Voznesensk in European Russia; self-educated teacher of religion in St Petersburg parish school; revolutionary and conspirator; active St Petersburg student movement (1868–1869); in exile in Switzerland with Bakunin (1869; 1871–1872). Founded secret organisation in Moscow, Narodnaya Rasprava (People's Judgement or Retribution); organised murder of one of members, Ivanov, on the unsubstantiated grounds that he was a police spy (21 November 1869). Fled to Switzerland, leaving behind his membership and contact list, which the police used to arrest many others. Visited London; arrested by Swiss police for murder, August 1872; extradited to Russia and tried in January 1873; sentenced to life hard labour; died in Peter and Paul Fortress, St Petersburg.

O'Donovan Rossa, Jeremiah (1831–1915). Leading Fenian, publisher of *The Irish People* (1863–1865), arrested and sentenced to life imprisonment (1865); amnestied (1870) and released (1871); emigrated to the United States.

'The Old One': Term of affection for Blanqui.

P2 Masonic Lodge. The focus of a long running conspiracy between the Italian secret service (Gladio), senior officers of the armed forces, Christian Democrat political leaders, and the US Central Intelligence Agency, to defeat Soviet and Communist activity in Italy. The Moro initiative to open politics to the Communist Party (see Moro) alarmed the group and a plan for a coup was prepared; selected assassinations were also undertaken; 143 died between 1969 and 1984 (including 85 in Bologna station – Bologna was a stronghold of the Communist party. In August 1980 P2 Masonic Grand Master Licio Gelli was tried but released on a technicality and fled to Argentina.

Peter and Paul Fortress. One of the older buildings in St Petersburg (in its church are buried the Romanov tsars); most notorious prison in Tsarist Russia.

Potato famine (1846–1851). Collapse of the potato harvest in British administered Ireland; it is estimated that the population of Ireland fell by half as the result of famine and the reactive emigration in the second half of the nineteenth century.

Proll, Astrid (1947–present). Baader-Meinhof gang; participated in attempted bombing of two Frankfurt department stores (1968); arrested May, 1971; escaped to Britain; arrested 1977 and extradited, but legal fault in original court decision led to release.

Proudhon, Pierre Joseph (1809–1865). French journalist, economist and anarchist; leading intellectual; major influence on the Left in the middle years of the century and on the leadership of the Paris Commune.

Pumps. Nickname for Mary Ellen Burns (b. 1860), niece of Engels' partner, Lydia Burns, and daughter of her sister, Engels' first partner. She was at this time about 12 years old.

Qutb, Sayyid (1906–1966). Egyptian Ministry of Education; teacher and inspector; study tour of educational facilities US (1948–1950); joined the Muslim Brotherhood (1952), and as prodigious author, became part of the leadership. Failed attempt on Nasser's life (1954), arrested and tortured. Published most famous work *Milestones* in 1964, declaring Egypt no longer Islamic. Seen as founding document justifying Islamic terrorism. Died in captivity.

Red Brigade (Brigate Rosse). Formed in 1969 from a split in various student organisations; undertook numerous kidnappings, murders and acts of sabotage to overthrow the Italian State and end Italy's role in NATO. Most notorious act: the kidnap and murder of former Prime Minister Moro. Severe repression and group disintegrated after 1984 (although in the twenty-first century, some attribute new acts to them).

Richard, Albert Marie (1846–1918). French journalist and leader of the Lyons section of the International; member of the Alliance for Social Democracy; active in Lyons uprising (1870); after suppression of the Paris Commune, became a Bonapartist.

Rimini Conference (4–6 August, 1872) Conference of those Italian groups claiming to identify with the International (although only some of them were formally affiliated); strongly influenced by the Bakuninist International Alliance of Social Democracy. The conference voted to boycott the Congress of the International in the

Hague in protest at the centralised power of the General Council (and the domination of Marx). It was proposed to hold an alternative Congress at the same time as that of the IWMA in the Hague, in Neuchâtel, Switzerland.

Sadat, Mohammed Anwar Al- (1918–1981). Attended Military College, 1936. Key follower of Nasser, with Free Officers in seizure of power (1952). Succeeded Nasser as President (1970), and realigned Egypt with US (expelled Soviet advisers); began open economy and under US pressure, recognized Israel and offered peace in return for Israel giving up Sinai (seized in the 1967 war). Assassinated by Islamist group (1981).

Sandinistas (FSLN). Group engaged in armed struggle in 1970s to overthrow dictator Somoza of Nicaragua, and begin a social revolution; won and governed country (1979–1990) in the face of great difficulties: US cancelled loans, instituted trade boycott, ended sugar quota and financed guerrilla opposition (from 1984). Sandinistas ultimately defeated in 1990 elections.

Schnappy (1868–1872). Nickname for Charles Etienne Lafargue (1868-72), Marx's only grandson, child of Paul and Laura Lafargue.

Sendero Luminoso (Shining Path). Group formed to precipitate revolution in Peru; their politics married nativist revolutionary tradition and Maoism. Group set up by University teacher Abimael Guzman (Chairman Gonzalo) in late 1960s, armed struggle from 1980. Guzman captured under Fujimoro regime and group disintegrated (although some claimed later incidents).

Shigenobu, Fusako (1945–present). Leader of the Japan Red Army. Lived in exile until 55; arrested November 2000.

(All-India) Sikh Student Federation. The leading organisation fighting for an independent Sikh State, Khalistan, in northern India. Prime Minister Mrs Indira Gandhi attempted to dislodge the political dominance of the Akali Dal in the state of the Punjab by promoting the religious figure, Jarnail Singh Bhindrawale, who in turn launched terrorist campaigns for Sikh independence. Gaoling Bhindrawale prompted an intensification of agitation and repression, culminating in the 1984 Indian army attack (Operation Blue Star) on the centre of Sikh worship, the Amritsar Golden Temple, and an act of reprisal in the murder of Mrs Gandhi by her Sikh bodyguards. There were major anti-Sikh riots following this and the massacre of many Sikhs.

Stauffenberg, Claus, Graf von (1907–1944). German army officer, initially pro-Hitler, but increasingly hostile to the brutality of the regime; General Staff Colonel from 1944; conspired to assassinate Hitler; placed bomb beneath table in Hitler's conference room (in the Prussian bunker at Rastenberg) on 20 July, 1944, but failed to kill Hitler; shot the following day.

Tamil Tigers. Sri Lankan group formed in 1976 to establish independent Tamil State in north and east Sri Lanka. Specialised in suicide bombings, one of which killed Rajiv Gandhi, then Prime Minister of India. Leader Velupillai Prabhakaran.

Terror, The (French Revolution) (1792–1794). The most radical phase of the revolution, under the Jacobins – Danton, Robespierre and the Committee of Public Safety; possibly 40,000 guillotined.

Thiers, Louis Adolphe (1797–1877). Prime Minister of France (1836; 1840); chief of the executive power (1871); brutal suppression of the Paris Commune; President of the Republic (1871–1873).

Third Republic (of France). Set up on the collapse of the Empire of Napoleon III under Prussian invasion, 1871.

Tupamaros. National Liberation Army of Uruguay, named after Tupac Amaru, Inca opponent of Spanish conquest of Latin America. Active in early 1960s, redistributing wealth to the poor from robberies, with number of spectacular attacks on government. Major military repression culminating in mid-1970s coup and military regime until 1985. Tupamaros since opted to become a legal political party.

Umkhonto we Sizwe. Armed wing of the African National Congress, formed 1961 by Nelson Mandela as Commander-in-Chief; Mandela organised guerrilla training abroad (1962), although was then sentenced to life imprisonment at the Rivonia trial. Organisation active in acts of sabotage throughout the period up to the end of apartheid.

Universal Federalist Council. Set up by disaffected French members of the International, claiming to be the International; Congress September 1872 before disappearing.

Vaillant, Edouard Marie (1840–1915). French socialist, physician and engineer, Blanquist; member of the Paris Commune, and, in exile, of the General Council of the International (1871–1872); after the decision of the Hague Congress (1872) to transfer the General Council to New York, left the International.

Zasulich, Vera (1849–1919). Joined the Narodniki and in January 1878 shot General Trepov, head of the St Petersburg *gendarmerie* for insulting and beating a political prisoner. Exiled in London (1880); worked with Lenin and the Russian Social Democratic party in exile in London (on editorial group of *Iskra*).